KAAJAL OZA VAIDYA is a prolific writer and orator, actor and model, teacher and social worker. Her columns are widely read amongst the Gujarati readers. Her work touches upon the untold and unheard stories of youth and women in the context of family, tradition, race, class, gender, culture and the politics of living in today's challenging postcolonial societies. In a short span of twelve years, she has published eighty books including a gamut of novels, short stories, translations, essays, plays and collections of poems along with many audio books. Some of her notable works are *Krishnayan* (2006), *Yog-Viyog* (2007), *Draupadi* (2011), *Madhyabindu* (2007) and *Maun Raag* (2007). Her works have been translated into more than five languages including English. She has travelled across the globe for speaking engagements. She delivers her talks in Gujarati, Hindi and English, on reshaping and transforming public consciousness.

SUBHA PANDE has worked as a professor of Pharmacy in RGUHS Bangalore. Her flair for languages drew her to translation. She has translated Kavita Kane's bestsellers *Sita's Sister* and *The Fisher Queen's Dynasty* into Hindi. She works between multiple languages. Her English translation of Girish Kuber's *Yuddha Jeevanche*, a Marathi bestseller on biological warfare, will be released in 2021. She has also translated four novellas by iconic Tamil writer Sivasankari into English. They have been released as e-books by Pustaka.

Krishnayan

KAAJAL
OZA VAIDYA

TRANSLATED FROM THE GUJARATI BY
SUBHA PANDE

eka

eka

First published in Gujarati as *Krishnayan* in 2006 by Navbharat Sahitya Mandir, Ahmedabad

First published in English as *Krishnayan* in 2021 by Eka, an imprint of Westland Publication Private Limited

1st Floor, A Block, East Wing, Plot No. 40, SP Infocity, Dr MGR Salai, Perungudi, Kandanchavadi, Chennai 600096

Westland, the Westland logo, Eka and the Eka logo are the trademarks of Westland Publications Private Limited, or its affiliates.

Copyright © Kaajal Oza Vaidya, 2021
Translation copyright © Subha Pande, 2021

ISBN: 9788194879008

This is a work of fiction. Names, characters, organisations, places, events and incidents are either products of the author's imagination or used fictitiously.

Typeset by Jojy Philip, New Delhi 110 015

As Krishna lay under the peepal tree with his eyes closed, myriad thoughts flooded his mind ... the palace of Dwarka, the battle of Kurukshetra, Draupadi's swayamvar ceremony, the abduction of Rukmini and the look in Satyabhama's eyes on the way to Prabhaskshetra ...

The pendulum of time swung back and forth as random thoughts flowed back and forth in his mind. The peepal tree, below which he lay, appeared like the mythical seven-headed serpent, Sheshnag, spreading its hood and sheltering Krishna. The three rivers—Hiranya, Kapila and Saraswati—flowed serenely from multiple directions and formed the sacred confluence near the temple at Somnath. The place, known as Prabhaskshetra, was famous for appreciation of art, literature and culture.

Krishna had completed the renovation of the Somnath temple recently, embellishing it with silver and gold.

Krishna, with eyes shut, reminisced every moment of his life with happiness and satisfaction. His body shook with waves of pain intermittently, as if a thousand scorpions were stinging him. The hunter Jara sat near him with folded hands; a small puddle of blood had formed on the ground where the arrow had pierced Krishna's foot. Reaching the confluence of the rivers from the jungles of Prabhaskshetra had felt like ages for Krishna.

Gandhari's curse ...

Durvasa's curse ...

How could they ever fail!

One by one, his brothers, uncles, sons, grandsons, nephews, friends and loved ones had perished in the flames of time, and he too was headed in the same direction. Despite being aware of the situation, Krishna watched everything dispassionately. Even now, the last screams of the Yadavs echoed in his mind. How could they kill each other so barbarously and push the Yadav race to the brink of extinction?

It was true that Krishna hadn't picked up weapons and killed anyone during the battle of Kurukshetra but the bloodshed and devastation he had witnessed continued to torture his mind.

Had Arjun spoken the truth? Was the kingdom won by killing one's own brothers, friends, uncles and other relatives really worth it? If it was so, why couldn't the Pandavs or any of the other victors sleep in peace after the war? Righteousness and good had won over evil in the battle of Kurukshetra, but had sin and immorality been truly vanquished?

Millions of such questions rose like waves in Krishna's mind. Why was he plagued by these unending questions? Why was his mind unable to calm down?

Yet another thought arose in Krishna's mind. Is this how the last moments of one's life are? Innumerable words, thousands of moments and countless emotions did not allow even for a moment's peace.

All he wanted to do was to contemplate and go into deep meditation. He desired to concentrate his soul on the universal One and facilitate his final journey, but every thought that arose distracted him and shook his very being. Even before one thought subsided, another one sprang up, creating chaos.

Why was this soul, which constantly focused only on purity, meditation and acceptance, so disturbed and distracted today? What was troubling him so much? He, who was revered as Ishwar or God and recognised as the supreme being or Poorna Purushottam, was struggling to achieve his own state of completeness.

How could Krishna save himself?

Even gods, born on this earth as incarnations in human form, become powerless in the face of their destiny. What could be said of ordinary human beings then?

The Yadav race had been wiped out just a while ago and the mangled bodies of his friends, brothers, sons and grandsons still lay scattered in the jungles of Prabhaskshetra. In the distance, the sun was getting ready to rise at the confluence of the Hiranya, Kapila and Saraswati. The sky was a deep red and the leaves of the peepal tree swayed in the sweet breeze that carried the message of Krishna's pain in all ten directions. The melting darkness and blazing red hues in the sky looked like flaming pyres. It seemed as though thousands of priests were chanting the Vedas and their chords echoed everywhere.

Mamaivamso jiva-loke jiva-bhutah sanatanah
Manah-sasthanindriyani prakrti-sthani karsati

The living entities in this conditioned world are my eternal, fragmental parts. Due to this conditioned life, they are struggling very hard with the six senses, which include the mind.

A life full of death or a death full of life—a dilemma that the common man could never fathom. Krishna too, waiting to dissolve into the absolute, was faced with the same tussle. During the great battle of Kurukshetra, he had revealed to the world his immortal self sans beginning or end. The same supreme being that had sent him to the world as a mortal was now beckoning him. Krishna was reminded of Draupadi's words:

Twadiyam vastu govindam tubhyamev samarpaye

Whatever I have belongs to you and I surrender all of it to you

Krishna lay with his eyes closed, reliving his life. He still couldn't fathom why Draupadi had said those words.

It was all of a sudden, while travelling from Dwarka to Hastinapur, that she had uttered them. She was choked with emotions but her voice was firm, and despite her dry eyes, Krishna could sense their moistness.

'You yourself had said, *sanshayatma vinashyati*—indecisiveness leads to destruction—didn't you?' she had asked.

'My dear Sakha, it is true that knowledge creates doubt, and my whole life has been full of questions, each one piercing me like an arrow. My questions impaled and hurt my loved ones ... my doubts and my indecisiveness led my soul towards destruction ... they traumatised my near and dear ones ... Please liberate me from indecision, questions, doubts and this anguish ...'

Like a high tide, a surge of thoughts crashed into Krishna's mind, foaming. But why were these memories tormenting him now, in these circumstances? Why was he reminded of his bondage in the countdown to his liberation?

When Draupadi came to him seeking liberation, was Krishna himself free?

There were so many questions to be answered ...

One by one, everyone who mattered would come seeking their rights ... each one just waiting to bind him and he would have to seek liberation from each one of them.

Had the process of emancipating everyone before he could liberate himself possibly begun?

'You will suffer a beastly death—lonely, helpless and aggrieved,' Mata Gandhari had cursed him after the battle of Kurukshetra. The heart-wrenching pain and anguish in her voice haunted him. Gandhari's cries had reminded him of his own mother Yashoda's wails when he was leaving Gokul. The pain of separating from one's children is felt the same way by mothers of every age and era.

Gandhari had said, 'I have lost ninety-nine sons. My feet are still stained with the blood from Duryodhan's bleeding thighs ... I am tired of washing my feet time and again ... Dushasan's severed hand still calls out to me in the middle of the night ... Krishna, you failed to do justice.'

Despite knowing everything, Kunti too chose to blame Krishna for the carnage. 'Krishna, my sons might have emerged victorious, but you have rendered so many mothers of Hastinapur childless and ruined so many families. How can I rejoice amidst so much grief? Krishna, you will never understand the agony of Gandhari bahen, because you yourself are not a mother ...'

It wasn't that Krishna couldn't understand Gandhari's grief, but all this was predestined; it had to happen. Having taken the trouble to come this far, how could Krishna leave without completing the task? He had always known that he would have to witness such devastating slaughter. Not only did he have to count the bloodstained and ravaged bodies of his kinsfolk, but he also had to face the situation with courage and equanimity.

abhyutthanam adharmasya tadatmanam srjamyaham

For the preservation of the good, I manifest myself.

How could this vow be rendered futile?

It is true that even God, born as a human being, has to follow the moral codes of the mortal world. He has to experience all the emotions born of love, attachment and relationships that bind him. The mind, concealed by the body, gets enslaved and, as a result, every human suffers its travails.

That is why Krishna was distraught on witnessing the misery his own siblings, friends, nephews, grandchildren and great grandchildren had inflicted on each other.

Draupadi's words still echoed in his mind ... '*twadiyam vastu govindam tubhyamev samarpaye*'.

'I cannot continue carrying the burden of this knowledge any longer ... Where am I going? I am not sure. I don't even know if I am even going anywhere; yet, I would like to return everything you have given me and become free of debt.'

What freedom or liberation was she referring to?

Both Krishna and Draupadi understood the meaning of the words bondage and liberation.

It was time. Though the exact moment was still unclear, it was certain and fast approaching. Draupadi and Krishna were preparing each other for that moment.

While he was the one who was bestowed with the prowess of understanding people and reading their thoughts, Krishna wondered whether Draupadi too could read his mind ...

'Was my relationship with Draupadi so deep that she could decipher even my innermost thoughts? Had she probably decided to free me before she liberated herself? Did she know that until she liberated me, she wouldn't be able to free her own mind that so intensely identifies with mine?' Krishna asked these questions of himself.

'While men are incapable of understanding the difference between the mind and the intellect, women understand the mind much better!' she had said.

He recalled Draupadi saying, 'Is there actually something called the mind, Sakha? Where in the body does it lie? Can you tell me what colour and shape it is? We don't know so many things about it; nevertheless, the mind rules over this huge body, the past, present and the future ... As women, we have a strange comradeship with our mind. Not only are we able to hide a lot of things in it, we also understand it better than men do. The mind controls the body as per its will. While women dance to its tunes, men are slaves to intellect, they measure and weigh everything by it and behave accordingly. A man's intellect and a woman's mind never think in the same direction, and that, my dear friend, is the root of all complications.'

Krishna had asked, 'But how do you segregate and manage the variety of thoughts that arise?'

'O Sakha! Doesn't a mother manage five sons who are all different? Each one's behaviour, thoughts, words, likes and dislikes, expectations of affection and expressions of love are different. Yet, doesn't she handle them? When we spin thread from cotton, sometimes, the threads do get entwined and tangled; similarly, our thoughts too can sometimes get tangled ...'

'I have always seen you behave with restraint and express yourself clearly. Of course, I wouldn't say you were always balanced, as I have seen you lose equanimity at times. Yet, your clarity constantly keeps your tone, behaviour and thoughts tied together. How are you able to achieve this, Sakhi?'

'Well, I don't know how, but you do exactly as you say; is it any surprise that I too behave in a similar manner?'

'Sakhi, sometimes I am bewildered by the way you became five different women while relating with your five husbands ...'

'All those five women have become one and are surrendering to you—the man who holds the most exalted and singular place in my mind. The one who is my friend, my brother, my companion ... and ...'

'And what else, Sakhi?'

She added hesitatingly, 'You are my all—my honour, my identity, my femininity ... I have truly run out of words, my dear ... I dedicate to this man, whom I hold in the highest esteem, everything that he has bestowed upon me and even all that he did not ...'

Draupadi's eyes seemed vacant and forlorn. Those flaming and ever-vibrant fiery orbs were unusually listless.

Was this the final moment of parting? Who was going away? And from whom ...?

Had Draupadi realised that her life purpose was over?

Krishna wondered, Is that why she had come to me? To seek liberation ... or to grant me mine? Is that why she had said: *Twadiyam vastu govindam tubhyamev samarpaye*'?

❖

When Draupadi and the five Pandav brothers came to Dwarka, little did they realise that it was the last time they were seeing Krishna there.

Just before leaving, Draupadi came to Krishna's chamber early in the morning. Even his wives and his brother Balaram hesitated to visit at this hour because this was his time for daily prayers and meditation. Krishna loved his solitude in the morning, but Draupadi couldn't help meeting him because what she had to say to him could be said only in utmost privacy. Draupadi feared that he would get busy later with his rajya sabha. She had to meet him first thing in the morning!

Krishna looked resplendent in his silk dhoti. His face was radiant with a sandalwood paste tilak on his forehead. Bare-chested, slender-waisted, broad-shouldered and devoid of any jewels except the sacred thread, his sinewy body looked arresting. His hair was freshly washed and combed back, with a few strands of grey peeping from behind his ears. His eyes were full of compassion and tenderness.

Draupadi wondered as she stood looking at him, 'Is this the human form of God?'

Krishna wasn't surprised to see Draupadi. Welcoming her with a sweet smile, he said, 'Yagyaseni! The arrival of the Goddess herself immediately after my pooja is an auspicious sign indeed!'

Draupadi softly said, 'Sakha ...'

She stayed silent for a long time. She had come fresh from her bath, water dripping down her wet hair, her face soft and aglow. Even though age had caught up with Draupadi, she was so beautiful, statuesque and slender still, that she could make a lot of young women envious. She wore a beige bodice and a saree to match. Yet her face gave away signs of having spent a sleepless night. She opened her mouth to say something several times, but hesitated. She didn't know where to begin. Sitting in awkward silence, she looked intermittently at Krishna and the sky visible through the window opposite her. She seemed to be struggling to gather her thoughts and feelings and kept playing with the end of her saree.

Krishna asked her gently, 'Do you want to say something? Is there a problem?'

'Yes, I want to tell you something, but I am not sure how.'

Krishna said, 'Just start speaking; everything will flow on its own.'

'I have never been at a loss for words with you, Krishna. You come to know of my thoughts and words even if I don't express them, but today ...'

'Come now ... tell me without hesitation. Don't be shy.'

'Oh, Sakha! Why would I feel shy? I hesitate because once I tell you, there will be nothing of mine left with me.'

'I am completely yours. I am always with you. So how will you lose anything by telling me?'

'That is all I came to tell you, Sakha ...' Draupadi said, looking into Krishna's eyes.

Krishna had perceived an unseen torrent in Draupadi's eyes, for the first time in the time that he had known her. Her eyes welled up and tears streamed down her cheeks, her voice choked as she quietly turned her face and walked away.

Her unsaid words seemed to echo in the room, long after she had left:

Twadiyam vastu govindam tubhyamev samarpaye

Not just Draupadi, everyone says, 'Accept whatever Govind gives you and offer it back to him; that is what life is all about. If you accept him wholeheartedly, how can he ever abandon you?'

Uddhav, Arjun, Balaram and everyone else was aware that non-acceptance was never a part of Krishna's character. He had never learnt to despise, disregard or abandon anyone. He had always said, 'Truth and untruth, evil and virtue—they are two sides of the same coin. If you accept one side, the other is naturally accepted. Sunset is inevitable once the sun rises. One is the harbinger of the other. Accepting every person, thing or idea wholeheartedly and absolutely is what makes our existence complete because it is only our acceptance that can lead us to completeness.'

That which is unpleasant and false becomes beautiful and true by Krishna's mere touch. The one who had lived his life experiencing joy in every moment and making it meaningful was now accepting and welcoming death with open arms. Though he had accepted death naturally and was peaceful, the pain in his heart was far more excruciating than the wound in his foot. Maybe that is why he was being reminded of Draupadi's words.

'Madhav, it is not in your nature to reject or abandon anything, and you have always unconditionally accepted me with all my happiness and sadness, my pride, anger and my hatred. I am certain about this because you are complete and there is no place for any inadequacies and misgivings. But Govind, I do feel like asking you this question. When you accepted me completely, hadn't you wished for your own acceptance? Didn't we accept you with all your happiness and sadness, deprivations and abundance, truths and untruths? I have lived my life taking everything you offered me. Today, I surrender everything to you ... and I believe with all my heart that you will not reject me either ...'

Krishna accepted all situations, pleasant and unpleasant, with equanimity and looked at questions and answers objectively. His give and take was fair. No one had ever embraced life with an intensity as fierce as Krishna's. His unconditional acceptance of everyone unshackled the chains that bound their hearts. His completeness was truly multifaceted. That is why he was bestowed with the title of Poorna Purushottam or the complete being. He had never looked at life with sorrow, seriousness or leniency. To him, it was a celebration with all its music, dance and love.

Life isn't just a source of entertainment, a procession or a carnival that can be merely witnessed by looking out of a window, or standing on the street side; it is a celebration one needs to participate in. The steps in the journey from Aham or I to Param or Absolute have to be taken by individuals themselves. The attitude of identifying the self and surrendering to it was Krishna's life ethic. If one is focused on the Atman—the inner self—life inevitably becomes a celebration. In the true sense, a life of karma yoga, detachment and stoicism is Krishna.

He belonged to everyone; he had accepted everyone.

But he was all alone today.

The wound in his foot throbbed excruciatingly.

He was in a state of complete acceptance, at peace with himself, as he approached his last moments.

Yet, Draupadi's words, rising and falling like waves inside him, created a whirlpool, leaving residues of moistness and salinity behind.

The moistness and the salinity—were they Draupadi's tears?

Were they the tears she had swallowed all her life, the tears she had brought along from the sacrificial fire she was born of?

They had been singeing and choking her right from the swayamvar, from when she was disrobed in the rajya sabha, since the battle of Kurukshetra, but they had never found their way out.

Today, those tears were struggling to flow; instead, all that came out was a stream of words.

'Govind, I surrender to you everything that you have blessed me with. Yet, I am unaware of the meaning of surrender even today. In all these years that I have spent with you, I have often wondered what I would be left with if I placed all my happiness and woes at your lotus feet. I feel the need to let go of all my positive and negative experiences for my own good ... but despite letting go, nothing ever leaves me. Every human being's fate and their circumstances in life are predetermined and hence our accepting them or otherwise cannot change our destiny in any way.'

When the buoyant and cheerful Yadavs left Dwarka on their golden chariots, little did they imagine that not one of them would return alive. Once they reached the shores of Dwarka, the Yadavs sailed towards Somnath. Blissfully unaware of their impending annihilation, they bathed in the sea before praying at the temple.

It was Krishna's desire that the Yadavs worship at the Somnath temple, before proceeding on their last journeys, and get liberated from the cycle of births and rebirths. Somnath was considered the most significant Shivling among the twelve holy Jyotirlings. According to legend, Chandradev had performed a penance there to free himself from the curse of Daksh Prajapati. Lord Shiv had revealed himself to Chandradev and freed him from the curse.

When Krishna reached Prabhaskshetra with his brother Balaram and the Yadavs, he knew that none of them would return to Dwarka. The Yadavs, after a dip in the sea and prayers at the Somnath temple, went to the jungles of Prabhaskshetra for celebrations. A serious argument broke out among them, and soon, the situation worsened. They came to blows. Since they weren't carrying any weapons, they began using sharp-tipped grass blades called erka, which grew there, as weapons. Most of the Yadavs died in the fight that ensued while all Krishna could do was sit and watch their doom with a heavy heart. A few Yadavs who were still alive started hitting each other with pots and pans ... It was a pathetic end to the Yadav race, a race which held pride of place in the annals of the history of Bharatvarsh.

Krishna, who despised weapons completely, was forced to take control of the situation, just to ensure that his kinsmen stopped fighting, and put an end to their misery and pain. He was deeply saddened to see the Yadavs spewing venom against each other and destroying their own brothers.

Krishna and Balaram tried their best to stop the Yadavs from self-destruction, but in vain! The erka grass, the very fate that the Yadavs had tried to run away from, became an instrument of their death.

The Yadav land had perished.

Durvasa's curse had come true.

It was now turn for Gandhari's curse.

Krishna walked determinedly but with a laden heart towards the forest along the river Hiranya and sat under a peepal tree.

The Hiranya glistened like silver in the distance. There wasn't a soul for miles. The sun was about to rise. The confluence of the three rivers was where his elder brother had breathed his last.

Balaram had sought farewell from Krishna soon after the Yadavsthali episode. With a stricken heart, Krishna had consented that his brother take the path of nirvana. Balaram sat there in meditation near the confluence of the three rivers. Later, a cowherd was heard telling his friend, 'A man transformed into a seven-hooded serpent and disappeared into the river ...' It was Sheshnag, having done his duty on earth, going back to his lord.

Before Krishna made his way to the bare and unadorned forests of Prabhaskshetra, he had ensured that all his kinsmen were given an appropriate funeral. His head was devoid of the peacock-feather crown and his neck was without his vaijayanti flower garland. His handsome and captivating face was as before but his eyes reflected the immense pain he was going through. They were moist in expectation of the impending moment. He sat motionless under the tree with his left foot crossed over his right knee and went into a state of meditation. Though his eyes were open, they were unmoving, like stones. Those twinkling, mischievous and smiling eyes had now transcended far into infinity, crossing the endless skies.

In a fit of rage, Rishi Durvasa had cursed the Yadavs. Now the curse was coming true, and it seemed to be boasting of its victory to the rising sun. While the Yadav race had met its end at Yadavsthali, their crown jewel, Krishna, lay waiting for his last breath. There was an unexpressed pain in his heart. The rising sun looked lacklustre and seemed tormented by the fact that the lord, born in human avatar, was bidding his farewell to earth. In the meanwhile, a hunter named Jara had reached the bank of the river on the other side in search of prey. In the darkness, the way Krishna was seated, it appeared to him as though a deer was sitting there.

'You will suffer a beastly death—lonely, helpless and aggrieved, the same way my sons died. You too will be a witness to the collapse of your race—your sons, grandsons, friends and family members will all die a miserable death!' Gandhari's anguished voice had seemed to echo all over the palace in Hastinapur and reverberate across the universe.

'You will suffer a beastly death—lonely, helpless and aggrieved …'

Gandhari had repeated her curse several times and had articulated her words in such a way that they seemed to have got etched on the walls of the palace forever. Yet Krishna had greeted her with folded hands, accepting her curse with humility. Who other than Gandhari had the power to curse Krishna.

Gandhari, who had spent all her life with her eyes covered, was blinded by love for her sons. Though her sacrifice for her blind husband had given her the exalted status of a sati, she never found any solace in the greatness thrust upon her. She, who was incapable of seeing the flaws in her sons, had declared Krishna guilty of being responsible for the destruction of her family. As an aggrieved mother, she had inadvertently wished for Krishna's liberation through her curse.

Krishna himself had never desired war or destruction. He had always preached acceptance and reconciliation. Enlightenment or samadhi was the pinnacle of complete acceptance. He had spent every moment of his life in a state of samadhi and that is why he was called Yogeshwar and Sthitapragya, one untouched by external circumstances. Despite this, it appeared as if he was destined to bear witness to terrible devastation and carnage.

Was this necessary for the destruction of evil or was Krishna himself in search of a reason to abandon his mortal form?

Something had to be done to deliver him of the burden in the aftermath of such carnage.

Maybe that is why he had himself created the situation for Gandhari's curse.

After listening to Gandhari, he had stood with folded hands and said, '*Tathastu* ... so be it.'

Who else but Krishna could accept his own death so willingly and placidly.

It seemed as if death had finally arrived! It was Krishna's wish that when he left his body, the Yadavs too should leave the earth. It would be best if the Yadavs didn't have to witness the immorality and impropriety of Kaliyug, and Durvasa's curse on the Yadavs was the first step in that direction.

Sage Durvasa used to perform penance at the Pindara shrine, near Dwarka. The Yadavs were infamous for their debauched and frenzied behaviour, drunk on youth and power. They lost good sense and sobriety under the intoxicating influence of wine, women, wealth, and gambling, and indulged in all kinds of sins.

Samba was Krishna and Jambavati's son and known to be naughty and frivolous. One day, Samba and some of his Yadav friends decided to test the powers of the sage. Samba was dressed up as a pregnant woman. They went to the sage and without so much as a greeting, laughed aloud and said, 'This is Babhru Yadav's wife and she is pregnant. She wishes to have a son. Will her wish come true?' The sage saw through the prank and, riled by the audacity of the Yadavs, cursed them, 'Whatever Samba gives birth to will end not just his existence but the entire Yadav race.'

The Yadavs were so petrified that they chose not to tell Krishna about what had transpired. Samba gave birth to a pestle. In order to destroy the evidence, the Yadavs ground it into a fine powder and scattered it over the sea. The powder washed upon the shore at Prabhaskshetra and grew as the erka grass. With time, it turned into sharp, strong and ramrod-straight blades. Weapons were being readied for the Yadavs.

The Yadavs continued to live their lives drunk on power, blissfully unaware of what was happening far away from Dwarka.

A small piece of that pestle which had remained uncrushed was swallowed up by a fish that got trapped in a fisherman's net. The fisherman gave the metal piece to a hunter named Jara.

Jara fixed the same piece to his arrow.

Who but Krishna would know that the same arrow was set to become the reason for the end of his life on earth.

Jara aimed that arrow at a deer.

A sharp whizz pierced through the air. The toe which had been bathed by Uddhav's tears, caressed by Rukmini's hair and anointed daily with sandalwood paste, was now bathed in blood. It seemed as if a spark of fire had entered Krishna's body through the toe and left it at lightning speed through the sole.

Jara's arrow hit Krishna like a deadly weapon.

Gandhari's and sage Durvasa's curses had come true and led Krishna towards his last moments.

Elated at having hit a deer, Jara emerged out of the chest-deep waters and waded towards the bank of the river. Instead of a wounded deer, he was astounded to see the lord himself.

Jara was terrified. All the poor hunter desired was prey, but there lay in front of him the life-giver himself, wounded by his arrow. He hurried and tried to pull the arrow out of Krishna's toe.

'Let it be, my friend,' said a feeble voice. The same voice which had echoed loud and clear on the battlefield of Kurukshetra.

'Niyatam kuru karm tvam karm jyayohya karmanah
Shareera yatrapi cha te n prasiddhayed karmanah'

'Performing your prescribed duty for action is better than inaction. A man cannot even maintain his physical body without work.'

The hunter, Jara, had performed his prescribed karma. He could perceive a great pain and a deep silence setting in, in that voice.

A hint of grey near the ears, exhausted eyes, his head devoid of his crown and peacock feathers—despite all this, Krishna's dark and handsome face was still alluring and radiated immense compassion.

Blood began trickling from the wounded toe and the pain worsened. Krishna's body readied itself to renounce life. The supreme being was preparing to merge with the divine. Just then, Draupadi's words began to echo in Krishna's ears:

Twadiyam vastu govindam tubhyamev samarpaye

Why? Why were these words repeatedly echoing in Krishna's mind? What bonds were shackling his body and refusing to let go of his mind? When his soul was fluttering its wings to take flight and soar freely, was this voice reminding Krishna of his earthly duties?

And what were those duties?

Krishna's reverie was broken by Jara's sobs.

The dark-skinned Jara, attired in a loincloth and feathered headgear, sat with folded hands, pleading tearfully to his lord.

Jara begged Krishna for forgiveness. After a long time, a smile broke out on Krishna's face, as if he had just emerged from a sea of pain—soaked, and yet, charming, handsome and marvellous.

Krishna asked Jara, 'Who are you, my friend?'

Jara replied trembling, 'J ... J ... Jara ...'

Krishna continued with a smile on his face, 'Jara, I have been waiting for you. What took you so long?'

Jara mumbled, confused, with folded hands, 'My lord, this arrow ...'

Krishna said, 'I know it is yours. I recognise this piece of the pestle. I have been remembering sage Durvasa and Ma Gandhari since morning ...'

Jara stared blankly.

'You are the harbinger of my liberation!'

'Please forgive me, my lord,' Jara's eyes welled up with tears.

Krishna said, 'You have nothing to fear. You will go to heaven. You have liberated God from the prison of the human form. It is I who should be indebted to you.'

Krishna folded his hands and shut his eyes. His face glowed with a mix of relief and pain. Jara sat mesmerised, staring at Krishna's beatific face, his all-forgiving, half-shut lotus eyes and his bleeding toe. Krishna's smile continued to play on his lips, despite the intense pain. Jara, blissfully unaware that he had found a place for himself in heaven for having wounded Krishna with his arrow, just sat watching the lord's final spectacle with folded hands.

Krishna, the one who could alleviate all suffering, was himself in terrible agony. As he prepared to relinquish his human form, all the events of his life flashed before his eyes.

After the annihilation of the Yadavs, Krishna had requested his charioteer, Daruk, to leave. Daruk wasn't ready to leave Krishna's side even for a moment. He stood stunned, watching all the divine weapons that had won Krishna his numerous battles—the Sudarshan Chakra, the Kaumudi mace, the Sharang arrow, two quivers, his Panchajanya conch, the Nandak sword and his chariot—as they circumambulated Krishna before disappearing towards the sun. Daruk's eyes filled with sorrow as he took leave of his lord. He wondered how many more moments were left before the anchor of his life, his lord ... He knew the answer and so did Krishna.

Krishna knew that he would be gone before Arjun arrived. Arjun would be left with the challenging task of narrating everything to Ugrasen, Devaki and Vasudev. Each one of them would bear the pain of his loss in their own way.

The lord himself could now feel the anguish that human beings felt at the loss of their loved ones.

Krishna requested Daruk to escort Arjun to the confluence of the rivers. Perhaps, he desired for his mortal remains to be cremated appropriately.

Krishna was saddened at the prospect of relinquishing his human body. His attachment and the bonds of love that had developed over a lifetime were tugging at him him, not allowing him to let go.

He sat under the aswattha tree with Draupadi's words resonating in his mind.

Were feelings of incompleteness and imperfectness plaguing the supreme being himself?

Perhaps Krishna desired that his soul merge with the divine at the same place where his brother had breathed his last. Despite the excruciating pain, he stood up and started walking towards the Triveni Sangam.

It seemed as if his brother Balaram was calling out to him, 'Come, Kanhaiya, it is time to depart. How long will you sleep? I have been calling you for such a long time. Get up, Kanhaiya, and come with me ...'

Krishna gathered all his strength and began walking towards the confluence of the holy rivers. His toe continued to bleed, and the pain felt like the sting of a thousand scorpions. Yet his gait was steady.

Jara walked slowly behind Krishna, not wanting to let go. Krishna paused and turned around. He said, with a charming smile, 'Mitr, please stop. Why are you wasting your time following me?'

Jara's eyes were full of tears. 'You are all alone ...'

Krishna laughed even in those grim circumstances, 'Oh mitr, this is the final journey; where is the question of anyone's company? This journey has to be completed alone ... I am eternally grateful to you ...'

Jara stood there nonplussed.

Krishna resumed his walk. His face contorted in pain with every step but his pace was steady and determined.

Slowly, Krishna reached the confluence.

He lay down under the wide canopy of a peepal tree. The confluence of the three gurgling rivers was right in front of him. He could see the brown Hiranya, the green Kapila and the clear waters of the Saraswati as they merged and drifted towards the sea. In any case, the sea was the final destination for all rivers. Just the way the soul gravitates towards the universal being and merges with the divine cosmos to become one with it, a river merges with the sea and becomes the sea.

Krishna closed his eyes.

The chants of *Aham Brahmasmi*—I am Brahman—echoed all around.

Lying under the tree, Krishna was experiencing an amazing mental state. This was a wholehearted acceptance, not negation, but pure existence.

Jara pleaded once again. 'My lord, your toe is bleeding profusely. Please allow me to apply some medicine and bandage it, you will feel better ...'

Krishna smiled, 'Don't worry. Everything is going to become all right for everyone.' The shanti mantra being chanted at his guru Sandipani's ashram reverberated in Krishna's mind—

antarikshah shantihi ... vanaspatayah shantihi
Prithvi shantihi ... deva shantihi

May harmony rule over the earth and the Supreme being.
May harmony rule all over this world, in water and on
all herbs, trees and creepers.

Serenity pervaded all over ... inside and outside ... it was time for his mind and body to be at peace.

The lilting melody of the flute began to echo in Krishna's ears, the gurgling waters transformed into the Yamuna, the branches of the kadamba tree drooped over him, and the sweet breeze from the trees on the banks of the Yamuna wafted all around. Thousands of peacock feathers fell on Krishna and straggled all around him.

The narrow bylanes of Gokul and cows with their tinkling bells appeared in front of Krishna's half-shut eyes. It seemed as if every lane, every street was appealing to him with open arms—come Krishna, come ...

Krishna's mind suddenly reverberated with the chirping of birds at dawn, the sounds of cows from every household and the melodies of daybreak being sung by the women of Gokul!

He could clearly hear his mother singing her morning bhajans. He desperately wanted to open his eyes, but for some reason he couldn't. It felt as if a heavy weight had been placed on his eyelids; they just refused to open.

Draupadi's face, riding on the waves of the Hiranya river, was saying, 'Sakha, I accepted wholeheartedly the sorrows, happiness, respect, disgrace and this life that you bestowed upon me, and now, I dedicate everything back to you.'

Krishna had immense respect for Draupadi's will to battle through all her torment, her struggles, her repeated defeats and her ability to bounce back and fight back each time. Draupadi's self-respect defined her personality, her identity. Krishna knew what a woman of her stature could offer when she surrendered her all.

For the first time a thought crossed his mind, 'Will I be able to accept everything this woman has dedicated to me? Am I even worthy of such an enormous offering? When a person dedicates her identity and her rights to you, what can you offer to her in return? When I am myself readying to go, where is the time left for acceptance and surrender? Despite that, the burden of her surrender weighs heavily on my heart. 'Sakhi, why do you bind me with this great responsibility in my last moments?' The moment he asked the question, her flaming eyes brimmed with tears that spilled over like a stream.

'Have I faltered in my role as your wife?' A gentle face gazed at Krishna. He was at a loss for words as he watched the gushing waters of the Kapila vanish into the sea. He could see Rukmini's tearful face floating over the waters of the Kapila. Despite the passage of time, the same question tormented Krishna to this day. 'Why? Aryaputra, why did you carry this burden all alone for all these years? You did not allow me to accompany you, but the least you could have done was to stay for me ... just for a few moments ...' Rukmini's eyes reflected her pain more than her reproach. 'I would have never, even for a moment, stopped you ... I would have cleared your path of thorns and laid it with flowers. I would have dispelled all darkness and brightened it like a flame. Why did you undertake this arduous journey all alone? Didn't I deserve it, being your wife?' Never before had Krishna seen such hollow eyes. He was shaken by their desolation.

'Prabhu, I have always walked hand in hand with you through all worldly affairs, whether dharma, artha or kama—in duty, prosperity or desire. But now, when it's time for liberation, why have you chosen to travel alone?' Rukmini repeated her question but Krishna remained speechless. His heart felt burdened. These were the women who had given him their everything—their identity, essence and their individuality. All of them had lived their lives dissolved in him. But why were their eyes so vacant, so forlorn today? Hadn't he lived up to their expectations? Krishna was deeply saddened by the thought.

'Whenever you feel sad, lonely or confused, remember me. Close your eyes and take a deep breath—you will feel my presence beside you. Though I have never left your side even for a moment, it is you who leaves me alone time and again ... but Kanha, remember ... in your moments of solitude, in times of isolation and confusion, there is only one name that you will recall, and that will be mine. Even if you choose to leave me behind, I am always with you. It is not possible for you to detach yourself from me. I dwell in you, Kanha. Just breathe deeply and call out my name, and I will appear beside you ...'

Two pained, longing, devoted eyes floated on the clear waters of the Saraswati. 'Will you still ignore me and embark on your journey all alone? Please let me accompany you. Your existence is incomplete without me. I am your shadow—how can you go without your shadow, Krishna?'

Krishna's mind was now meandering along the lanes of Gokul. Hordes of gopikas were leaving for Mathura to sell butter. They would greet Ma Yashoda on the way. The sweet tinkling of his mother's bangles as she churned butter echoed in Krishna's ears.

His mother would wake up at the crack of dawn, feed the cows, milk them and then sit down to churn butter. The constant sound of the churning reverberated through the house. The cows, tied in the courtyard, were busy fondling their calves. The smell of dripping, frothing, fresh milk and the strings of bells tied to the necks of the pots of curd created an intoxicating melody.

A voice called out to Krishna over the tinkling bells of his mother's churning pot.

'Kanha ... o Kanha! Kanha ... aa ... aa ... o Kanha ...!'

The three merging rivers seemed to be churning his memories as they flowed together.

Sakhi, wife and lover ... all three had melded into a seamless womanhood. By becoming one with Krishna, the complete one, they too had become embodiments of completeness. Just like the three rivers that were eventually merging with the sea.

Despite its vastness, all that the magnificent sea manages to bequeath the rivers that merge into it is its salinity. Had Krishna done the same with the three women who had come to him expecting greatness?

God, in his human incarnation, develops relationships owing to his birth. Man has no liberty in choosing his parents or siblings. But there are three women that a man chooses to be with—his wife, his lover and his friend. He chooses them, nurtures them, creates them or destroys them. Could Krishna offer anything at all to these three women who came into his life?

Their faces flashed in front of Krishna's eyes yet again.

Radha had said while he was leaving Gokul, 'Don't make false promises, Kanha. I won't leave Gokul, and you are not going to return to Gokul ever. The waters of the Yamuna, the branches of the kadamba and these lanes of Gokul will never forget you, and I will ensure that I never think about you.'

Krishna had replied, 'Radhike! One remembers someone who has been forgotten ... It is impossible for you to forget me, and if I ever forget you, I will cease to breathe ...'

Draupadi had once asked him very casually, 'I get thrilled at the very thought of asking you if you ever loved me. What would have been your response had I asked what my place in your life was, whether you ever desired me, even for a moment?'

She continued, not waiting for Krishna's answer, 'Sakha, don't say anything. I haven't asked yet because I am afraid that once I hear your answer, I will not be myself any more.'

Krishna said, 'Ask only if you expect an answer. I will have to reconsider calling you my Sakhi if you need to look for answers outside when you know them already. There are bound to be numerous questions, but all the answers exist within your mind. It hardly matters whether you ask me or your own self. We are not separate, are we, Sakhi?'

Rukmini, after having waited for several nights on end, had asked her husband in one of those rare happy moments, 'Have I married the king of Dwarka or the lover whom I wed simply on the basis of faith and the promise of a spontaneous life? You seem to constantly worry about others and never once about your better half! You have never asked me about my aspirations or my desires.'

Krishna had replied with a smile, 'Whenever I think about one half, won't I be thinking of the other too, my dear? You are seated on the throne of Dwarka and the crown that sits on your head has innumerable thorns; they prick only the person wearing it. To the viewer, it is a beautiful, golden crown, nothing more.'

Rukmini stared at Krishna in awe.

'Only the head that bears the weight of the golden crown deserves the exalted status, Rukmini. Buried under the foundation of the throne are sacrifices of personal desires. It is because of the sacrifices that the throne remains unshakeable.'

So saying, Krishna had pulled Rukmini into a tight embrace. Rukmini had fallen in love with Krishna all over again.

Krishna's mother had pleaded with him when he was leaving Gokul, 'Please don't go! I haven't even finished cuddling and loving you ... you have barely left my lap, Kanhaiya, and you say you are going to fight, against that evil Kansa—why Kanhaiya? Think about your mother. When I grow old and my eyes become weak, who will guide me? Who will take me to the Yamuna? Who will light my funeral pyre, Kanhaiya? Don't go ...'

In response, Krishna had simply hugged his mother tight and remained silent.

Yashoda stopped crying and her sobs subsided after a while. It seemed as if Krishna's hands, stroking his mother's back, were saying, 'I am nobody's son, lover or husband ... I have come to complete my mission and that is my only goal ...'

Yashoda's eyes flitted in front of Krishna and disappeared. Myriad images flashed before his eyes ... Yashoda berating him for stealing butter, then affectionately serving it to him, Yashoda weeping on the shores of the Kalindi and ... Devaki's eyes yearning for Krishna. All these memories merged into one another and glistened as tears in Krishna's eyes.

He remembered his father Vasudev's dejected eyes as he bid him farewell on the banks of the Yamuna before returning to Mathura.

And now, many pairs of eyes stared fixedly at Krishna—those of Sudama, Rukmini, Subhadra, Draupadi and Karna. Bheeshma's eyes, as he lay on his bed of arrows, and Duryodhan's defeated gaze, in his last moments—all of them were boring intently into his eyes.

Ma Gandhari's eyes that very few had ever seen reminded him of the curse. Uddhav's tearful eyes moistened Krishna's even today.

All of them began to haunt Krishna. He lay there, trying to assimilate all these moments from his past, and waited to merge with the setting sun. It was as if a child locked up in prison was struggling for freedom.

Krishna closed his eyes. The memory of the fateful evening he had spent with Uddhav in Rukmini's palace still scourged Krishna's heart. Krishna had made up his mind, but he had waited for the right moment to arrive. The site for departure had been decided; all that was left to be decided was the time.

Finally, it was time.

Krishna stood in his verandah watching the setting sun spread its saffron hues across the sky. Krishna, in that moment, decided that it was time for Durvasa's prophecy to come true. Just as the sun rises and sets at the assigned time, it is only appropriate that the human body too depart at its destined time.

kalo 'smi loka-ksaya-krt pravrddho
lokan samahartum iha pravrttah

rte 'pi tvam na bhavisyanti sarve
ye 'vasthitah pratyanikesu yodhah

Time I am, destroyer of the worlds, and I have come to
engage all people. With the exception of you (Pandavs),
all the soldiers on both sides will be slain.

It was only a day ago that a messenger of the gods had
come to Krishna in disguise, carrying a missive from the
Vasus, Aadis, Ashwini Kumars, Marut, Rudra and other
deities. 'Oh Almighty, you have fulfilled your duties on
earth, but if you still enjoy being there, you may stay on.
I am but a slave and have come to remind you of time.'
Krishna had replied, 'The earth will not be unburdened
till the Yadavs are demolished.'

Yada yada hi dharmasya, glanir bhavati bharata
Abhyutthanam adharmasya, tadatmanam srjamyaham

Whenever and wherever there is a decline in religious
practice, o descendant of Bharat, and a predominant
rise of irreligion, at that time I manifest myself.

'This pledge of mine remains unfulfilled. I cannot
leave this universe till I have reinstated every piece of
my creation to its rightful place. Only after I free this
earth from death, decadence, suffering and diseases, and
return this planet designed by Vishwakarma back into
the ocean, will I depart for my abode.'

The messenger dutifully left for heaven with Krishna's message.

One night, the sea was stormy, its waves crashing loudly on the shores, spreading white froth far and wide. It was unusually dark and it seemed as if the sea, carrying the future in its womb, swept over Dwarka anxiously. Krishna sat all alone by a window of his queen's palace.

It wasn't rare for Krishna to sit alone and ruminate for hours on end. Rukmini was used to seeing Krishna sit meditatively for long periods ever since they had married. There wasn't much difference between loneliness and solitude for Rukmini. It seemed that the queen of Dwarka was destined to wait for Krishna.

Rukmini was wise and erudite, having studied politics and the scriptures keenly. The king of Kundinapur had not discriminated between his son Rukmi and daughter Rukmini in any manner, and both siblings were well-versed in the art of politics and the use of arms. It would frequently occur to Rukmini that it would have been better if she too were an ordinary woman and not a scholar. Krishna rarely had a chance to spend time with her, and even in those rare moments when he did visit her, he would discuss matters of the court and politics with her. Rukmini had often complained to him: 'I am seeing you after two long weeks. I don't want to waste these moments discussing Dwarka, its politics, Duryodhan or

Hastinapur.' She would sometimes tell Krishna candidly, 'My lord, I am your wife, not your minister. Just love me!'

It was just a day ago that Rukmini had spent the whole night awake, on the terrace of her palace. For the past several years, every balcony, every window and every single door and sentry bore testimony to her eternal wait. They were no longer surprised to see the palace lamps burning all night.

Everyone was aware of her abiding wait and dejection. All the lanes, every citizen and mansion and deities of each and every temple in Dwarka knew of the sleepless nights she had spent. When she had left the green and verdant Kundinapur, set on a triangular piece of land between the Veena and the Bhadra rivers, and come to Dwarka for the first time, she was not Krishna's consort but his sixteen-year-old fiancée. Blinded with love for Krishna and mesmerised by his magnetism, his voice, eyes and laughter captivating.

When Krishna had stretched out his hands towards her on the ghats of Kundinapur, Rukmini had closed her eyes for a moment, silently prayed to her God, and gave her hand to him.

Krishna had gently picked her up in his arms, like a flower, and raced away with her in his chariot at lightning speed.

That was her moment of union and surrender. Krishna had transformed into her husband, her God from that moment on. Her brother Rukmi had chased them from Vidarbha, vowing to separate her from Krishna. He had attacked furiously but was defeated. The fierce, broad-chested warrior, with his leonine waist, who fought back the colossal Vidarbha army and defeated her brave brother Rukmi, was now her husband. The very thought filled Rukmini with delight and pride.

She had alighted on the shores of Dwarka with Krishna. Rukmini had heard a lot about the golden city and was enchanted by its beauty. The white sands sparkled like a vast carpet of silver. She picked up a fistful of sand and watched it slip away from between her fingers, forming irregular figures in the air. Krishna turned back to look at her and broke into a captivating smile. She didn't realise then that what had slipped away from her hands was not sand but time.

She couldn't even recollect the number of years that had flown by since Govind had married her formally and brought her to this palace. There was no difference between her first night at the palace and today. That night, Krishna hadn't even entered her chamber, and though he was with her tonight, he was far away, lost in his own thoughts.

She could still vividly recall her first night at this magnificent palace. It was a night meant for festivities, celebrations, dreams and desires. The room filled with the intoxicating fragrance of perfume, the floor adorned with floral designs, the silken sheets on the flower-bedecked bed and columns of flower garlands ... she could still clearly visualise everything.

That was the night she had waited for all her life. The cool breeze wafting from the sea rattled every window and with every knock, it seemed to announce the arrival of Govind. The chimes of the bells attached to the silk curtains reminded her of the melodies of Krishna's flute.

Yet, Rukmini's wait had not ended—her beloved, adorned in his peacock-feather crown and vaijayanti garland hadn't come.

Some boats were stuck on the shores of Dwarka and Krishna had to be there, leaving her stranded in a vast sea of solitude. This was her wedding night, and despite years of devotion, she had not attained him.

Her lord, her beloved, her husband was not hers alone. He and his time belonged to everyone. He first belonged to others, and only what remained belonged to her.

Govind was her husband, and she, the queen of Dwarka. But this wasn't what she had ever asked for. She was neither his first, nor would she be the last! She loved him, pined for him and had surrendered to him, but she wasn't the only one. There was Gokul, Dwarka, Hastinapur, the Yadavs, Ma Kunti, the Pandavs, his brother Balaram, his mother Devaki, sister Subhadra, Uddhav, Akrur, Vidur, Narad ... and ... and ...

Her heart skipped a beat and with great struggle, came the name—Radha. How many names could Rukmini recall? Each one of them was immersed in Krishna and possessed by him. And he too was ready to give his life for each one of them without a moment's hesitation. Just as she had written to Krishna, asking him to save her from marrying Shishupal, others too sought him in their times of distress, and Krishna had obliged, just the way he had obliged her.

Rukmini lamented, 'When did you ever have time for me, my feelings, aspirations and dreams?'

Even today, it is Radha-Krishna that people chant, not Rukmini-Krishna. 'Why?' Rukmini would wonder. 'Wasn't she his wife, the queen of Dwarka? He had wed her and yet ...'

An event from a few years ago flashed in Rukmini's memory. Krishna had promised her that he would celebrate his birthday, Janmashtami, with her in the palace. He had returned to her that evening after day-long celebrations. Rukmini had gifted him a gold flute with diamonds and pearls set in it and sapphire peacocks and parrots carved into it. Two beautiful silk thread tassels dangled at one end of the flute. Krishna gazed fixedly at Rukmini for a few moments, kept the flute aside, picked up the gift-wrapped Panchajanya conch and blew it in the most sorrowful tone.

Later, Rukmini would jam her ears at the mere memory of that anguished sound. She could still recall the tears in Govind's eyes when he blew the conch.

Lying under the peepal tree, Krishna recalled the turmoil in his heart while blowing the Panchajanya conch. The pain of betrayal and the disaffection in Rukmini's fierce eyes haunted him. He wondered how he would explain to his beloved wife the pain he felt on seeing the flute. The pain was real but had nothing to do with memories of Radha. It was the anxiety of the impending battle.

On the eighth day of the waning moon in the month of Shravan, the ghastly events of the full moon day of Kartik echoed in Krishna's mind. He could hear the frightful sounds of the bloodbath, the loud trumpets of elephants and the neighing of innumerable horses ... And his dear, innocent wife was presenting him with a flute ... she was gifting him the melody of life. That divine music was a recollection of his pure and blissful childhood. The flute was reminiscent not only of Radha but also Ma Yashoda, Nand baba, brother Balaram and his cowherd friends. It brought with it the banks of the Yamuna, its dense trees and their vast shade. It contained mischief; it carried happiness and celebration. It was a celebration, a festival when he had blown the Panchajanya conch. The bugle of death was going to echo in all directions, countless sleepless nights were going to be haunted by the heart-wrenching screams of the dying ... Innumerable widowed women and orphaned children ...

He would stand witness to all this, a mute witness! That was his karma, his irrefutable destiny. And at a time like this, his wife was gifting him a golden flute!

Rukmini's dejection, her hurt eyes, haunted Krishna to this day. His eyes welled up with tears.

The reminiscence of this incident filled Rukmini with pangs of jealousy.

'I am the Goddess of fortune for the Yadavs, their empress, their queen, but not his Kanupriya—his beloved—only Radha can be that! I am not his friend either; that privilege is Draupadi's alone! I am not Satyabhama, who can sulk and throw tantrums and compel Krishna to beg, plead and cajole. I am not even Kubja or Trivikra, who blossomed into beautiful women merely at Krishna's touch! I am neither like Charuhasini, Shaibya or Jambavant's daughter, Jambavati, who are ready to give up their lives for Krishna.

'Then, who am I? What is my place in Krishna's life?

'Krishna is God ... the lord who gave Arjun the knowledge of the Gita, the lord who revealed his supreme form of Vishwaroop, the one who showed his mother the entire cosmos in his little mouth, the one who lifted the Govardhan hill on his little finger, and the charioteer during the Kurukshetra war! I am but an ordinary woman. I just wished for "my" Govind to be my husband. A husband who would love me, be angry with me, chide me, fight with me and plead with me; who would return home at dusk, take me in his arms at night ... someone I would wake up with every morning after nights of ecstasy. This wasn't too much to ask for, was it?'

Rukmini's eyes fell on Krishna who stood lost in deep thought. Today, even she was lost in contemplation.

In the wedding vows, the wife is described as the *sahadharmacharini*, an equal partner for life. What a deceitful description that was! Sahadharmacharini means someone who walks the path of dharma, righteousness and duty.

And what was dharma? Was it waiting for Krishna endlessly? Or waiting for him to invite her to join him on his journey?

Krishna stood all alone, watching the sunset from his queen's palace.

'What would he be thinking?' she mused.

Ever since Krishna had returned home from the Kurukshetra war, he watched the sun set every day. Rukmini had started getting used to his silence and self-isolation. But today was different—his silence was troubling Rukmini. Portends of inauspicious events rose like waves and crashed in Krishna's eyes. When Rukmini couldn't take it any more, she sent her maid to call Uddhav.

Despite the late hour, Uddhav arrived without a moment's delay. Both Rukmini and Uddhav sat watching Krishna's still form melt into the darkness. Just by looking at Krishna's back, Uddhav had a strange premonition of forthcoming events. His heart skipped a beat. He felt this was the last time he would see his friend, his lord and life-giver. Uddhav never disturbed Krishna during his time alone, but today, he rushed to the window. He fell at his lord's feet, his eyes brimming with tears.

'My lord, what do you have in mind? Why do you torment me so?'

A salty gust of wind blew away Krishna's shawl, and it landed smoothly on Uddhav's head. Gently pulling back his shawl, Krishna held Uddhav by his shoulders and drew him into a tight embrace. Uddhav broke down and sobbed uncontrollably. It seemed as if he was living some forthcoming moment right then.

'My lord, what is happening and why?' Uddhav asked, his voice choked. Krishna stroked his head without replying. Uddhav felt as if the cool breeze from the Himalayas had enveloped him. When he looked into Krishna's eyes, they seemed a little moist.

'What?' Krishna asked with a gentle smile. Uddhav stared at Krishna imploringly, with hundreds of questions rising in his mind. Was the thought that had crossed his mind just an aberration or a premonition? Uddhav struggled to fight back tears and simply stared at Krishna.

Holding Uddhav's hand, Krishna closed his eyes for a moment and pursed his lips, as if he were making a decision. Suddenly, a deep, grave voice seemed to emanate from the depths of the Himalayas and echo from the pillars in Rukmini's palace:

'There is no more time left; you must leave for Badrikashram immediately. The annihilation of the Yadavs is certain! It is my wish that once the high waves of the ocean swallow the kalash on the highest domes of the Dwarka palace, you attain peace in the lap of the Himalayas.'

What was his loving friend, his companion and lord saying? What would happen after Krishna? Why should he go to Badrikashram or the Himalayas? This world would be worse than hell for Uddhav without Krishna.

Unable to speak, he prostrated himself at Krishna's feet.

Rukmini stood a little distance away, watching the scene. Krishna's eyes glimmered even in the dim light. For a moment, she felt like running to Krishna and embracing him. She would have to stay awake the whole night awake till she found out the cause of Krishna's anguish.

Rukmini had spent countless years, days and nights absorbed in Krishna. She was familiar with his every nerve and cell, his likes and dislikes, ups and downs, and considered his worries and dreams her own. But, today, he felt like a total stranger.

Rukmini's heart started thumping. What was it that her husband couldn't share with her but found Uddhav worthy of? For a woman who had no great objection to sharing Krishna with 15999 co-wives, Rukmini, for the first time, felt her power over Krishna weakening.

Uddhav found his voice and said, 'No, my lord! I won't go anywhere, leaving you alone. I cannot, for a moment, live without you.'

'Uddhav, have you forgotten my words? Do I have to repeat what I told Arjun on the battlefield of Kurukshetra? Everyone who takes birth has to die.'

Uddhav interrupted angrily, 'Even I have taken birth, then why ...?'

Krishna just smiled. That one smile had answers to hundreds of Uddhav's questions. It embodied every word of the Gita that Arjun's charioteer had spelt out in Kurukshetra. 'Accept everything. The way you accept pleasure, accept sorrow too. Uddhav, if you have accepted birth, then it is your duty to accept death too. There is nothing that is possible without the consent of time, there is nothing beyond it. It is Mahakaal—it embraces one and all equally, and the same Mahakaal has opened its arms to welcome me. I have to go, Uddhav.'

'What about me, prabhu? When will Mahakaal accept me?'

'Time is under no one's control,' Krishna said compassionately, washing away Uddhav's despondence. 'A person who accepts happiness and sorrow with equanimity and doesn't begrudge anyone, receives all situations in his life as my blessing with reverence, is my true devotee.'

Uddhav's face brightened up with a smile like the sun peeping out of a monsoon cloud. He bent down on his knees with folded hands and moist eyes, accepting every word of what Krishna had said.

Rukmini stood watching the scene.

'What was it that Krishna was explaining to Uddhav?'

Uddhav got up gently, as if he were a body without a soul, and slowly walked out of Rukmini's room. Never before had he ever walked out of her room without greeting or wishing her. Rukmini stood in astonishment, watching Uddhav walk past her. There was an ethereal glow on his face. A smile was dancing on his lips and tears were streaming down his face.

Rukmini ran after Uddhav, but he had left the palace as if he were walking on air. It seemed as if the guards, the maids and everyone else didn't recognise Uddhav; his eyes seemed to be locked with the infinite in a trance, trying to prepare him for some impending journey.

Rukmini returned to find Krishna still watching the sea. It was almost dawn and the sea had turned calm. Gentle waves were soundlessly crashing on the shores. The early rays of the sun were visible on the eastern horizon, ready to announce the arrival of a new day. They were being reflected in Krishna's eyes. The exhaustion of a sleepless night mixed with tears gave his eyes a strange crimson hue. Rukmini stepped forward and stood next to him. A few moments passed in silence. Then she gently placed her hand on his shoulder. Krishna turned to look at her. It seemed as if the colour of his eyes, their moistness and the expression on his face were completely new to Rukmini. The person who looked at Rukmini was not her husband Vaasudev. This was not the cowherd who had abducted her in his chariot from Kundinapur. This was not the beloved with whom she had spent nights of ecstasy, neither was he the king of Dwarka. Who was he? Rukmini stared at him in bewilderment. She wondered whom this distraught, unfathomable and distressed face belonged to.

'What is it?' Krishna asked in a weak and sombre voice.

'It's you who has to tell me, prabhu.'

'Me? What am I to tell you?'

'Whatever you told Uddhav ... If it is something confidential and meant only for him, let it be,' she said.

'Do you really want to know?' A fleeting smile played on Krishna's lips and disappeared instantly.

'Why not? I am your wife, your *ardhangini*, not only in good times, but also in bad ...'

Krishna slid his hands up Rukmini's back to her shoulders and pulled her close. He leaned in and whispered, 'My dear, the time for such beautiful intimacy is coming to an end. Perhaps your touch and your companionship was meant to be with me only up till here ... Time beckons yet again ... I have to go now.'

Rukmini stared at him wide-eyed. His face beamed with the usual beatific and serene smile. She shook Krishna by his shoulders and asked, 'What do you mean? Are your duties as a human avatar over?'

'Devi, everyone is committed to fulfil their duties. Completeness is the only truth and is Krishna possible without truth?'

'But, prabhu, is this the only truth?' Rukmini's eyes were filled with disbelief and irreverence. For the first time in her life, she had doubted the words of the person with whom she had walked away from home, purely out of trust and devotion.

'Do you know what you are saying, prabhu?'

'My dear, you are my better half, my companion. You know I have never said anything without serious deliberation.'

Rukmini's eyes brimmed with tears, 'Do you mean now ...?'

'My duties as a human being are over, my dear.'

'And what about me, my lord?' Rukmini's voice was choked. Her eyes were no longer able to stem the flow of tears.

'Is it possible for a part of me to survive when another part of me leaves? You are an inseparable part of my body and my soul ... but ...' Rukmini had so much to say, so much to ask Krishna, but the incomprehensible expression on his face forced her to stop mid-sentence.

Krishna wrapped his beloved wife in a tight embrace. Rukmini could no longer hold back her pent-up feelings and burst out crying. Her wail shook the whole palace and her tears flowed down Krishna's chest, moistening his shawl. Krishna's eyes, fixed far away on the horizon, seemed to hold a message for all celestial beings:

'My time has arrived. I am coming.'

The battlefield of Kurukshetra materialised before Krishna on the banks of the Hiranya and Kapila rivers. The armies of the warring Kauravs and Pandavs stood facing each other. Arjun stood in his chariot right in the middle, refusing to pick up his bow and fight. It was there that Krishna had revealed his divine form. The sound of the Panchajanya conch echoed all around and Krishna's voice reverberated as he said, 'Only those who have recognised their true selves are free from kama, krodh—desire, anger—and other emotions, and only those who have conquered their minds are capable of attaining enlightenment or being in perpetual *Nirvikalp Samadhi* ...'

It was as if Krishna wasn't addressing Arjun alone but the whole universe. 'A person who harbours no bitterness or hatred, is free from expectations and has conquered his senses, is effortlessly able to free himself from worldly attachments. A person who has control over his mind, whose conscience is clear and considers all forms of creation as one attains freedom from the cycle of birth and death.'

Why was it so difficult to let go of one's mortal body? Must every human go through the same anguish and pain?

Krishna's closed eyes were experiencing an inexplicable, excruciating pain. The darkness he had sensed all around in Ma Devaki's womb, the agony that he had suffered while being born in his human avatar on the eighth day of the month of Shravan and the pain that he was experiencing today—was human life nothing more than a journey that began and ended in pain?

na hanyate ... hanyamane shareere ...

For the soul there is never birth nor death.

In other words, 'Anyone who is born has to die, only to be born again!'

Krishna found his own words hollow. Had he succeeded in freeing himself from his own worldly attachments? Was his term on earth truly over? Had the earth been unburdened and was he free to leave? Had Ma Devaki, Vasudev baba, the bylanes of Gokul and the currents of the Yamuna agreed to let him go?

What had made Krishna bind himself with these ties and suffer so much? Blood oozed continuously from his wounded toe. A small puddle of blood had formed near his feet. Jara asked, 'My lord, what can I do to alleviate your pain?'

'By design, that very act of yours will cause pain and suffering. Your duty is to liberate me. Your attempts to bring me relief will only augment my sorrow.' Despite the pain, Krishna smiled. Heaps of peacock feathers lay scattered all around him. The music of the flute hadn't stopped yet.

Suddenly, a soothing voice was heard in the distance, as if someone was singing a lullaby. It merged with the sound of the flute.

'Kanhaiya ... o ... Kanhaiya ... Kanhaiya ...' It was Ma Yashoda calling out frantically. Little Krishna was hiding behind the large tree in the courtyard, watching his mother fret and fume. This little game had become a daily occurrence. Yashoda would continue playing hide and seek. She would have to go out in search of him and drag him back home by his ears.

Though Krishna had come home, he wouldn't let go of a chance to annoy her. Ma Yashoda was exhausted, yet, she stepped out of the house to look for him. She could see the ends of his yellow dhoti from behind the tree. She ran from the other side, grabbed little Krishna, brought him home and sat him down for lunch.

'Open your mouth, Krishna.'

'Uh huh ...'

She stared at Krishna for a moment. Her eyes were indignant.

'You don't want to eat, do you?'

'Uh huh.'

'Beware! I won't give you anything to eat the whole day.'

Krishna simply shrugged. 'If you dare come asking for food, you will get a royal spanking.' Even as she was saying this, Yashoda knew she didn't mean a word of it.

'Fine.' Kanha sprinted out of the house and out of sight before Yashoda could call out to him again.

'Kanha ... o Kanha ... Kanhaaa ...!' A sweet voice reverberated along the banks of Yamuna for a long time. Krishna could hear the voice, but refused to respond because he was angry. Irate and fuming, he sat by the river, throwing stones into the water. The moment he threw the stone, it would settle at the bottom of the river with a glug. The waters of the Yamuna gurgled peacefully. The chirping of the birds seemed to match the rhythm of the flowing river. The sun moved slowly towards the western horizon.

'Kanhaiya ... o Kanhaiya ... Kanhaiya ...!' The sweet voice seemed to move closer by the minute and suddenly was right next to him. Radha had been looking for him all over and had finally found him on the riverbank. 'Where have you been? I have been looking for you since morning.' Radha demanded.

'Why?' Krishna was still angry and irritated, and his hunger only enraged him further. His tricks had failed and he was caught in his own game.

'Why!' Radha asked, staring at Krishna wide-eyed, as she sat down beside him on the bank. This time, before the stone that Krishna threw fell into the river, she caught it mid-air.

'Why do you think I search for you every day?' she asked.

'Go away, stop annoying me.'

'Annoying you?' Radha said, ruffling Krishna's hair. 'You look angry.'

'Yes,' Krishna said, snatching the pebble from her and flinging it into the river, '... and hungry too!'

Radha chuckled, 'I see! You should have eaten when your mother asked you to. Why didn't you?'

'Because I hadn't asked *you* if I could eat.'

'I am asking you to now ... go and eat,' Radha laughed aloud, splashing her feet in the water.

'Will you just go away?'

'Yes, but with you. Ma Yashoda sent me here to get you home.'

'Why didn't you tell me all this while?'

'Because you didn't ask!' Radha said teasingly.

'Now, just get up.' Kanha stood up and began pulling Radha by her hand. 'Come on, let's go.'

'Let's sit for a few minutes. What's the big hurry?' Radha said mockingly.

'Will you come or shall I go?' Kanha hadn't let go of her hand yet.

'Alone? What will you tell Ma Yashoda? That you came home because you were hungry?' Radha was still sitting with her legs dangling in the water and laughing. She seemed to have no intention of moving from there.

Kanhaiya thought for a moment and pushed Radha hard. She was taken by surprise and fell right into the water. She was drenched from head to toe, and Kanhaiya turned around and stomped away.

'Kanhaiya ... o Kanhaiya ... Kanhaiyaaaa ...' The sweet voice followed him all the way.

The gushing Yamuna then and the calm, serene waters of the merging rivers now were a study in contrast, just like the impudent, conceited and short-tempered Krishna of yore and the meditative Yogeshwar Krishna of today.

The faint sound of somebody calling out to him was still audible, 'Kanha ... o Kanha ... Kanhaaaaa ...!'

Krishna opened his eyes all of a sudden and looked around, perplexed. There was no one there except Jara.

Who was calling out to him, then? Krishna strained his eyes but couldn't sight anyone.

'My lord. What can I do for you? Do you want some water?' Jara asked with folded hands.

Krishna's eyes continued to search desperately. The voice still echoed around him.

'Kanhaiya ... o Kanhaiya ... Kanhaiyaaaa ...!'

Who could it be? Who was trying to hinder his departure? Had he failed in his duties towards someone? What was it that remained unfinished and prevented him from relinquishing his human body?

The day of the journey had been decided and Akrur was seated in Nand baba's courtyard. The message from Mathura had arrived. Krishna's maternal uncle Kansa had invited them for a yagya. Yashoda had fought tooth and nail with Nand baba and had finally given up. Nand baba had left the decision to Krishna. Despite the fact that he was yet just a young boy, Nand baba had immense faith in Krishna's intelligence and powers. He believed that whatever Krishna did would be correct.

Radha stood teary-eyed under a tree on the banks of the Yamuna. Her hair was dishevelled and her saree was draped carelessly. She had reached there at the crack of dawn. Krishna finally showed up after finishing all his tasks. He gathered Radha's loose hair and began tying it into a bun.

'Are you leaving?' Radha asked, her eyes flooding with tears. Krishna understood how she felt, but her words did not elicit any response from him.

'Please don't go, Kanha. What on earth will I do without you?' She must have said the same thing a thousand times since morning.

'Go sell milk, fill grains and ... take care of your husband, Ayan.' Krishna's voice sounded hollow.

'Is that so?' Radha stared at him and retorted, 'You have made up your mind to go, haven't you? You don't care about me. Do you?'

'Radha, you know very well that Gokul is where my life began, where my roots are. I have innumerable journeys to undertake. How will I be able to go anywhere if you bid me farewell with these tearful eyes each time?'

'Then don't go. What work do you have in Mathura anyway?'

'Don't you know?'

'No, I don't. I know nothing!'

'Oh! You look so lovely when you sulk!'

'You look so lovely ... my foot!' Radha was livid. 'Is that why you want to go away?'

'Yes, that is exactly why I am going away from you. If you continue to love me so, I will never be able to go anywhere. I will be bound by the shackles of attachment forever!'

Radha was confounded. 'What are you saying?'

'Never mind!' Krishna chuckled. 'Akrurji will be here any moment. Can I take your leave? I still have to console my heartbroken mother.'

'Must you forsake the love of so many people to go meet that tyrant Kansa?'

'Yes, everyone has a right to freedom ...'

'I can never comprehend a word of what you say ...'

'Me neither ... where have I understood anything? That is precisely why I have to undertake this journey. Shall I leave now?'

'Go! Go away and never come back again,' said Radha, turning her face away.

Kanhaiya moved close to her and lifted his hands to touch her shoulder, but hesitated for a moment. 'Say that again.'

'Yes, yes, go away and never come back here again.'

Kanhaiya's eyes welled up with tears. He looked at Radha in torment. He stuck his flute into his waistband and raised both his hands upwards, '*Tathastu* ... so be it!'

He turned around and walked away. Radha could hear his retreating footsteps. She had made up her mind not to stop Kanhaiya this time. But right the next moment, she turned around and ran behind Kanha at lightning speed: 'Kanhaiya ... o Kanhaiya ... Kanhaiyaaaa ...!' That sweet voice trailed behind Krishna. The same voice seemed to have followed him right here, years later, to the banks of these rivers.

The sun spread its dazzling light all over the banks of the Hiranya-Kapila. The silvery waters of the Hiranya had

turned a molten gold. Jara sat on his knees with folded
hands. The sun's bright rays fell on Krishna's face and the
branches of the peepal tree swayed gently in the breeze,
creating myriad patterns on his visage. His anguished
eyes remained shut and the smile on his face was intact.
The image of scattered peacock feathers danced in front
of his closed eyes. The strains of his flute blended with
the sound of the Panchajanya conch and created a strange
melody. The traveller, who had taken the first step in his
great journey, was hesitating to take the next one. What
was holding him back?

Krishna murmured, 'Why do you tie me down so,
Radha? Let me go—my journey is still incomplete.'

Having completed his daily ablutions, Krishna entered
Rukmini's room. The shadows of the previous night
were still visible on his divine face. And yet lines of
determination, firm as a rock, to embark on the final
journey were clearly etched on it.

Rukmini's hands trembled as she stood before Krishna
with a ceremonial lamp and tray. The flame of the lamp
flickered for a moment. She had to stretch her hands high
to reach Krishna's forehead to anoint him with vermilion
and grains of rice. She stared into Krishna's eyes for a
moment as tears welled up in her own.

'My dear, this was destined, wasn't it? Then why this
trembling and fear?'

'This is not fear, it is attachment.'

'You? And attachment?'

'My lord, as there are some laws and duties of human life, so are attachments. Our bodies are controlled by our senses, my lord!'

'I am surprised you are saying this.'

'You shouldn't be. Who knows women better than you?'

'Are you being sarcastic?'

'Can't I?'

'Not at this time.' Krishna held Rukmini's face in his palms. 'There is hardly any time left anyway.'

Rukmini's eyes brimmed with tears. 'This love, affection, compassion and these relationships ... leaving all this ...?'

'One who is born is destined to die, priye.'

'But you are ...'

'I am Krishna, born of Devaki's womb, Ma Yashoda's son, your husband and the king of Dwarka ... that is all, devi!'

'I can very well understand, but cannot accept this destiny.'

'Think about your dharma; it will make acceptance easier.' Krishna placed his palm on Rukmini's head. She closed her eyes and the drops of tears that she had held back for so long rolled down her cheeks. Krishna too closed his eyes.

It felt as if all her grief, rage and pent-up feelings had calmed down at his touch. She prostrated herself at his feet, surrendering her body, mind and soul. She then said in a feeble voice, *'Twadiyam vastu govindam tubhyamev samarpaye ...'*

Krishna was stunned.

'Why is everyone surrendering their selves to me? Unacceptance would be immoral, but where would I take them with me even if I accept? I will have to break these shackles of attachment.

He was dumbstruck!

'Despite being so close to them, I failed to understand their feelings, whereas these women know me from head to toe. Not only can they read my desire for liberation but they have also accepted it wholeheartedly. Have I been able to recognise and acknowledge the desires, expectations and aspirations of my wife, who has thought about nothing but my happiness all her life? Even if I have known them, have I ever tried to fulfil them?'

Krishna stood looking at Rukmini's closed eyes, her bent body, her hair caressing his feet, and her tears. Krishna had been mesmerised by the human body, its relationships and attachments.

Rukmini and Draupadi—despite being so different and far away from each other—had a similar sense of enquiry and the same desire to surrender. How was this possible? Krishna wondered in awe.

While I have only been contemplating seeking moksha and preparing myself for it, these two dearly loved women have read my mind and shown immense courage and come forward to liberate me from this cycle of life. Only women can do this. Only a woman can control her heart and mind and fulfil her moral duties. Forgiveness, acceptance, spontaneity and love are characteristics unique to a woman. She endures pain to give life, and that is why she is always a step ahead in the circle of liberation.

And only she has the magnanimity to accept a co-wife and give true meaning to the word life-partner, Krishna thought, and said hesitatingly, 'Rukmini, permit me to take your leave ...'

'Permission? Only you have the authority to command, my lord! I am but your mere servant ... it is my duty to follow your command.'

Krishna held her gently by the shoulders. Tears flowed unabated down her cheeks. She tilted her head back and raised her chin. Krishna gently held her raised chin between his thumb and fingers, and kissed her intensely on the lips that were wet with tears.

This was the kiss of farewell, the final one.

The riverbanks seemed to be spilling over with peacock feathers and the heaps were getting larger by the minute. Their myriad colours were creating a variety of patterns in Krishna's eyes. With every pattern, a new moment, a new relationship was emerging.

For one who could not spare a moment for himself all his life, Krishna was waiting for death to come and claim him. But it appeared to be testing him.

Krishna licked his lips. Oddly, it felt prickly and tasted of salt. He hadn't realised when his lips had become wet with tears.

Taking leave of Rukmini had been the most intimate moment for both of them. That was how it was meant to be. The dreadfulness of the parting of two people who have spent a lifetime together can be understood only when the moment of separation looms large. Humans living under the blissful illusion that such moments will never come to pass are ignorant of its truth and lack the emotional maturity to accept it. It is not necessary to negate the here and now just because the day of parting is destined in the future. And by turning a blind eye to the imminent moment of separation or becoming apathetic to it, it cannot be avoided or postponed. It is a certainty. Any event that has begun has to reach its logical conclusion. Anyone who is aware of this and accepts it enjoys the present with happiness and satisfaction. A person who approaches the future with open eyes, lives in the present without any delusions and accepts the present as real without any expectations of permanence, is able to guide every moment of his life towards the future.

'So, my dear ...' Rukmini's parted lips were still trembling after the kiss. Krishna broke her stupor: 'My dear, I would like to take your permission to leave.'

'Will you get permission just by asking?' Rukmini's eyes were filled with despair.

'That is certain, even if I don't ask for it, isn't it?'

'My lord, can I ask you for something?'

'Is there anything left even now? I have given you my body, my soul ...' Krishna placed his hand on Rukmini's shoulder.

'I know, I am fortunate to have been your consort. But my lord, in all these years, you have, not once, shared with me your mind.' Rukmini's anguish was expressed more by her tears than her words.

'Really? Is that what you feel?'

'Is it not true? Have you ever shared your worries, sorrows and inadequacies with me?'

'But, my dear ...'

Rukmini cut him short, 'Now, don't tell me you have never experienced any of these feelings ... they are an integral part of human life.'

'Why this sadness now?'

'If not now, then when?'

There was silence for a few minutes. A chain of restless moments passed between the two of them. Rukmini gazed into Krishna's eyes, as if the answer to her question was written in them.

Rukmini's intense gaze became unbearable for Krishna. She hadn't fixed him with such a look even when he had brought Satyabhama into their lives. Although Rukmini had, without a fuss, accepted Jambavati and all his other queens, she had resented him for marrying Satyabhama.

Krishna broke away from Rukmini's gaze and said, 'May I leave, my dear? Do I have your permission for my journey, now?'

'Journey? Is the journey still due? The last journey, right?' Rukmini asked.

'You are capable of understanding the journey as well as the destination.'

Krishna folded his hands, 'If I have ever hurt you knowingly or unknowingly, I seek your forgiveness.'

Rukmini held both his hands in hers. They stood with their eyes closed. 'Priye, now ...' Krishna seemed to be searching for words. 'Please don't stop me ... not even for a moment. Otherwise, this moment will become centuries-long; do you understand? Please let me go.'

'What about me?'

'Time will take care of one and all. What is destined to happen will happen, my dear.'

'As you say, my lord. There is no path other than liberation.'

'Even liberation is not a path; it is also only a direction. The path is to walk tirelessly, with consistent effort; that is destiny ... *tathastu* ... so be it.'

Krishna walked out of Rukmini's chamber without waiting another moment. Rukmini stood rooted, looking at his retreating figure.

She knew very well that his departure was certain. It was time to return all the elements that had accompanied

Krishna to his temporal life to their rightful places—even Lakshmi and Sheshnag.

Krishna waited for Arjun's arrival with a heavy heart. Daruk had already left for Prabhaskshetra to bring him. Krishna knew that this news would be unbearable for him. Arjun, also known as Phalgun, hadn't loved anyone more than Krishna. He fought the Kurukshetra war purely on Krishna's willpower and morale.

Waves of pain rose in Krishna's body. A multitude of images floated behind his closed eyelids. Hordes of peacock feathers were floating up and down on the waves of the Yamuna. Someone was playing the flute, hiding among the branches of the kadamba tree. The whole tree was shaking. Who was shaking it? Was Balaram standing beneath the tree and doing it? Or was it the mighty serpent Kaliya? The sacred chants of *Aham Brahmasmi* were echoing in the ears of the supreme being. The one who had proclaimed 'I am the peepal among trees' was himself lying incapacitated today, under the shade of the same tree, his breath slowly waning. Was he really waiting for Arjun or ...?

When the Yadavs were fighting each other at Prabhaskshetra, Balaram looked at Krishna sitting sedately under the tree. What was that in Krishna's eyes that made Balaram shudder?

He went close to Krishna and shook him violently. 'What are you doing sitting here calmly, Kanha? The Yadavs are getting decimated ...'

'I know ...' Krishna's face was chillingly calm. Balaram looked at Krishna's eyes. They were cold as stone.

'Kanhaiya ...'

'Bhai, do you remember Rishi Durvasa's curse?'

'Yes ... yes I do,' Balaram said in a faltering voice. 'That means we too ...'

'Why not? Are we any different?' Krishna's eyes were morbidly cold, and his voice sounded like the Panchajanya conch. He looked at Balaram with still and grave eyes and said:

'Dehino 'smin yatha dehekaumaram yauvanam jara
Tatha dehantara-praptir dhirastatra na muhyati'

'The passing of youth, old age and death are not to be mourned.'

'I don't want to listen to all that ...' Balaram became uneasy. Krishna embraced him gently and pulled him close, without saying a word. When the brothers moved apart, Balaram felt as if all the doubts and questions plaguing him had disappeared. But it wasn't as if he had been freed of all anguish.

An uncanny, overwhelming feeling encompassed them. Balaram closed his eyes, folded his hands and fell at Krishna's feet. His tears were wetting Krishna's feet. As Krishna caressed his brother's head, a deep voice rang out all around.

'Yathakasa-sthito nityam vayuh sarvatra-go mahan
Tatha sarvani bhutani mat-sthanity upadharaya'

'Like the sky remains in its place and the wind, despite moving, doesn't leave its origins—eventually, all beings become one with me. Please understand this and unite.'

Tears continued to flow from Balaram's eyes. Krishna's words echoed like a shanti mantra over the tumultuous cries of the Yadavs. Here was his brother, who was going to relinquish his life in a few moments; this was the brother with whom Krishna had shared the sweet memories of his childhood, this was the person that Krishna loved more than his own life.

'You can leave ...' Krishna said.

Balaram was anguished at the horrifying condition at Yadavsthali. 'And you?' he asked.

'Me?' Krishna's face and voice were restrained, but his eyes were moist.

'Me?' he repeated. 'I have to stay here, till all this comes to a close. And then ...'

'Why, Kanha, why? Is this all about you? Is this all your responsibility?' Balaram's heart cried out and Krishna seemed to be echoing his voice when he asked, 'Why should you stay here?'

'I am the one who said that indecision leads to destruction, but I am myself plagued by doubt.'

The Yadavs were fighting like beasts right in front of Krishna's eyes. The sight seemed to blur because of the tears brimming in them.

'You must go now,' he said to Balaram again, wiping off a teardrop before it reached his cheeks.

Balaram hugged Krishna as if he wanted to merge Krishna into himself. Then, he turned around and walked away towards the Triveni confluence, where the sun was getting ready to set. It could be seen going down behind the Somnath temple. Balaram looked like a golden statue slowly moving towards the glimmering, amber rays. The terrifying shrieks of the Yadavs could still be heard in the background. Balaram quickened his stride, as if he wanted to get away from the shrieks that were pleading him to turn back. He seemed to be holding himself guilty for what had happened. The root cause for the destruction of Dwarka was alcohol. The Yadavs had been given a free rein to drink by Balaram himself.

'May I come in?' Krishna asked before entering Balaram's chamber.

It was evening and the salty winds blowing from the sea were rustling the curtains violently. The saffron hues of the setting sun bathed the room in light. Balaram's fair body looked as if it had been dipped in saffron-milk.

'O Kanhaiya, at this hour?'

'Why, isn't this a good time?' There was a hint of bitterness in Krishna's voice unheard of before.

'No, nothing of that sort. Tell me ...'

'Bhai, you will be hurt if I tell you the truth.' Krishna looked right into Balaram's eyes.

Balaram maintained eye contact. 'I know ... I know that I will be hurt by what you are going to tell me, but I also know that you have been saddened by what you have heard about me. I realise that despite listening to what you have to say, I ...' Balaram turned towards the window.

'Kanha, there are several things that are beyond our control ...' he murmured.

'Bhai, these are lame excuses. There is no bigger weakness than accepting one's own failings.'

'Kanha, if you have come here to give me advice, then just go away. You are welcome if you desire to join me for a game.' Balaram took some silver coins and began arranging them on the table.

'Bhai, you are responsible for the upliftment and protection of the Yadavs, and if you yourself start to ...'

'Protection! Responsibility!' Balaram said in a pained voice. His voice had the emptiness of a desperately lonely person, frighteningly hollow. 'Kanha, you are the king of Dwarka. You are the creator, builder and protector of this city. Then why torment me with this sermon?' Balaram filled a glass with wine and took a sip.

'Bhai ...' Krishna's face and voice reflected deep anguish. 'What on earth you are doing?'

'Bhai ...!' Even before Krishna could say anything, Balaram cut him short with his loud voice.

'I am your older brother, yet, everything in Dwarka happens according to your wishes ...'

'What can I do? Do I have the liberty to accept or refuse anything!' Krishna's voice had the pain of a defeated commander. 'I don't even have the independence to decide where I will have my supper. I am but a prisoner of time who has no freedom of expression whatsoever.'

'Is that so?' Balaram asked sarcastically. 'So now you are using words to play with me as well!'

'Bhai, have I hurt your feelings in any way? Have I erred somewhere?'

'You? And make a mistake?' Balaram's voice was filled with acid. 'Can you ever go wrong? You are, after all, a great man, and the whole world bows before you.'

Krishna looked at Balaram's dejected eyes and said, 'You know they don't bow before me but before my power and strength. You are my strength, bhai ...'

'You seem to have realised that only today.'

'Sometimes, it is difficult to accept reality. I can very well understand your bitterness and your pain, but ...'

'Is this you, the narrator of the Gita, the omniscient friend of the Pandavs and charioteer of Arjun, speaking? I am surprised.' An intoxicated Balaram's voice was slurred, loud and dramatic:

'Yato yato niscalati manas cancalam asthiram
Tatastato niyamyaitad atmanyeva vasham nayet'

'When the mind wanders, you need to restrain it and refocus it on the soul.'

'Isn't this true?' asked Krishna.

'You know better, you are the wise one! We are all Shudras—poor and lowly creatures. We are forever indebted to you for saving our lives in the Kurukshetra war.'

'Bhai, I am your servant. I will do as you say. But I can't bear to see this anguish, this despondence and pain any more.'

'Oh, the king of Dwarka can't bear agony ...'

'I am your younger brother,' Krishna pleaded.

'And yet, you are the ruler, the prosperous, wealthy king of the Yadavs, the lord of Bharatvarsh ... the most popular and loved man of this era, and the narrator of Kurukshetra.'

Krishna sat down near Balaram's feet. Holding them with both hands, he said, 'So much pain? Why are you holding on to all this misery? You never thought of sharing it with me?'

There was so much grief in Krishna's voice that Balaram's eyes welled up with tears. He placed his hand on Krishna's head and closed his eyes. 'Kanha, this is neither a grievance, nor jealousy ...'

'I understand,' said Krishna and shut his eyes.

The brothers sat still for a few moments, reminiscing about their childhood adventures, escapades, quarrels, animosities, love, loyalty and trust. Tears flowed unabated from their eyes as they sat lost in memories. They didn't know how much time had passed, but for Balaram it was as if centuries had gone by.

Krishna stood up gently and asked, 'May I take your leave?'

Balaram continued to sit, dazed.

'Please forgive me, Kanha,' he said with folded hands.

'Please don't embarrass me,' Krishna said, holding his hands. Balaram couldn't control his tears.

'Kanhaiya, I have erred. I have let you down.'

Krishna clasped him in a tight embrace. His shoulders were drenched with Balaram's tears. Krishna decided then and there that he would never reprimand Balaram for his drinking habit, nor stop him.

This was the same brother who had saved Kanha innumerable times from his mother's wrath. The siblings were partners in crime, in teasing gopikas and playing pranks on them.

They would race to swim across the wide expanse of the Yamuna, and Balaram would deliberately lose, lest his little brother created a scene. Whether it was pestering gopikas on their way to Mathura or climbing trees on the banks of the Yamuna and breaking the pots of the village women, the two brothers were always together.

Balaram loved Krishna more than his own life. He couldn't bear to see tears in Krishna's eyes. He loved his little brother so much that he would tie the cowherds, who annoyed Krishna, to the trunk of a tree and shake it vigorously. The cowherds would scream in fear but Balaram wouldn't relent till they asked Kanha for forgiveness.

But whenever Ma Rohini took Krishna's side, Balaram would get perturbed. The fact that Ma Rohini found the little, innocent but mischievous Krishna adorable irked Balaram no end. It wasn't as if Ma Yashoda didn't love Balaram, but he hated sharing two things—his mace and his mother, Rohini.

Balaram had been looking for Krishna all morning. God only knew where he was hiding—it was almost noon, but there was no sign of Kanha. Balaram had looked everywhere—on the banks of the Yamuna, on the branches of the kadamba tree, on the road to Mathura, in the cowshed and behind Radha's house—Kanha was nowhere to be seen.

'Kanhaiya ... o Kanhaiya ...!' Balaram shouted.

Suddenly, Balaram heard a *shhhh* sound. It had to be Kanha. Little Kanhaiya was standing outside the window of their house and peeping in. He was waiting for a hand to come out of the window and give him food. He had been punished by his mother yet again.

Kanhaiya and his friends had entered Kokila's house, eaten up all the butter and turned her house upside down. When Kokila came to Yashoda to complain about Kanha, she was already annoyed about something. Her anger knew no bounds when she heard Kokila's complaint.

'Balaram ... o Balaram!'

Balaram had been waiting for this call ever since he had overheard the conversation. He dropped his mace and ran to Krishna's mother.

'Yes, Ma.' Balaram knew exactly what was going to follow.

'Go, find Kanhaiya and get him here.'

'But Ma ...'

'Didn't you hear me? Go and get Kanha. I will straighten him out today. I am tired of these daily complaints. I am going to teach him a real lesson. Go, bring him here!'

Rohini, who was returning home from the cowshed, heard Yashoda's words and said, 'Let it go, bahen. He is just a little boy ... bound to make mischief!'

'Rohini, let me handle this.' Balaram smiled when he heard Yashoda say this.

'But ...' Rohini tried to come to Kanhaiya's rescue yet again.

It was common for the womenfolk of Gokul to come to Kanha's rescue time and again, but for some reason, Yashoda wasn't ready to listen to anyone this time.

'Balaram, get him here. I am going to lock him up and starve him till evening.'

Balaram broke into a grin. It was Kanhaiya's turn to get a scolding!

Usually, it was Balaram who saved Kanhaiya from the wrath of his mother and lied to save him. But Rohini had ruined everything by stepping in.

Balaram looked everywhere, in every possible hiding place, but couldn't find him anywhere. How could he, when Kanhaiya had been hiding right behind his own house all morning! Ma Rohini had already seen Kanhaiya. For some reason, she took pity on the naughty little boy every time Yashoda refused to give him food.

It was Rohini who had signalled to Kanhaiya to come and stand quietly behind the house and given him food.

'Shhhh ...'

'What are you doing here?' Balaram asked, as if he knew nothing.

Kanha placed a finger on his lips and beckoned him closer to share his secret. 'I am hiding. That Kokila has gone and told Ma everything ...'

'Is that so?' Balaram put on an act.

'And now, Ma is looking for me. I am surely going to get spanked today. She may even lock me up in my room or put me in the cowshed,' Krishna said pitifully. 'I haven't eaten anything since morning.'

'Why, didn't you eat a potful of butter?'

'Well! Anyway, I am very hungry now.'

'So what do we do?'

'Ma Rohini has gone to get me some food. I will run away with it and come back home only after sunset. By then, Nand baba will be back and there will be nothing to worry about,' Kanhaiya announced his grand plan.

'Hmm ...' Balaram nodded and stood up.

'Where are you going?' Kanhaiya asked.

'To see what is taking Ma so long,' Balaram said and entered the house.

Kanhaiya stood watching with expectant eyes.

A few minutes later, a hand extended out of the open window. There was a hot roti with a big blob of delicious butter on it. Kanhaiya started drooling. Just as he extended his hand to take the roti, the other hand came out and grabbed Kanhaiya's hand. They then tied

Kanhaiya's hands to the window. Ma Rohini! He couldn't believe that Ma Rohini would do such a thing.

Even before he could understand what was happening, Ma Yashoda came charging at him with a long stick. It was a sight to behold! Her eyes were red with rage.

'Ma ...' Kanhaiya said in a pitiable voice, trying to assuage his mother's anger.

'Quiet! I won't hear another word. You are going to remain tied all day.'

Who was that behind Ma Yashoda? Balaram! His own brother! Was he capable of doing something like this? Did he squeal to Ma? Kanhaiya couldn't believe his eyes!

'My brother Balaram? He did this?' Krishna couldn't accept it. Krishna closed his eyes in pain. Uddhav stood in front of him.

'I don't mean to cause you pain, but it is my duty to tell you about everything that is happening in Dwarka,' Uddhav said.

'I had my own suspicions, but my elder brother ... I had never thought my own brother would do something like this.' Krishna's heart was filled with sadness. 'If Balaram consumes liquor in Dwarka, how can I stop the other Yadavs?'

'My lord, your elder brother is encouraging everyone to drink. When Duryodhan visited Dwarka, both of them sat on the seashore and drank in public.' Uddhav continued to speak and Krishna just listened with his eyes closed.

'The Yadavs will follow their example, and it will be extremely difficult to stop them. If the Yadavs, already intoxicated by power and wealth, drink like this, there will be nothing left ...'

Krishna closed his eyes in despair. 'Who can stop fate, Uddhav? Despite trying everything in my control, I failed to slow down the passage of time. What is written has to happen ...'

'What is written? What is destined to happen?'

A wistful smile spread on Krishna's face. 'Uddhav, the seeds of the future have been sown. We just have to wait for them to take root ... the roots of a terrifying future.'

Uddhav couldn't understand all of what Krishna had said, but it was clear that the Yadavs were faced with some severe calamity.

Once Krishna made his decision to go to Prabhaskshetra, he went to Balaram's palace. There was a sense of urgency in his gait. Uddhav was accompanying him, but couldn't keep pace and fell behind.

Although Krishna was his younger brother, Balaram was strongly influenced by him and well aware of the fact that drinking was causing him harm. Yet, he was unable to get rid of the addiction. Krishna had reasoned with him time and again, but instead of discussing his problem, Balaram began looking for ways to avoid meeting Krishna in the evenings. He always managed to complete all his administrative duties during the day.

'May I come in?' Krishna asked before stepping into his chamber.

Although the sun was overhead, Balaram had just woken up. His mornings were usually late and steeped in laziness and haze. The silk sheets on his bed were crumpled, and he appeared hung-over. His handsome face looked swollen, and his eyes were sunken and red.

He was a little astonished to see Krishna in his room so early. He hadn't even completed his daily ablutions. Krishna sat down before saying anything.

'Krishna? So early in the morning?'

'Early? It's almost midday. Even the roof tiles are shining like gold.'

'The tiles of these palaces are made of gold and don't need the sun's rays to shine. Besides, the sun and time function as per your command in Dwarka ...'

'Bhai, time never runs on anybody's command.'

'Kanhaiya, is this *you* saying this? The king of Dwarka, the protector of fifty-six crore beings, the creator of an earth free from death, old age, disease and sorrow—time runs as per your orders, directions change as per your wishes, seasons come and go according to your desire ...' Balaram's eyes flashed with arrogance.

'Don't be under such illusions, bhai. Lord Shiv's ways are mysterious. When we feel that everything is going just fine and as per our wishes, it might just be the beginning of terrible times ...'

Balaram asked, 'Have you come to talk about all this, first thing in the morning?'

Krishna chuckled and said, 'No. Such things should be spoken about only in the evenings. Isn't that so, bhai?'

Balaram was taken aback. 'Krishna, let's not talk about my weaknesses ...'

Krishna said, 'Is there anything worth discussing?'

'Krishna, don't try to trap me with your words. The very fact that you have left all your tasks and come here when the royal court is in session tells me that there is certainly something important ...'

Krishna remarked with a beautiful smile, 'You are perceptive, bhai, and you know me well.'

Balaram got up from his bed. Krishna looked at his bare body, strong arms, wide chest decked with pearls and precious jewellery, dishevelled curly, black hair and intoxicated eyes reflecting admiration and compassion.

'I wish that we move to Prabhaskshetra with all the Yadavs.'

Balaram, standing by the window, was taken by surprise. The sun's rays were glistening over the rising and falling waves of the sea. The waters softly caressed the sands and receded. Balaram turned around and stared at Krishna, as if searching for something in his eyes. Krishna shut his eyes, as if he wanted to hide something from his elder brother. For some time, the room was filled only with the sounds of the sea.

'Prabhas? Why Kanha?' There was a quiver of fear in Balaram's voice. It was filled with dread about the times to come. Krishna opened his eyes and looked at Balaram silently.

'You mean to say that our time has come?'

'Who am I to say, bhai? What was destined is about to come true.'

'Can't it be deferred, Kanhaiya?' Balaram pleaded. It was as if he was imploring Kanha to save him from his mother's wrath.

'Time?' A sombre smile spread on Krishna's face. He looked straight at Balaram, 'Who can possibly change the course of time, bhai?'

'Prabhas ...' Balaram's voice became feeble. He asked in an aggrieved voice, 'All right, Kanha, when should we leave?'

'As soon as possible.' A mysterious smile played on Krishna's lips. He looked at Balaram's eyes. They were moist. Krishna stood up and embraced his elder brother. The tides of time moved steadily in front of their closed eyes. The gurgling sounds of the Yamuna echoed in the ornate palace room along the seashore ... and the two men locked in a tight embrace knew what was in store in the days to come. One heart was insecure and jittery while the other was eagerly waiting to walk the path of liberation.

The urn on the pinnacle of the palace of Dwarka glistened in the noon sun. The streets were overflowing with people as if it was a celebration of sorts. The golden chariots with their fluttering flags, the neighing horses and charioteers gave the city an air of prosperity

and well-being. Krishna had invited all the Yadavs to
Prabhaskshetra for a celebration and the entire race was
getting ready to leave for the occasion. Dwarka city which
had usually in the past been in celebration mode had
become sullen and deathly following the Kurukshetra
war. There wasn't a single household that hadn't lost a
loved one to the war. It had stood witness to the terrible
dance of death. Krishna himself had become a recluse for
some time after the war. He was someone whose entire
life was a celebration; he lived life to the fullest and
believed in helping others to grow and bloom. If such
a person becomes reclusive, it is natural that the same
feeling resonates all around.

The Yadavs, living in the shadows of death for so long,
had forgotten the meaning of celebration and revelry.
Dwarka hadn't celebrated Janmashtami with pomp and
gaiety for several years now.

Krishna had gone to every Yadav house personally and
invited them for Janmashtami. Every single Yadav man,
child, youth and elder, was invited to Prabhaskshetra.

They were ecstatic. They wore all the ornaments that
the Yadav women owned. Boys danced in merriment, and
the young men looked forward to enjoying moments of
happiness to the fullest.

Krishna watched these scenes from his palace window.
He sighed deeply and wondered if what he was doing was
right. The divine person, who had lived with undisputed

truth, was plagued by doubts about his decision and behaviour. So many people were going to go with him purely because they trusted every word he said. They were blissfully unaware that none of them were going to return.

What had the Kurukshetra war achieved? Could the victory be called a true victory? Had anyone been able to celebrate the victory? Had dharma and righteousness truly won? Had he fulfilled all his duties? What had the victorious Pandavs achieved? Dead children? Lifeless men amidst the shadows of death? Wasn't this too another Kurukshetra? Was adharma or evil going to be truly vanquished?

Krishna was inundated with doubt and uncertainty as he readied for the second phase of carnage and destruction. He had contemplated and questioned his decision several times. Since the scene hadn't unfolded before him yet, it hadn't felt too terrifying. But now that the moment had arrived, it was quizzing his mind about truth and untruth, right and wrong, and for once, Arjun's charioteer was shaken to the core.

'Let's go, I am ready.' It was Satyabhama's voice. She had called out to Krishna as she walked out of her room.

Satyabhama was delicate and petite, like a glass doll. She was beautiful and loved to dress up.

Krishna gazed at her for some time. She had tied up her long hair in a bun and bedecked it with fragrant white flowers. She wore beautiful earrings and a matching necklace studded with precious stones. Her soft, wheatish skin shone from under her dress. She wore a white silk bodice and a white stole, and looked radiant like a white lotus blooming in the blue waters of the Yamuna. Her teeth were glistening like the pearls in her long necklace.

Krishna's eyes filled with tenderness. 'I may not get to see this beautiful smile any more ...' Krishna pulled her close.

'What are you doing, my lord?' Satyabhama asked shyly but came close to him nevertheless.

She loved Krishna's passion and fascination for her. Satyabhama always tried to ensure that Krishna remained captivated by her. The self-assured Rukmini ignored Satyabhama's childish attempts and laughed them away, but Satyabhama didn't like any of Krishna's queens. She knew Krishna well enough not to express her feelings openly, but every night that Krishna didn't spend with her, she would refuse to sleep. She would lie awake on her silk mattress and dream about her time with Krishna, sulk and get angry with him. Krishna would have to come and pamper and cajole her till she relented.

Krishna was surprised to see Satyabhama ready.

'You?' he asked.

'Yes, what will you do without me? If I don't come with you, the celebrations will be lacklustre. Won't they, my lord?' she asked, flashing a captivating smile. There was a childlike innocence and curiosity in her eyes.

Krishna pulled her close once again. This time she came to him with a hint of protest. She placed one hand on Krishna's chest and began fiddling with his arm band using the other. Her eyes were fixed on his face. He was almost a foot taller and her head seemed to fit perfectly in the crook of his arm.

Krishna started caressing her back, his touch on her young, soft as a petal skin felt very different today. This wasn't the touch of a lover; it was that of a mature, father-like figure.

Krishna smelt her hair. The fragrance of the jasmine flowers and sandalwood in her hair sent his mind into a whirl. He took a deep breath and without saying a word, pushed her away.

Satyabhama looked at Krishna in bewilderment. What was in that touch? Pain? Stoicism? Agony? Her lord, for whom she had dressed up so much, had hardly paid any attention. Even otherwise, Krishna had become temperamental ever since the Kurukshetra war had ended. He would be remorseful and seek solitude and on some nights, he would wake up Satyabhama so that he didn't feel lonely. At times, he would lie awake all night without saying a word, staring at the ceiling. Occasionally, he would spend the night on the palace terrace watching the sea. His eyes would well up for no reason. He would go silent for days on end. It wasn't as if she hadn't noticed these changes. She had tried very hard to get him out of his state—sometimes with her body, and sometimes with empathy.

It was tough for Satyabhama to handle the changes Krishna was undergoing. It was difficult both to understand and to accept them. She had always seen Krishna as a lover, an amazing lover who constantly thought about her happiness and fulfilled all her wishes even before they occurred to her.

She was immersed in his love from head to toe. This new facet of him was alien to her. She would become even more childish at such times. The more dispassionate he became, the more she tried to draw him out. Once in a while, Krishna would go to Rukmini to extricate himself from the tangle. Rukmini, who was wise and mature, would understand his state of mind and let him be.

This arrangement seemed to be working for Krishna, and so he began spending more nights at Rukmini's palace. On the other hand, Satyabhama found it unacceptable and unbearable. In the past, Krishna would indulge a sulking Satya for hours, but nowadays, it was nothing like that. Satyabhama, angry at Krishna's having spent the night with Rukmini, would spend the whole night just lying on her bed alone, while Krishna would stay up all night without speaking a word. The moment the sun rose, he would head for the seashore. This had happened several times lately. Krishna's indifference was worse than death for Satyabhama.

'Maharani, there is a celebration in Prabhaskshetra.' Manorama walked in with the news. She was Satya's favourite maid and would get her eyewitness accounts of all that transpired in the rajya sabha and Rukmini's palace. Till today, not one piece of news that she had brought had proven untrue, but somehow, Satya couldn't believe what she heard today.

'Are you sure?' Satya asked again.

'I swear by you, Prabhu Krishna has personally gone to every household and invited the Yadavs. They will be leaving for Prabhaskshetra tomorrow, around noon,' Manorama declared.

Satya held Manorama by her shoulders and twirled her around. As if the news filled the palace with happiness; as if every pore of her body pulsated with immense joy.

'Manu ... Manu ... I will gift you with pearls ... drape you in silk ... give you my gold bangles ... you have no idea what great news you have given me! Happy days are certainly back again! Finally, my lord, my life, my lover's heart has been freed from the circle of grief. Those wonderful days will come back Manu ... they will come back!'

Overjoyed, Satya didn't bother to completely hear what Manorama had to say. She wanted to communicate that the celebration was only for the Yadav menfolk, but Satyabhama didn't allow Manorama to speak. Seeing her queen's elation, Manorama decided to keep quiet.

❧

On the banks of the Triveni confluence, Krishna lay with his eyes closed. Satyabhama's beseeching and pleading eyes floated before his mind's eye. When Krishna tried to convince her that the celebration was meant only for the Yadav menfolk, she wouldn't hear any of it.

Satyabhama had no idea about the realities outside her palace. She lived in a dream world and created ways and means of recreation. She wasn't ready to listen to Krishna at any cost. The very thought that Krishna could be happy without her was intolerable and false for her; her definition of happiness began and ended with Krishna. Perhaps, making your emotions reverberate in someone else's heart is called love. To see the person in front of you as a mirror is the nature of love.

Had Krishna told Satyabhama that they were embarking on their final journey, she would have collapsed then and there. But karma was above all else for Krishna; it was the ultimate truth. And Satyabhama wasn't destined to be liberated as yet. Her karma was tied to Dwarka, and she would not be liberated till she completed all her karmic duties.

Krishna pulled her close and smelt her hair.

'My dear Charusheela ... only the men are going for the celebration.'

'Why? What is our fault? Why not us women?'

'Only because women have done nothing wrong, can they not come to the celebration ...'

'I don't understand, my lord ...'

'Even when you are not with me, you always are ... I am taking you with me ...'

'Swami!'

'You are my wife ... a part of you is etched in my soul, isn't it?'

'Only words ... a wicked web of words ...!'

'Priye, if I could take you with me, I would.'

'Who can stop you?'

'Me? Who can stop me? But it is not time yet ...'

'Time?' Satyabhama was stunned. 'Time for what?'

'The appropriate time. Priye, there is a right time for everything and today is not the right time for you to come with me ... you have to be here a little longer.'

For some unfathomable reason, Satyabhama did not throw a tantrum. She was suddenly reminded of what Krishna had said in the past:

'Yo mam pasyati sarvatra sarvam ca mayi pasyati
Tasyaham na pranasyami sa ca me na pranasyati'

'One who sees me everywhere and sees everything in me, I am never far away from such a person and he is never far from me.'

'Devi, you are constantly with me, everywhere ...' Krishna's eyes were filled with compassion and perhaps the grief of having to go away from this extraordinary woman.

The thought that he couldn't tell Satya the truth about leaving rankled in Krishna's mind in the last moments. Now her resentment and agony would not let her rest in peace. Krishna, who had very effortlessly explained death as 'just another event' to Arjun was in a deep quandary. He sat with his eyes closed in intense pain. Satyabhama's eyes looked at Krishna reproachfully ... The passionate nights spent in Satyabhama's palace ... the touch of her warm, dark body felt strangely cool and soothing. She had surrendered her body and soul to Krishna completely. Yet, he had betrayed her ...

Yam yam vapi smaran bhavam tyajatyante kalevaram
Tam tamevaiti kaunteya sada tad-bhava-bhavitah

Whatever state of being one remembers when he quits his body, he will attain the same without fail in his next avatar.

I was the one who said this and now ...

Krishna was perplexed. Who could tell Satya that the one who cajoled and pacified her ... her lover, was now ... Why should she be told? If Satya's soul is truly connected with mine, she will naturally come to know. The emptiness in her heart will divulge my absence. Can Satya survive without me?

The very thought of her brought a smile on Krishna's lips. Maybe not ... she might struggle and experience death every living moment. Yet, would that change his decision?

Then what was the point of all these thoughts? Wasn't this attachment? Did he desire in the heart of hearts that once he was gone, someone, especially the women in his life, pine for him endlessly? Was he also thinking like any other ordinary man? Krishna was stunned. What were these thoughts indicating to him? These human emotions and feelings were so strong that even God couldn't be easily freed from them.

It was Arjun's turn to spend the next twelve months with Draupadi.

It was late in the night and Indraprasth was deep in slumber. The lamps in the palace struggled against the breeze. Arjun woke up to find Draupadi standing by the window. Her long, dark hair was glistening in the dim light. Despite her advanced age, Draupadi's body was still beautiful and statuesque. Arjun found the dark-complexioned Draupadi just as captivating now as the time when he had first set eyes on her at her swayamvar.

Arjun too came and stood by the window. Draupadi turned around, startled.

'Are you not able to sleep, Yagyaseni?'

'Sleep? My sleep vanished ages ago. Now I am just waiting for eternal sleep to come and claim me.'

'It's the same for everyone,' Arjun said sighing deeply.

'Parth, my heart is heavy. I don't know why my hands and feet are limp. I stammer ... and break into a sweat.' She looked at Arjun with a strange expression.

Arjun pulled her towards himself affectionately.

'This has been happening often since the Kurukshetra war. I am fearful of sunrise ... the sound of the conch and drums. I am frightened of the war cries of attacking soldiers and of vultures and eagles circling overhead in search of dead prey. I am mortified by the ravenous messengers of death. I am frightened, Draupadi ... that the sun will rise and I will have to pick my bow and arrows again and kill my near and dear ones. I am scared that I will have to listen to the heart-rending screams of my dying kinsfolk; my heart sinks at the very thought, Draupadi.'

'That isn't fear, Parth.'

'Then what is it, Yagyaseni?'

'Parth ...' Draupadi hesitated. She wondered how to tell Arjun about her decision.

'Parth, I want to go and meet my Sakha. Now ... at this very moment.'

Arjun continued to gaze into Draupadi's eyes. Her eyes were sullen, filled with a nameless fear. He guessed that she had had a premonition.

Arjun shook her by the shoulders and asked, 'Why all of a sudden, priye?'

'I don't know why, but I want to just meet him now. My heart is beating fast in anticipation of some forthcoming event. Phalgun, I have been feeling as if Sakha is calling out to me ... his voice is echoing all around this chamber.'

Draupadi clenched her fist as if catching something from the air. 'See?' She opened up her fist in front of Arjun.

Her palm was empty. Arjun looked at her face. There was a strange crazed look in her eyes, and she appeared confounded.

'Here is Sakha's voice. Listen to it. I have been trying to capture it since morning, but it refuses to get trapped. I don't know what my Sakha is trying to tell me, but I am sure he needs me, Parth ... he is calling out to me. Please get the chariot ready. I have to leave for Dwarka right away.'

'But sweetheart, we don't know whether he is in Dwarka or elsewhere ...'

Draupadi cut him mid-sentence, 'I am sure he is in Dwarka. I can see him standing teary-eyed by the window of the palace. I can hear the sound of the crashing waves. Please take me there before it is too late, Parth!'

'Priye, I am not able to understand your agony, but I can feel it ... We will leave at daybreak.'

'Daybreak? By the time the sun rises, it ...'

'Why do you have such ominous thoughts, Yagyaseni? He is God incarnate! So many lives are dependent on him. What can happen to him?'

'God? I haven't seen him in his divine form. For me, he is human. Taller than all of us ... yet human. Parth, everything I have seen in his eyes is the same as every other ordinary human being. Possibly, the lesser human beings living around him have given him the exalted status of God. Otherwise, he ...'

Arjun looked at Draupadi in disbelief. 'Are *you* saying this, Yagyaseni? You, of all people? You are the one who has been witness to most of his miracles, you have experienced his divinity the most, you have been closest to him and experienced his benevolence, and yet ...?'

'Yes, I am saying this. Who else but I can say this? What you call miracles are for me a power, an indomitable desire to reach the other person, an unparalleled power that makes him extraordinary.'

'And what about the way he rescued you in the Kuru palace?'

'That was his love ...' There was a strange purity in Draupadi's eyes. Seeing the ease with which Draupadi was expressing her feelings, Parth felt like agreeing with her. Draupadi continued, 'Just think, Parth. If he was indeed God and could perform miracles, would he have allowed me to come out of my chamber and be taken to the rajya sabha? Would he have even let Dushasan touch me? If my Sakha was really God, Dushasan would have been burnt to ashes even before he caught hold of my saree. And why even go that far, Parth—would he have let Yudhishthir lose the game of dice?

'He has a very pure mind, purer and cleaner than all of us! Just like the waters of the Mansarovar, in which you can see the clear reflection of the sky. What appears to be a miracle to you is nothing but the purity of his subtle consciousness.'

'Yagyaseni, you are such an astute observer and judge of people. And you articulate your insights so sharply.'

'It is all due to Sakha's influence ... Whatever I am today is only owing to all the love I have received from him.'

Arjun's voice became a little rough: 'Only to the love you received from him? Then what about us? Who are we, Yagyaseni? The husbands who did not protect you in the rajya sabha? The ones because of whom you spent twelve years in exile?' Arjun lowered his eyes as he spoke.

'You are the ones who gave me Indraprasth too.' Draupadi's voice became soft as she placed her hand affectionately on Arjun's shoulder. 'Are you feeling jealous of Sakha?' She looked straight into Arjun's eyes.

Despite all the tenderness, the question shook Arjun. She had asked the question very tactfully, ensuring that their relationship remain unaffected. Yet, Arjun's face changed on hearing it.

'Me? Feeling jealous of Sakha? What are you saying, Yagyaseni? He is my life. I breathe because of him. I eat because he is there. I am alive because of him. I am not separate from him. I am his reflection ... a part of him.' Draupadi looked into Arjun's eyes. He was telling the truth. 'Then why did you ask that question? Don't you know that our lives have been possible only because of Sakha?'

'My dear Yagyaseni, I know that. If he hadn't fought on our side in Kurukshetra ... Perhaps, I get disturbed by your attachment to him. As it is, I am sharing you with my four brothers.'

'Attachment? The Gita was addressed to you. If the first listener of the Gita can't differentiate between attachment and devotion, who else will? And Parth, there is no attachment left for anything—this body, the

ornaments, the luxury, the splendour—do you think
I enjoy all this? No, Parth. No! This is what Sakha has
taught me. Absolute acceptance. The dharma taught
by Sakha means accepting everything wholeheartedly,
accepting all of humanity with a smile. It is possible to be
detached despite being tied in relationships. It is possible
to live the life of an ascetic amidst all material wealth.
Sakha's ultimate mantra is, *tyena tyaktena bhunjhithaha*—
enjoy with a sense of renunciation.

'And I too am enjoying life after renunciation ...'
Draupadi laughed. 'Or maybe I am trying to renounce life
after experiencing it to the fullest!'

'Krishnaa ... it seems like Krishna himself is speaking.
Everything you say is so meaningful!'

'Yes, Parth! These are his words. Because my
relationship with Krishna is like that of a child attached to
his mother's umbilical cord. All the thoughts the mother
thinks reach the child. Her hearbeat and her thoughts are
hers but they influence the child's instincts and attitudes.
It is the same with me, Parth.'

Draupadi's eyes welled up with tears. 'Parth, please
take me to Sakha before it's too late.'

Arjun held Draupadi's hand reassuringly and caressed
it lovingly before leaving the room in rapid steps.

Dawn was nearly at its end and the sun's rays had begun
to get straighter and warmer. The sands on the banks of
the confluence had slowly begun to get hotter. Krishna

lay there watching the changing hues of nature with delight. His open eyes were filled with compassion. As he lay pondering about Lord Shiv's mysterious play and the constant journey of life, he was struck by a thought. Life is like a tight-rope walk. It's walking back and forth from one end to the other. Although one is walking constantly, it leads nowhere. The tight-rope walker has to take care that he doesn't lose concentration. After having walked with so much care, precision and skill, if a person doesn't reach anywhere, it makes one wonder! A smile spread on Krishna's face.

Jara asked with folded hands, 'My lord, if you are uncomfortable, please lie down for some time. Your back might be hurting after sitting for so long ...'

The smile on Krishna's face widened. 'Jara, my brother, don't worry about me so much. You were hungry since yesterday. Today, your arrow found me instead of a deer ... Think about your meals.'

'My lord, my hunger and thirst have vanished on seeing you in this condition. Till you feel better, I won't be able to think about anything else.'

'Jara! You care so much for me?' Krishna looked at Jara and closed his eyes. Jara stared at Krishna, perplexed.

Suddenly, Jara heard a sound coming from the riverside. A deer was drinking water. Jara saw the deer and turned his face away. The deer walked away slowly.

Krishna opened his eyes and saw the deer in the distance.

'Jara, didn't you notice that deer?'

'I did, my lord; it was very close.'

'Then why didn't you kill it?'

'My lord ...' Jara muttered, looking at Krishna with a strange, enchanted expression.

'Jara, I am on my last journey. Please stop worrying about me. You still have a life ahead of you. Think about yourself.'

'I will, but only after I complete my unfinished task! Hunting is my livelihood. How will I eat if I don't hunt? I understand that. But at this moment, I am only worried about you—nothing else but your well-being. Not about myself, my hunger, or my hunting.'

Krishna closed his eyes yet again. He had told Arjun, 'Only he who is free from doubt and attachment, and resolutely absorbed in me and works selflessly for the benefit of others will attain moksha or liberation. He whose actions are offered to the lord and whose apprehensions and doubts have vanished because of love may not be a learned person but is certainly a yogi.'

Arjun returned faster than he had gone.

'Yagyaseni, the chariot is ready. How long will it take?'

Draupadi looked up at the sky. The sun wasn't fully up but the sky was a crimson red. It was close to Brahma Muhurta—an hour and a half before sunrise. Draupadi kept looking at the sky as if she was asking, how much time will it take?

The one who was omniscient and could control time was himself watching the dance of time as a spectator. The sun too seemed to have become sullen on seeing Krishna's bleeding foot and hid behind the clouds, waiting for the lord to begin his journey. Unable to bear the brightness of the sun's rays, Krishna closed his eyes. Mata Gandhari's lustrous, pure eyes swam before him. The eyes were without their blindfold, and there were tears streaming from them. Krishna couldn't believe what he was seeing. Was Mata Gandhari crying? She seemed to be asking him, 'Son, are you in terrible pain?' Krishna could feel her soft hands stroking his head.

'Ma! This is a blessing from my mother, a blessing for liberation.'

'Krishna, why did you accept my curse?'

'Ma, who says it is a curse? It's a blessing! Who but you could have wished for my liberation? This is a heartfelt blessing from a mother to her son. Ma, I feel that my time on this earth is over. I just need your permission to leave. Who other than a mother can understand her son's deepest desires?'

'Krishna,' Gandhari couldn't control her tears, 'it will be a sin!'

'You yourself have granted Krishna liberation and the liberator can never be called a sinner.'

'Krishna, please don't go! How will we all live without you?'

Did this voice belong to Gandhari or to Yashoda weeping on the banks of the Yamuna? 'My son, perhaps my mind was clouded; how could I have otherwise cursed you thus? Wasn't I aware that it was my son Duryodhan's liberation too? I have cursed the one who released my son from the cycle of birth and death.'

'Are you repenting for it, Ma? All your words were always acceptable to me.'

'That is what hurts me most, my son. If only you had refused my curse, I wouldn't be alive to see this. How am I going to answer Devaki, Kunti and Yashoda?'

'Please understand that this is not your responsibility. You are venerable, the pride of the Kuru lineage.'

'A mother has a responsibility towards another ... and what about the Kuru family? What am I going to gain by being called the pride of the Kuru race which embarked on the path of destruction and gave birth to the likes of Duryodhan and Dushasan.

'If you can ... please ...' Gandhari lowered her eyes.

'Ma, weren't Vidur and Sanjay born in the same race as Duryodhan and Dushasan? The water that cleanses our feet is the same that becomes slush when it mixes with dirt. The mind is also called water, Ma ...'

'Son, can I ask you for something?'

'What can I give you, Ma?'

'I know. You have given to this world every bit of everything you had. You absorbed all the defilement, accepted it and in return gave purity, love and morality. I wish ...'

'Tell me, Ma. Only the very fortunate get a chance to serve you, don't they?'

'Will you give me whatever I ask for?'

'How can I promise? I have nothing left ... Even my breath is no longer mine.' Krishna sighed deeply.

Gandhari's eyes glistened with an unearthly glow. 'Please take birth from my womb in my next life, son ...'

'That means you are forcing me to take birth again? Won't you liberate me, Ma?' He could see flashes of Devaki and Yashoda in Gandhari's eyes.

'*Tathastu* ... so be it.' Gandhari raised her hands in blessing. Krishna's gaze was fixed on her hands. Her lifeline extended from the edge of her palm to the ends of her fingers. She had a long way to go.

Gandhari's heart-rending wails echoed from the domes of the Hastinapur palace. Kunti sat caressing her back and consoling her, but nothing seemed to work. Gandhari couldn't control her tears.

'I have committed a heinous crime, Kunti ... God will never forgive me.'

'What do you mean, Gandhari?'

'Krishna ... Krishna ...' Gandhari said between her sobs. Her tears fell unabated.

'Krishna? What about him, Gandhari?'

'Kunti, my soul stings me time and again. The reverberations of my own curse are echoing in my ears. I have been audacious enough to curse the greatest man of all time!'

'He accepted your curse, didn't he?' Kunti caressed Gandhari's back. 'That too with such grace.'

Gandhari continued to cry uncontrollably. The blindfold on her eyes was drenched with tears. 'That's his greatness! And I cursed this great soul, the narrator of the Gita, with a beastly death. My karma and my misdeeds will not spare me. After witnessing the death of my hundred sons, what more is left to be seen? What is holding me back here in this defeated and desolate land of Hastinapur?'

Kunti mustered a distressed smile. 'Have you even seen anything, Gandhari? You have lived your whole life blindfolded ...'

'That doesn't mean that I have stopped seeing. On the contrary, the sights in my imaginary world are far more terrifying than those seen by the naked eye.'

'That might be so, Gandhari. Please don't repent what happened in the past. Once a word has escaped your mouth, it is futile to regret it. The curse has been given and it has hit its target. The echoes from the universe are coming back to us, Gandhari, and we are bound to listen to them.'

'This is what karma is, I suppose. Krishna could have liberated me had he wished—by refusing my curse ...'

'Krishna's dharma is to accept—he never refuses or rejects anything.'

'I am really saddened by this,' Gandhari said and began crying loudly yet again. 'Krishna, please forgive me ... please liberate me ... I don't want to live on this earth any more. I don't want to imagine terrible things with my blindfolded eyes. Please liberate me, my lord, please ...'

Jara poured some water from his mud pot into Krishna's mouth. As the water trickled down Krishna's throat, a smile of satisfaction spread on his face.

The worth of water can be realised only when one is thirsty. Water consumed without thirst has no value. Krishna was reminded of his own words.

Seeing Krishna smile, Jara asked, 'Are you at peace, my lord?'

'Yes, Jara. I am really peaceful after having water from your hands. Parth will be here the moment he gets the message.'

'Lord, Arjun is your closest friend, isn't he?'

'Yes, Jara. He is very close to my heart.'

'Lord, what if he takes long to reach here?'

'Then?'

'Then would you ...'

'Then I ...' Krishna smiled with contentment. He continued, after a pause, 'Then maybe I will not wait for him. Time and fate don't wait for anyone.'

Arjun's chariot raced rapidly. Usually, he had a charioteer with him, but today Arjun had decided against it. He was in a hurry to fulfil Panchali's wish. His mind was racing at twice the pace of his speeding chariot.

What had caused Panchali so much distress? Was it her imagination or was Krishna really remembering her? How could only Panchali hear his call? Why couldn't he hear it? Was Panchali truly so close to him? Why couldn't he reach the place where Draupadi had reached?

Krishna had always treated Arjun as his friend. But Arjun was his disciple. Also an indecisive individual who had dropped his weapons in the Kurukshetra war—a broken and shaken man, Arjun thought to himself, being brutally truthful about his actions in the battlefield. While Draupadi was Agniputri—the daughter of fire. After severing Dushasan's arm, when Bheem had asked Draupadi to soak her hair in Dushasan's blood, she wasn't shaken one bit. She smeared her hair, forehead, cheeks and even her lips with his blood. The blood had flown down her chest; her saree and bodice were drenched in blood. When Bheem ripped Duryodhan's thighs, she stood there watching and laughing aloud. Her eyes shone with the derangement of a crazy person. There was a terrifying detachment on her face. The satisfaction of revenge pervaded every cell of her body. What a chilling scene that was! A woman who always looked beautiful, delicate and seductive now looked hideous and frightening. Arjun was reminded of that blood-smeared face every time he held Draupadi's face in his hands.

When Arjun had mentioned this to Krishna, a mysterious smile had played on his lips. He had asked Krishna in distress, 'You, who is ever-forgiving and considers acceptance his dharma, do you think that was justice? Was it dharma?'

'Justice and dharma are two different things, Parth,' Krishna had said with an enigmatic smile. He said, 'Instead of saying blind son of a blind father, had Draupadi said the sighted son of a sighted man, the meaning would have remained the same, wouldn't it have? But Krishnaa puts things as they are—she says the truth. Truth can't always be palatable.'

Arjun stuck to his point and said, 'I am not talking about truth-untruth or palatable-unpalatable. I am talking about justice and dharma. We were equally culpable for the sinful actions committed by Duryodhan and Dushasan; yet Draupadi pardoned us and held them guilty and sentenced them to death. Then, what is the difference between Dhritarashtra and Draupadi? Dhritarashtra constantly discriminates between the Pandavs and Kauravs and Draupadi too is doing the same. So which one is justice and which is dharma?'

'Arjun, you forget that Panchali loves you the same way Dhritarashtra loves Duryodhan. Many a time, we turn a blind eye towards the shortcomings of our loved ones. Panchali feels that if there is anyone who is to blame for all these situations, it is me. She also believes that I could have prevented all this.' Krishna sighed.

A deep silence pervaded the air. Krishna placed his hands on Arjun's shoulder.

'Parth, women and men think differently. Their notions and thoughts about ethics and dharma are very different. One thinks from the heart and the other with the intellect. A woman is far more capable of giving love than a man. For a woman, love is devotion, service and companionship. But for a man, love is, for a large part, only a physical necessity. For a woman, love is an exalted feeling and predominantly a psychic and spiritual experience, while for a man it is but a fleeting emotion. While a woman believes in being faithful to one man all her life, a man can be a polygamist and love all his wives equally. A woman can easily pardon the most heinous crimes of her man whereas he understands only the language of dharma and revenge.'

'Then why is Panchali so different? She could have forgiven Duryodhan? If we behave with a sinner the way he does, how are we different?'

Krishna looked at Arjun as if he was addressing an innocent child, and said in a gentle voice, 'Draupadi thinks like a man. She is also polygamous. Forgiveness and compassion are not part of her ethics ... it will be a mistake for us to expect forgiveness from this Agniputri, born from the flames of vengeance. It is in her nature to seek revenge. It is our fault that we see her as a woman and evaluate her sentiments as one.'

'But the scriptures have laid down rules and regulations for women, and according to them ...'

Krishna cut Arjun mid-sentence. 'And I am telling you that women are far stronger than men and have a very intense relationship with life and nature. Draupadi is exceptionally strong and equally sensitive and refined, Parth.'

Arjun was awestruck. Every word that Krishna said about Draupadi was so true! She had truly been able to detach herself. She had cried inconsolably after she had drenched her hair with Dushasan's blood.

'And anyway, blood is not something frightening for a woman. She sees herself bleed every month, Parth; how can she be afraid of it?'

Arjun was reminded of how Draupadi had completely forgotten about Duryodhan and Dushasan immediately after the Kurukshetra war. She never spoke about them. It was as if they were never part of her existence. She had erased them from her memory so effortlessly. She had not only forgotten the entire episode, she had actually gone to console Bhanumati and Vrishali, Duryodhan and Karna's wives, and like an elder sister and the queen of Hastinapur, provided them shelter.

'Krishnaa—an appropriate name indeed!'

She too, like Krishna, believed in her karma and her individual dharma. She could easily accept every situation with equanimity. She had been stoic even when faced with the death of her sons! When Ashwatthama killed her adolescent sons and consigned them to the flames of death, her heart wailed and she had tears in her eyes, but her face reflected acceptance! When every household in Hastinapur and Indraprasth was losing their brave loved ones to the war, Draupadi set aside the grief of the death of her own sons and stood as an example for all women.

The same Draupadi was distressed today and rushing anxiously to meet Krishna. As the chariot raced ahead, Arjun kept thinking, were Yagyaseni's fears real? Was her Sakha, her guru and the charioteer of her life in some kind of trouble? Had she really heard his call ...?

Draupadi's eyes were getting clouded as she stood on the speeding chariot. A strong breeze blew as the sun readied to rise. The saffron ball was slowly moving upwards.

What is this sky like? Does it belong to dawn or to dusk? It looks the same at both times. Human life is also the same ... Yagyaseni's mind was in turmoil.

Where was the warrior who had been on her husbands' side in the war, the one who hadn't picked up weapons himself but motivated them to? Where was he today?

Why am I so fearful? What kind of pain must Sakha be in now? He was adept at understanding others' pain. He could accept their pain and make it his own. He knew very well how much I loved him; yet he had me married to his friend Arjun ... had me divided among five brothers to keep them united. His eyes were so aggrieved when he came to meet me before the disastrous gamble. But I couldn't read the message in them. He himself had devised everything. He knew that I would call out to him, didn't he?

When Krishna went to Hastinapur with the reconciliatory message from Upalavya, he knew it was futile. Despite knowing that he would be humiliated, he went to Hastinapur with the settlement offer from the Pandavs. And when Duryodhan said, 'Forget five villages, I will not give the Pandavs land even the size of a needle-tip', it was he who had gone to meet the eldest Pandav, hadn't he?

He knew well that Karna would reject Mata Kunti's plea; yet he went to meet Karna, and perhaps that was the reason why Karna was able to embark on his final journey, from the battlefield, a contented man.

Everyone knew that owing to Lord Parashuram's curse, Karna would lose all his skills ultimately. Karna was brought up as a *sutaputra*—a low-born. This man had to bear humiliation from every quarter.

Lord Parashuram, Guru Dron ... and ... and me. Even I hadn't spared him.

When Karna, born wearing the glistening golden armour and earrings, walked like a lion to pierce the fish's eye with his arrow and win my hand in marriage, I had said, 'I will not marry a low-born *sutaputra*.' I hadn't meant to humiliate him. In my heart, I had wished for every prince to fail to fulfil the task and wished for Krishna to be forced to pick up his bow to protect my father Drupad's reputation.

I was sure that if Karna took aim, he would surely hit the target. He was an exceptional archer, unparalleled! Because the news of Arjun and the other Pandavs perishing in the wax palace had spread far and wide by then. I could have said anything else and prevented Karna, but I don't know why I called him *sutaputra* and humiliated him in the rajya sabha. That humiliation tormented him till his last breath, like a thorn in the heart.

When Sakha went to Anga just before the Kurukshetra war to persuade Karna not to fight on Duryodhan's side, the issue of my insult was bound to come up.

The one whom I loved and respected all my life ... And the other who I desired all my life ... What would the two of them have spoken about? Sakha never told me anything but he was filled with pain and sorrow.

After I asked him several times, he just said, 'Sakhi, Karna has encountered so much injustice and tolerated so much discrimination that he has begun to enjoy injustice. He has sent a message for you.' He took a breath and stared at me for a few moments. It seemed as if they were Karna's eyes.

He began to narrate Karna's message with moist eyes: 'Vaasudev, please tell the most beautiful, enchanting, sensuous and exquisite woman that I have pardoned her. And also tell her that if I had pierced the fish's eye as the eldest Pandav and won her hand in marriage, I would never have, under any circumstances, agreed to share her with my other brothers. Please tell her that she should forget the abusive words she said to me in the rajya sabha if she can. Because I can understand her loyalty, fidelity, truth and mettle ... but it is just too late ...' Draupadi's eyes filled with tears thinking about those words even today.

Sakha too seemed to be experiencing Karna's agony while giving her his message. What kind of empathy was this that made Krishna accept everyone's suffering as his own?

Draupadi's mind was whirling with scenes from the past. She was reminded of the day Subhadra had set foot in Indraprasth. Sakha? Could he do such a thing? Draupadi had found herself, unable to accept what had happened. Sakha is well aware of how much I love him. He knows everything about me—and how important self-respect is to me. How could he still allow something like this to happen?

Draupadi had never imagined in her wildest dreams that Krishna would allow his own sister to be kidnapped by Arjun and force her into their lives. Her pride had been crushed on seeing Arjun's affection for Subhadra. While there was merriment in the rajya sabha below, and the melodious strains of the shehnai reverberated all around, Draupadi's chamber was drowned in darkness and a chilling silence.

'Sakhi ... Sakhi, where are you?' Draupadi felt like screaming, shouting and throwing things around at the sound of Krishna's voice. Despite being so close to her, being her confidante, Krishna had humiliated her. Draupadi's anger knew no bounds.

'Sakhi, please say something.' Krishna's voice echoed all around Draupadi's chamber. Finally, Krishna lit a lamp and the room filled up with a soft light.

'You seem to be livid,' Krishna said with a smile.

'And you seem to be ecstatic.' Draupadi couldn't hide her bitterness.

'Why are you sullen?'

'Oh no! I am celebrating ...' Her hair was untied, she was bereft of any ornaments, and her face was red with rage and dark with sorrow.

'I can see that,' Krishna sat down.

'Why, Sakha? Why did you do this? Phalgun was not entirely mine anyway. Now you have ensured that I lose him completely. Why did you do this? I have always wished for your happiness. Why did you bring Subhadra like this?' Draupadi choked. She gulped down tears while wiping her eyes.

'Tears give us a lot of peace, Sakhi. We stop our breath by blocking our tears.'

'You are right, Sakha. You are with me only when I cry. You become aware of my existence only when I am miserable.'

Krishna laughed aloud and said in a gentle voice as if cajoling a child, 'It is not necessary to relate every small thing to our pride. Why are you associating this event with your self-respect, Sakhi?'

'Shouldn't I? A woman has entered my life as a co-wife. You know that I am a woman who has been treated as an object and divided among five men without a thought about her feelings and wishes. I accepted it as tradition. I am the one who has always prayed for her husbands' victory and their well-being, and fought for their rights. I am a woman who was exiled in the forests with her husbands and later lived the life of a maid, just to protect their respect and reputation. And now, a woman enters my life as a co-wife without any consideration for my self-respect. Who is this new wife? She is my closest friend's sister, and he is the one who has masterminded this conspiracy without my knowledge! I don't understand your mysterious ways, Sakha. If this is selfishness, then why is it necessary? If there is anyone's welfare in all this, then whom is it for?'

'Whenever doubts arise in the mind, faith and belief begin to fade, Sakhi.'

'I don't need words; I need to know the truth.'

'The truth? She is not your co-wife. Which brother wouldn't want the best groom for his sister? And is there a man better than Parth in the whole of Aryavart?'

'I am not against your desire for a suitable groom for Subhadra, but unfortunately this man happens to be my husband, Sakha. I was never fazed by Uloopi, Chitrangada and other women, but I am filled with envy seeing Subhadra's beauty. Phalgun is surely going to forget me.'

'Sakhi, what has happened to your wisdom and sagacity? Subhadra is a young girl. Are you going to compete with her?'

'She is young and beautiful; what else would a man desire?'

'A man looks for a lot more. I too am a man and I know. Despite having Satyabhama, Jambavati and many more queens, Rukmini's place in my life is eternal. She is an indispensable part of my life, though Radha never leaves my mind even for a moment. Am I being unjust with Rukmini? Am I being deceitful with my memories of Radha?'

'That is for you to decide, but I feel that if my husband is smitten by another woman, it would only be physical attraction. I take this as my defeat; what does a man look for in a woman other than her body?'

'A man looks for many things in a woman—a mother, a lover, a wife, a friend, a counsellor and sometimes, a strong enemy too. Subhadra will be none of these. She will be servile and devoted. You are strength personified.'

'That means a woman has to be devoted, doesn't she? Do you mean to say that only a woman who is helpless, dependent, dedicated and ready to be her husband's servant is acceptable? A woman who fights for her individuality, stands up for herself, has the gumption to question doesn't deserve love, isn't it?'

'Sakhi, the woman you described is a true *sahadharmacharini* or companion for life. She is the only one who deserves to sit on the throne and be called the queen; you are such a woman, Sakhi. Can any other woman match up to your natural superiority and elegance?'

'And that is why my husbands get Hidimba, Uloopi, Chitrangada and Subhadra, right?'

'I am a man and you are a woman. We are made differently. Although you may possibly not understand what I am saying, I feel it is important for me to tell you nevertheless. It is very easy for a man to get swayed by a woman's magnificence, but it is very difficult for him to come out of the sway unscathed. Sakhi, man is egoistic by nature and hence appreciates and loves women who are dependent, devoted to him and look up to him. A woman like you is rare and it takes more than one man to handle your intensity and prowess. The situation that you accepted grudgingly couldn't have been better for you. It truly turned out to be a boon. The arrangement of spending a year each with the five Pandav brothers too was a result of the inability of the men to stand up to your excellence. If the sun continues to shine with all its brilliance constantly, the earth and its beings will suffer immensely. Just watch the sun's rays at dawn and at dusk. If nature hadn't arranged for the sun to set and to provide us with cool nights, life on earth would have been impossible.'

'Do you mean to say that the sun's brilliance is not a virtue but a fault?'

'This discussion can be endless, Sakhi! Endless discussion is not the solution to any problem. And truly, there is no problem to be solved here. You shine like the sun in Parth's life and his life is unthinkable without you. Not just Parth, even your other husbands cannot imagine a life without you. You are the one who is keeping them together and you are the heart of this house and family.'

The tears that Draupadi had held back for so long flowed down her cheeks.

'I am getting burnt by my own brilliance, Sakha! Whom do I go to for some soothing? Where do I go for the coolness of the rising and the calming rays of the setting sun?'

'This is your destiny.'

'Call it misfortune, Sakha. Being like the sun is a curse. I have been doomed to burn constantly; I was born as Agniputri—the daughter of fire. People forget that I am a woman too.'

'No, it's just that your femininity gets masked by your fierce brilliance.'

'What is my offence—my femininity or my brilliance?'

'Being extraordinary is an offence. To be born before your time is an offence. It is an offence to know and to see something before its time. You have to pay a price to gain something, Sakhi!'

'Sakha, doesn't your brilliance ever burn you?'

'I am the moon. I am not illuminated myself. My effulgence is not my own. I reflect all the light that I receive from around me and hence it doesn't scald me. You are the source of your own brilliance, Sakhi, and hence, it is your destiny to burn.'

'Krishna, you never tried even once to give me a small part of your radiance and douse the constantly raging fire within me with your coolness and composure. Why, Sakha?'

'That's because it is my necessity. I have to incinerate adharma or immorality in these flames ... Subhadra is just a piece of wood which will keep the fire inside you burning for a little longer ...'

'I just don't understand you at times, Sakha!'

'Where do I understand myself?'

Krishna's eyes were glistening in the dim light of the lamps in that dark chamber. Draupadi decided to accept Subhadra. She called her maids and ordered them to illuminate the palace with lamps.

Why are women so similar to each other?

Sitting under the peepal tree, Krishna wondered as he remembered Draupadi's dark palace: Why do all women, of any period and age, think the same way? Why do they feel miserable about or get angry at the same things? And why is their way of expressing anger similar too? He chuckled.

Did these questions mean anything any more? His life had been lived. Why did the three most important women in his life feel the same compassion towards him, worry equally for him and love him with the same fierce intensity? The time to think about all this was long gone; only the memories of these women remained. They were not with him, but their eyes seemed to be looking at him with anxiety, ardour, warmth and immense love.

The three rivers flowed towards the sea, and the faces of the three women were reflected by the sun's rays falling unevenly on the undulating surface of the flowing rivers. Those were the faces of his lover, wife and Sakhi.

Their flowing faces seemed to be telling him, 'Our significance and worth lies in becoming one with you ...

you are the one who has blessed us with immensity. You have made us realise our limitless potential, absorbed our scorching brilliance and comforted us with your soothing presence. You have dignified our femininity while giving us love.'

The eyes of the three women seemed to merge together behind Krishna's closed eyes and reach his heart. A wave of pain radiated through his body, and he was reminded of that night in Dwarka. It was the night when Satyabhama had stepped into the palace, and Krishna's life, carrying the Syamantak diamond.

The palace of Dwarka had been illuminated with thousands of lamps. The streets were decorated with colourful rangoli patterns and sprinkled with rose water, and the palace entrances were festooned with flower garlands. At every single window in Dwarka stood men and women bedecked in finery and exquisite jewellery. Mata Devaki stood at the main entrance of the palace with the ceremonial tray, waiting to welcome the newlyweds.

The golden city of Dwarka was filled with the happy chatter of people. People joyfully threw gulaal at each other and waited with bated breath to get a first look of their king and his new bride.

But Rukmini's palace was drowned in darkness with a solitary lamp giving out a dim light. A beautiful young woman sat with red and swollen eyes, staring at the lone lamp. Her silk clothes, studded with exquisite gems, lay on the floor gathering dust, and her jewellery was scattered all over the room.

Her life seemed worthless. She felt as if she had no one to call her own in the golden land of Dwarka. The lover for whom she had walked away from her family and home, now belonged to someone else.

Krishna was surprised at not seeing a single familiar face among the innumerable people who had come to welcome them. He was reminded of the conversation with Draupadi regarding Subhadra.

After the welcome ceremony, Krishna went into the palace built exclusively for Satyabhama. He stepped out of the bedroom for a moment when she held his hand and asked, 'Where are you going at this hour?'

'To meet Rukmini.' He tried to extricate his hand gently. Satyabhama moved closer and placed her head on his chest. She wrapped her hands around his back and asked, 'Can't you avoid going tonight?'

'It will be fine even if I never go.' Krishna gently moved away. 'But my mind says I must go and meet her. Rukmini wasn't present at the welcome ceremony. She must be deeply upset.'

'Will you console her?'

'No, she is a very wise and mature woman and won't need any cajoling. I just have to clarify a few facts to her and she will understand.'

'You could tell her tomorrow as well?'

'No ... today's hurt has to be alleviated today itself, or else it will turn into a wound tomorrow.'

'My lord, didn't you know because of my arrival that this was bound to happen?'

'Honestly, no. I hadn't imagined that a woman like Rukmini would behave thus.'

'If I were in her place, I too would have done the same. It can't be easy to share you. Everyone wants you wholly for themselves.'

'But I always offer myself completely to everyone. There is no question of less or more. Everyone wants love, and more and more of it, my dear! There is no end to the amount of love you can pour into the sands of expectation. Every ounce gets absorbed, and yet it remains parched and thirsts for more.'

'Do you mean to say that the sand shouldn't expect rain? Should the desert always remain dry?'

'If you expect rain, you need to make the soil fertile. Even the clouds rain more over tree-laden forests.'

'My lord. I want to be your only wife and have sole rights over your love.'

'How can all the rain fall on a single piece of land? If that happens, it will be a cloudburst, and excess of anything is not beneficial to anyone. Only the right proportion of rain is needed for crops to grow ... even you will be able to digest only a certain proportion of love. Excessive love too can lead to ruin.' Saying so, Krishna walked out of the room. Satyabhama stood mesmerised at the intelligence and wisdom of the extraordinary man.

The realisation that she was the wife of such a great man filled her with pride.

Despite that, she couldn't bring herself to accept the fact that she had to share his love with others. She looked down her window to see Krishna hurrying towards the main palace, his shawl flying in the air behind him. Just the sight of his slender, leonine waist and broad, marble-like shoulders made Satyabhama want to lose herself in his arms.

God only knows when he will be back, Satyabhama thought in anger. Couldn't he have avoided going to console her tonight? She could see the discomfiture clearly in his hasty steps. Watching her husband's anxiety to meet Rukmini, Satyabhama decided, Rukmini may well be his queen consort, but it is I who will be his beloved and favourite wife and rule his heart. I may not be as well-read, and may be incapable of discussing politics and the scriptures with him, but I will bind him to my palace with my sensuality.

Satyabhama felt a hand on her shoulder. It was her maid, Manorama. She had accompanied Satyabhama to Dwarka and had known her since childhood. She had overheard every word of Satyabhama's conversation with Krishna. Manorama loved to gather information, gossip and report everything to her mistress.

'Maharani, feeling miserable will not help. You will have to fight for your rights here.'

'Fight? For what? She too is his wife after all. I would have behaved in the same way in her place.'

'That is your goodness talking. Otherwise, who can stand a chance in front of your beauty and love for Krishna?'

'Manu, I am not upset because he went to meet her. But he could have avoided going tonight, couldn't he?'

'That is exactly what I am trying to tell you, your majesty. Tonight was exclusively yours! How could he go tonight?'

'But I am not going to sulk tonight; I will carefully store this instance in my memory and ensure that the queen consort pays the price for having stolen time from this night.'

'You are not alone here, Maharani. There are sixteen thousand other queens.'

'Not sixteen thousand, sixteen thousand one hundred and seven to be precise. But he loves me ... that is enough. I know how to handle the rest.' Satyabhama glanced at her own dark-toned body. Her skin looked as if it had been made by mixing butter with kohl.

'Maharani, please be careful. What else can I say?'

'You are here with me. Just keep getting me information, and I will take care of the rest.'

Krishna climbed the stairs to Rukmini's palace and entered the main wing. It was completely dark, which didn't surprise Krishna. He was merely surprised at Rukmini's behaviour. He had certainly expected her to understand the situation. Patarani was aware of the battle that was fought for the Syamantak jewel and the pact with Satyaki. She was the one who had suggested that they reconcile with Satyaki and now she herself ...

How will I talk to her? What will I say? How will I explain to such a wise woman? She has so many answers for all my statements. She had suggested a reconciliation ... marriage was probably not what she had in mind. She wasn't this distressed about my weddings with Jambavati and the other queens. So, why now?

Krishna walked into Rukmini's chamber, lost in thought. A lone lamp fought valiantly with the darkness. Rukmini sat with her head bowed, crouched on a narrow seat. Her long, flowing hair reached the floor. Clothes and jewellery lay scattered all over the room.

'My dear Patarani, my queen!' Krishna said in a soft voice. Rukmini looked up. Krishna's heart ached on seeing her bloodshot eyes. He came close and sat down beside her. The moment he placed his hand on her shoulder, Rukmini burst out crying.

'My Dwarka will get swept away by your tears ...'

'So be it. Even I want to flow away with Dwarka and go back to Kundinapur along the Poorna river.'

Krishna smiled and said, 'The Poorna flows from Kundinapur towards Dwarka. Once you reach Dwarka, all roads to Kundinapur are blocked, my dear.'

'So what? I will give up my life in the vast seas of Dwarka.'

'But your life is tied up with mine. How can you decide anything about your life without my consent?'

'Are you joking?'

'Joking? Do I look like a jester to you, my dear? A bride is sulking out there, and a queen is taunting me here. One is angry because I came here, and the other will get angry when I go there.' Krishna burst out laughing.

'Go happily; I am not one bit angry.'

Krishna continued with a smile, 'I can clearly see that on your face.'

'What do you care about my sorrow or my anger?'

'Me? You are my wife, my *ardhangini*. When one half of me is sad and angry, how can the other half be happy? The half of me that resides in Satyabhama's palace is also angry ... she too is my *ardhangini*.'

'Then go and console her.'

'That is not possible till my first half is propitiated.'

'My lord! Your words cannot prevail upon me today.'

Krishna engulfed her in a tight embrace and said with a smile, 'If not words, what about touch?'

'Swami! All this is futile. My mind is disturbed. I don't know why, but ever since Satyabhama has come, I am ...'

'If a mother has two children and a third arrives, is she afraid that her love will get divided?'

'This is about man and woman, not mother and son.'

'I am talking about the divine relationships of the world. If Mata Gandhari can love all her hundred children equally, why can't I love and respect all my wives equally? My love is infinite. It can extend to whatever limit you want it to.'

'Then stay back here tonight.'

'What will you achieve by doing this? Victory? Against whom?'

He continued, 'True victory is one that is attained over the self. Victory over others is fleeting and transient, my dear. If I stay here tonight, you will surely win. Your femininity, your status as the queen consort will be proven superior in comparison to the new bride. But what about your personality? You will come across as small, shallow and ungracious. Have you thought about this?'

'Swami!'

'You are the queen consort. The queen of Dwarka, the destiny of the Yadavs! Your hands should rise to give, not to ask. Even if you consider me as an object, for a moment, and give me to Satyabhama, you will prove yourself to be greater. The giver's hands are always higher than the receiver's. Satyabhama is a child; she doesn't know politics and doesn't understand the language of giving and taking. She has been used as a pawn in the fight for the Syamantak jewel, but you are the conscious one. You understand politics, strategy and relationships. And you choose to behave like this?' It seemed to Rukmini as if her entire palace had been illuminated. She suddenly felt ashamed at her own behaviour.

Krishna was right. How could she have behaved like this? Why had she entered into this meaningless competition with a young girl? What was she trying to achieve?

She rested her head on Krishna's shoulder and said, 'Please forgive me, my lord!'

'It is I who should seek pardon from you for hurting your feelings. If I had known that you would be so hurt, I would have visited you immediately after the welcome ceremony. I would have gone to Satyabhama's palace only after seeking your consent. Sweetheart! Everyone is equal for me. For me, you and Satyabhama are the same. I love everyone dearly and accept everyone wholeheartedly. I absorb everyone within me and consider them as my own. Weren't you aware of this?'

'My lord, I don't know why I behaved thus. I am mortified.'

Krishna laughed aloud and said, 'After all, the wise and learned Maharani is also a woman. Till today, I have only debated with you and admired your erudition. But I feel truly blessed and fortunate to have met this affectionate wife, seeped in love.'

'Lord! Are you teasing me?' She covered her face with her palms. Krishna gently prised her palms open. 'As it is, there is only a lone lamp in this room. Do you know how dark it will be if you hide your face too?'

'My lord!' Rukmini blushed.

'I really don't feel like going from here.'

'Satyabhama will be waiting for you ... you have to go.'

'Do you mean it from your heart?'

'Yes, I mean it. This night belongs to Satyabhama, and I have to give you and her this right.'

'And you? What will you do? Sit all night morosely in this dimly lit room, stripped of all finery?'

'No, not at all. I will call the maid immediately and get a fragrant oil massage. I will have a nice shower, get ready and come to Satyabhama's palace to welcome her in the morning.' Then she said with a slight smile, 'You too will be there, won't you? I will get to see the glow that suffuses your face after spending the first night with your new bride.'

Krishna stood up laughing.

'Can't forget the first night spent with the bride, right?'

'Can you?'

'It is my duty.'

'And my dharma.'

'You are truly wise. It is impossible to win a game of words with you.'

'Then why do you play?'

'To lose the game. There is a unique pleasure in losing to you, my dear. Only the loser can understand this ...'

When he gave her a firm embrace and stepped out, Rukmini's palace came alight with lamps.

'Where is my queen? Still sad?' Krishna asked walking into Satyabhama's chamber, decorated with fragrant white flowers. The thick silk curtains hanging from the windows fluttered in the strong sea breeze. The tide was high and the sound of waves crashing on the shore could be heard distinctly in Satyabhama's palace.

'The queen consort will be here to welcome you in the morning! I believe you too will give her an appropriate welcome.'

'Anyone who steps into my palace will be welcomed appropriately. She is the queen consort! The queen of the king of Dwarka, protector of cattle and Brahmins, the greatest statesman, the mentor of the Pandavs and the one who is considered God.'

'Whom are you talking about, dear? I am from Gokul. Nand baba's son, Yashoda's Kanha and an ordinary cowherd.'

'A cowherd who drives the whole of Aryavart with the stick of his intellect, isn't it?'

'As you say. I have just returned after a very serious conversation and this happens to be the first night of our marriage. We will have several nights to talk about Aryavart and Bharat's politics. At this moment ...'

'What?' Satyabhama's voice quivered and her eyes shone. Her body became taut and her lips parted in anticipation.

'At the moment, I have to make my bride my wife. I have to give her her rights.'

'Rights?' Satyabhama asked.

'The rights to my love. The words "I love you" can be expressed without words too. I want to prove that to you.'

'Swami!' Satyabhama blushed and ran into Krishna's open arms.

Two palaces in Dwarka were lit bright that night. One was bathed in the abundance of love and the other was steeped in the light of devotion.

Kunti and Krishna sat without exchanging a word. The sky looked brown from the windows of the main palace of Indraprasth. Kunti's face was lined with pain and she looked distracted. Krishna stared at the sky silently.

'It's Karna's wish. He will conduct himself the way God wants him to.'

'Foi, you should talk to him once.'

'Me? Will he listen to me?'

'You are his mother, he may not refuse.'

'Kanha, what if he does?'

'Then he will fight for the Kauravs and brothers will kill each other,' Krishna prophesied. His voice sounded distant and grim. Kunti's eyes filled with tears.

'I am to blame for all this. I am the one who abandoned him. When the mother herself disregards life ...'

'Foi, I beg you, please talk to him once ... please try to convince him.'

Kunti stared fixedly at Krishna's face. Tears streamed down her face. She kept crying uncontrollably for a long time, while Krishna sat quietly staring at the sky.

'Kanha, if I talk to him, the Pandavs ...'

'The Pandavs will be enthused and Duryodhan's back will be broken.'

'But Kanha ...'

'Foi, I have promised you that your five sons will be safe. I am not asking you to request Karna to join the Pandavs out of fear or apprehension. But because I don't want to see a brave warrior and a great man lose. After all, he is my brother too.'

'Krishna, do you really think so?'

'Why? Why can't I? Foi, devastation is certain, but I want to try to save as many people as I can. History will stand witness to my efforts. That is why I went for peace talks.'

'Fine, Kanha. I will meet him if you so desire. But I know his answer already.'

'Whether he accepts you or not, it is important for you to accept and acknowledge him before he goes to the battlefield. It's important for both of you ... This is a battle for pride, acceptance and for existence. It is a fight for righteousness and dharma. It is a mother's duty to accept her son, and Foi, I can tell you from what I see that it is important for you to accept Karna once, for his peace and liberation.'

Krishna sat by the window in Rukmini's palace, worried and disheartened. Rukmini entered the room with a glass of hot milk.

'My lord, what are you thinking about?'

'As you are aware, dear, the situation is becoming grim.'

'What can you do? Brothers warring for property rights is nothing new. It has been happening from time immemorial.'

'But my dear, unfortunately, the whole of Aryavart will be burnt in the fire of this war. I will have to witness the miserable sight of innumerable war widows and the hopeless future of orphaned children.'

'You are certain about whose side you are going to be on, aren't you? And that side is bound to win the war.'

'But there will be so much bloodshed. There seems to be no way to avert this war.'

'Does your Sakhi have any ideas?' Rukmini asked.

Krishna looked at her aghast. 'Panchali? What can she do?'

'Politics dictate that when the enemy is afraid that they will lose the war, they become ready to surrender.' Rukmini said.

'Duryodhan knows that he will not win, but he is so conceited that he isn't ready to listen to anyone. You know very well that I had gone to them for reconciliation, but seeing the way Duryodhan humiliated me, the Pandavs are not going to sit quiet. And why should they? Tolerating injustice is injustice too.'

'There must be a way to get the Pandavs get their due while there is no bloodshed.'

'Please tell me, my mind is numb. If you have any such suggestions, I will welcome them.' Even as he asked the question, Krishna knew there was no way the war could be averted.

'Karna is Duryodhan's biggest strength and Draupadi is Karna's biggest weakness,' Rukmini said with an evocative smile.

'You don't mean ...'

'Yes, I mean exactly that and you have to do it. Your Sakhi will never disobey you. Mata Kunti and you failed in your efforts. But if Draupadi tries to talk to him, he might agree to fight on the Pandavs' side.'

'That is impossible. Karna will never do that.'

'Do you remember what he had said to you? It is not right for you to commit anything on Draupadi's behalf.'

'Yes, but ...'

'Irrespective of whether he chooses to fight from the Pandavs' side or not, Duryodhan's strength will be considerably weakened if Karna does not fight the war, just the way you aren't.'

'Your suggestion will only be an attempt. As far as I know Panchali, this won't be acceptable to her. And Karna's only goal is to kill Arjun.'

'Just give it a try. Panchali might agree, and Duryodhan and Karna's army might not have the courage to fight the Pandavs.'

'Patarani, I really respect your wisdom and intellect. Given the present circumstances, we must try everything possible, and I will surely make an attempt.'

'My lord, even though war looks imminent, time will certainly, gratefully validate the efforts you took.'

Draupadi's face was red with rage and her eyes were blazing.

She didn't know what to say to Krishna. Karna was her husband's sworn enemy. He had humiliated her by calling her a whore in the rajya sabha, and here was Sakha, wanting her to go and talk to him! He wanted her to put her self-respect aside and plead with him to fight on the Pandavs' side. For what? Purely in the hope of victory?

'Sakha, you are on our side; justice and dharma are on our side. Our victory is certain. Why should we belittle ourselves by pleading with Duryodhan's friend?'

'He is also the eldest Pandav.'

'For me, he is only my enemy's friend and an enemy's friend is an enemy too! Have you forgotten the way he humiliated me in the rajya sabha?'

'Sakhi, you too had called him a *sutaputra* in a very despicable manner.'

'At that time, he *was* a *sutaputra,* and you know that I ...'

'At a time when we are taking our first steps into this great crusade, it is your duty and your dharma to douse the fire in his heart and accept him.'

Draupadi's eyes were afire. 'And your diplomacy, I suppose.'

'If you say so, yes. You have to meet Karna once to ensure the safety of your five husbands.'

'You are saying this?' Draupadi asked, gazing intensely at Krishna.

'Yes. It is my suggestion that you make this one final attempt before the start of this war.'

'Your wish is my command. Do we have an option of not following it?'

'It is all right if you don't wish to; I was only thinking about everyone's welfare ...'

'Everyone's welfare? Their welfare is in this great war, my lord? Possibly the wails of grief from every household in Hastinapur and the helpless cries of orphaned children must be in everyone's welfare? I truly don't understand words like individual duty, politics and protection ... do I?'

'Your words are hurting me, Sakhi. I too agree that every person is correct in his own right. But the ultimate truth can be seen only when we trade places. If you don't even look in that direction, how will the light of the sun rising from there even reach you?'

'My lord, truth is like the light behind closed eyes. Even if the light doesn't reach the eyes, you can still feel its warmth. I am still keen to see whether your radiance and the power of your actions provide us with light or burn us with their intensity ...'

'Sakhi, you are sharp and can argue clearly, but you cannot understand feelings very well. Everything cannot be explained through numbers. The blooming of flowers, the falling of dew and its evaporation as soon as the sun rises are natural occurrences. Is there any logic to them?'

'Logic ...' Draupadi gave a bitter smile. 'If I had to look for logic, I wouldn't be living as the wife of five husbands. My father arranged for my swayamvar and organised the archery challenge without my permission. The Pandavs came to my swayamvar disguised as Brahmins. Despite knowing everything, you made Arjun attempt the task. As if this wasn't enough, Mata Kunti ordered for me to be shared between the five brothers. What was the logic in a woman being shared like an object? You talk about logic, Sakha? What was the logic behind dragging a menstruating woman to the rajya sabha? Was there any logic in staking one's wife? The rajya sabha, filled with the wisest of people, watched the horror in silence ... what was the logic, Sakha? What was the logic that made you wait till my dignity was crushed? If you had wished, Dushasan's hands would have been broken even before they touched me. What was the logic of putting me through all that pain and anguish?'

Draupadi's voice was choked with rancour. Her body shivered. Though tears weren't flowing from her eyes, it seemed as if her whole body was drenched in sweat and tears.

Krishna got up and filled a silver cup with water from an earthen pot nearby. He took Draupadi's hand in his and handed her the cup. He then gently held her face in his palms and said, 'Sakhi, in all of history, has there been any woman, who could curse Sati Gandhari's sons? And you, Sakhi, Agniputri, how is it possible for your tongue to spit fire without you being singed?'

'What do you mean?' Draupadi calmed down after sipping some water. She wiped the sweat off her face.

'Sakhi, there is logic in everything I say, but it may possibly not reach you. It is also possible that I may not allow the logic to reach you ... but logic is my duty, my objective.'

'Does this mean that we are mere pawns in your game of logic?' Draupadi said in a hurt voice.

'No, you are allies and companions—my loved ones, who help me achieve my goals.'

'Sakha, why did you do this? My humiliation will be remembered for thousands of years. I will be branded a helpless and weak woman for generations to come.'

'Helpless?' A smile spread on Krishna's face. 'You, the woman who takes care of five husbands, is helpless?' Krishna said affectionately, 'You will be remembered forever as a pure and sharp woman who struggled constantly to protect her individuality and self-respect. Relationships are never only about giving and taking. A relationship is about the union of souls wherein truth and words prove inadequate. Do you understand that anyone who is capable of helping me in fulfilling my duty should have a personality more magnificent and powerful than my own? When a woman is faced with the moment where she has to curse the sons of Gandhari—a woman who is revered for her chastity and faithfulness— her majesty and radiance have to be as bright as the sun. Agniputri, don't be under the illusion that the purpose of your birth is seeking revenge. The purpose of your life is the upliftment of dharma and it will erase the darkness of the times and spread the light of radiance in this world.'

'I will still not meet Karna. I don't want to have any part in this,' Draupadi said, as she swiftly walked towards the door. At the door, she turned around to look at Krishna, her eyes filled with a strange mix of affection and pride. She folded her hands and said, while looking into his eyes,

'Twadiyam vastu govindam tubhyamev samarpaye'.

Then she ran out of the room, sobbing silently, with the end of her saree stuffed in her mouth.

A private meeting had been arranged in Duryodhan's palace and Balaram had travelled all the way from Dwarka just for this meeting.

'Mama, do you think Balaram will agree?' a confused Duryodhan asked Shakuni.

'Why are you worried, my dear nephew? Even otherwise, Balaram is against Krishna. Being the elder brother, he is really annoyed at being deprived of the throne by Krishna.'

'How do you know this?' Duryodhan asked.

'Son, I am Shakuni. I can walk in and out of people's minds. We will convince Balaram that he will get the throne of Dwarka.'

'That is going to be difficult, Mama. He will not accept easily. I know him; he is my guru. He may have his problems with Krishna and resent him, but if that cowherd calls him Dau even once, this man will melt like wax.'

'Look Duryodhan, Bheeshma Pitamah, Guru Dron, Ashwatthama, your acharyas, your uncle, your father-in-law and numerous other princes are already on your side. And if Balaram joins you too, your army will become undefeatable.'

'Arjun's arrows are enough to eliminate all these people, Mama.'

'You are forgetting Karna, my dear. You have an archer to match Arjun on your side.'

'But, Mama, Krishna will certainly go to Karna and convince him that as the eldest Pandav he should be on their side. If that happens, Karna will not be mine any more. Being called a *sutaputra* has been the most humiliating experience of his life. You can't put it past Krishna to promise Karna that he will be given the status of the eldest Pandav and made king.'

'King? By assuming that Karna will be called the eldest Pandav and get the royal throne, you have conceded defeat even before the war has begun. Are you afraid that if that happens, Karna will desert you and fight the war on the Pandavs' side, and we will lose the war?'

'I can't be completely sure about Karna as yet. Also, his attraction for Draupadi might just pull him towards the Pandavs.'

'You are really stupid, my dear nephew. Why would Karna be interested in being the sixth husband? And which throne are you talking about? Karna knows his death is destined. He knows about Parashuram's curse. His golden armour and earrings have been taken away by Indra. Eldest Pandav, my foot!'

'Mama, do you agree that Krishna will surely speak to Karna once?'

'Let him, my son ... nothing will change. Karna is indebted to you for your benevolence. Karna is not so ungrateful that he will forget how you treated him with respect by making him the king of Anga. And more importantly, Karna will never let go of the first and last chance to torment Kunti for having abandoned him. He will never fight for the Pandavs, even if it means walking into his own death! He will reject and scorn them and create the fear of Arjun's death in their minds because if the Pandavs fear anyone, it is Karna.'

'I told you he won't agree,' Kunti said sobbing uncontrollably. Every word she had exchanged with Karna was piercing her heart.

'It is all my fault. A child abandoned by his own mother has every right to hate her. He humiliated me. I begged and pleaded that he should call me Ma just once. He refused my request and insulted me by calling me Rajmata.'

'But you accepted him, right? Don't worry, he will calm down now. He will not hold anything against you. He will leave behind all his thirst, desire and pain before he departs.'

'Which means that his departure is certain?' Kunti asked.

'Every person who has come is destined to go. Karna is no different.'

'He is my son. He will not attain moksha if he fights on the side of adharma.'

'Foi, don't take it personally. He has faced injustice since the moment he was born. A child born out of mere curiosity is brought up by a charioteer. He learns about injustice and gets cursed. He is unfairly disallowed from participating in the swayamvar and gets thrown to the side of adharma by deceit. Destiny has been unjust to him! How can he escape it?'

'It is entirely my fault. I failed to take responsibility of my child. I am being punished for my sins.'

'Punishment? Where have you been punished yet? You are yet to see devastating bloodshed with your own eyes. You have to experience numerous horrifying moments. You have to mutely watch the youth of Aryavart perish on the battlefields of Kurukshetra.'

'Kanhaiya, is my sin so grave?'

Krishna stared into the void silently, but Kunti got her answer.

The battlelines for Kurukshetra had been finalised at a private meeting in Duryodhan's palace. He had decided that he wouldn't give an inch of land to the Pandavs. Shakuni and Duryodhan seemed confident that they would be victorious. Besides, Shakuni's prediction of Karna's response to Krishna's ploy had turned out to be right. Even Duryodhan was right about Krishna. Krishna had decided to meet Karna once before the war. It was not as if he was unaware of the result of that meeting; yet, he had to try at least once.

It was common knowledge that Karna never refused anyone who came asking him for anything while he was praying to Suryadev at dawn. Indra had chosen the same time to ask for Karna's golden armour and earrings. Krishna too chose dawn to meet him.

The currents of the Hiranya and Kapila rivers gently merged with the Saraswati and flowed into the sea ... It was as if Krishna could see the events of the past in the gentle waves of the Saraswati. The Saraswati seemed to have transformed into the Ashwa river and Karna was standing in it, praying to the Suryadev.

Krishna could still visualise Aryavart's finest archer, with his broad, rock-like chest covered in golden armour, extending his powerful arms towards the sun to pay his salutations. But all of a sudden, the vision disappeared from his eyes. How many years had gone by? Yet, Krishna could still see Karna's pained eyes staring at him. 'Why Madhusudan? Why did you tell me? I didn't want to know the truth. The truth that has shattered my existence to pieces. I could neither become a Pandav, nor remain a *sutaputra*. You have left me stranded. You could think only about the welfare of the Pandavs.'

Krishna could hear himself telling Karna, 'Yes, the welfare of the Pandavs ... I consider you a Pandav! Hence your welfare too, isn't it?'

Karna's deafening laughter echoed all around the Triveni confluence. He had collapsed, laughing and then crying bitterly that day.

A lone tear rolled down Krishna's closed eyes.

Karna stood knee-deep in the Ashwa river, praying to the sun. His bare back, devoid of his golden armour, glistened with perfection. Even though he had lost his armour and earrings, his magnificence remained unchanged. Droplets of water gleamed like pearls on his golden burnished skin. At a little distance, his chariot and horses stood under a tree.

What Krishna intended to tell him was going to scar Karna for life. But it was necessary for Karna, stripped of his golden armour and earrings, to know the truth. Krishna was going to give him his new identity as a Pandav scion.

It was a very difficult task for Krishna. He had to tell Duryodhan's closest friend, Karna, who had made up his mind to fight the war from the Kuru camp, that he was a Pandav—the eldest Pandav!

Krishna walked slowly towards the river. He waited till Karna finished his prayers. Karna looked as brilliant as the sun as he stepped out of the water. His face changed the moment he saw Krishna, but he kept himself in check.

He had already guessed what Krishna would have come to say to him two days before the war.

Krishna moved forward when Karna greeted him with folded hands saying, 'Namaskar Vaasudev'.

'May you live long ... be victorious!' Krishna said.

Karna burst out laughing. 'Lord, how will you feel if your blessings prove to be wrong?'

'Not my blessings, these are my best wishes. And there are ways by which these can come true—only if you accept.'

Karna continued laughing. 'I should fight on the Pandavs' side, isn't it? You know that is impossible. My rivalry with Arjun is age-old. It's been continuing right from the princes' childhood days till Draupadi's swayamvar.' Karna sighed deeply.

'Such rivalry is quite natural between two brothers, right?'

'Brothers?' Karna's face reflected both bewilderment and a sense of hurt.

'Karna, look, I haven't come here to beat around the bush and trap you in a web of words. What I have to tell you is true and clear. There is only adharma, injustice and trickery on the Kauravs' side, and ...'

'And the Pandavs have dharma, truth, justice and you on their side ...' Karna laughed. 'Are you enticing me? Tempting me with life and victory?'

'You are complete by yourself. Nobody can offer you anything, Karna. All your life, you have only given to others. You gave away your armour and earrings too! What can I offer you?' There was a strange hollowness in Krishna's voice. 'I have not come here with any enticement; I have come to tell you a truth. After this, whether you get life or death, choose to be with dharma or adharma, decide to help your friend or your brothers ... it is upto you, o eldest Pandav!'

'Eldest Pandav ... Madhusudan!' Karna's voice was filled with disbelief. 'You too believe so?'

'I know it.' Krishna looked into Karna's eyes. His eyes were turning red. He said, 'So ... now what?'

The gurgling waters of the Ashwa crashing on the rocks were creating an eerie symphony. The birds chirping on the trees had gone silent. The sun's rays were searing, and the sands too had become hot. Karna's eyes were moist.

'Now what?' Karna asked again.

Krishna stepped forward and placed his hands on Karna's shoulders. 'Yes, you are Kunti's son—the eldest Pandav. I wish that you get your rightful place. When dharma wins and the victory procession reaches the gates of Indraprasth, I wish that there be six Pandavs, not five.'

Karna laughed so loudly that his laughter reverberated all around. Tears were streaming down Karna's face and yet, he continued laughing. Krishna looked at him without batting an eyelid. Karna slumped down disconsolately. Krishna sat down beside him stroking his hair and patting his back. Then, he said, 'You will get Draupadi too.'

'Draupadi? I will not accept Draupadi even if she is offered to me in charity. Everyone knows me as the most benevolent one! I don't want to beg for Draupadi.'

'I know you love her even today.'

'There is a big difference between loving someone and having their love, Krishna; who knows this better than you? She is known as Krishnaa even today, and you are the one who got her married to Arjun. You are the one who allowed her to be shared among five brothers, didn't you? And today, you are promising her to me on her behalf. Has Draupadi herself said that she will sit with me on my chariot on our victory procession to Indraprasth?'

'She has to accept this, eldest Pandav!' Krishna said and forcefully tried to put on his most charming smile.

'Rejecting once and accepting unconditionally later.' Karna's eyes looked dejected. 'Whether it is Kunti or Draupadi, what difference does it make to Karna's destiny? You are accepting me solely to protect Arjun and keep the Pandavs alive. I am not an ignorant fool! I am Duryodhan's friend. I don't need to be taught politics, Dwarkanaresh!'

For some time, the only sounds that were heard on the banks of the Ashwa were that of the gurgling of its waters and the intermittent chirping of birds. The sun was blazing hot. Karna's eyes looked bloodshot. How long could he keep his pain bottled up. Placing his head on Krishna's shoulders, he burst out crying.

Krishna continued to caress Karna's head and patting his back gently. Karna cried for a long time. Then, collecting himself, he said, 'It is getting late, Krishna.'

'I know you have faced a lot of injustice. All I want is for you not to face it any more.'

'How much more injustice can be meted out to me? I was called a *sutaputra* and thrown out of the Hastinapur court. Panchali humiliated me during her swayamvar in her father Drupad's palace. I get to hear only one word, day in and day out—*sutaputra*. This word has become an inseparable part of my existence, Vaasudev. I don't want to be a Pandav. I was born a *sutaputra* and I will die a *sutaputra*.'

'I can feel your pain, Karna.'

'No, you can't ... you are a king. You are a great man, an avatar—you cannot understand the pain of a *sutaputra*. You won't understand the feelings of a *sutaputra* who is told when he is nearing the end of his life that he is a Kshatriya, a prince! Krishna, I bow to you and beg that this truth be left here on the banks of the Ashwa. Please scatter its ashes in the river ...'

'Karna!'

'Enough! Don't say another word. I cannot handle any more truths. I have become used to untruth, living a life of adharma and tolerating injustice. Please grant this *sutaputra* permission to take leave.' Saying so, Karna greeted Krishna with folded hands and, with rapid steps, walked towards his chariot. The quick pace reflected his eagerness to move away from Krishna as soon as possible and also from the truth that he had just heard. Krishna stood staring at Karna's receding form.

Krishna mused: Two exceptional warriors, Karna and Arjun, born into the same family! Both brilliant and sensitive, but did only pain and heartache define Karna's personality? Deep in thought, Krishna began walking towards his chariot slowly.

The Kurukshetra war was scheduled to begin the next day. Warriors from all over Bharatvarsh were going to shed their blood in this war. Each one had chosen a side depending on his perception and definition of dharma-adharma. Tents had been pitched on opposite sides. Despite the presence of lakhs of warriors and animals, there was a queer silence all around; the slightest fluttering of leaves could be heard. The sun was about to set and the sky had turned blood red. Perhaps, even the earth would turn the same colour in a day's time.

Everyone knew that the next morning would bring with it the chilling message of death—deaths of near and dear ones, but it was only Krishna who knew who would be sacrificing their lives at the altar of Lord Shiv.

Krishna had promised Kunti that her five sons would survive. Every soldier in the Pandav camp was aware that Krishna would go to any length to keep his word.

On the evening before the war, Krishna assembled everyone in the Pandav camp. It was the first day after the new moon. Arjun sat disinterested in one corner. Yudhishthir was pacing the tent, lost in thought. His mental state was reflected clearly on his face. Bheem stood resolutely with his mace, ready for battle, and Yagyaseni stood gazing at Krishna. She wondered why

Krishna had assembled everyone. What might be going on in his mind on the eve of the war? Perhaps, Krishna wanted to apprise them of the calamities they would face in the days to come or maybe he wanted to inspect the weapons. Not the ones made of iron, wood and bones, but the mental weapons of his men! This war had to be fought with high morale and willpower.

Krishna's deep voice pierced through the tent like an arrow. 'The Dharmayuddh begins tomorrow. We are all soldiers of this crusade and cannot enter the battlefield with any kind of burden. We must go with a free mind, with full acceptance of the war. Only then can we be victorious.'

Draupadi looked at Krishna intently.

Arjun had been sitting silent for a long time and said feebly, 'I don't understand what you are saying.'

'Each one of us has to shed all our weaknesses right here, right now, in this tent!'

'What do you mean?' Yudhishthir stared at Krishna.

'All of us have accumulated so much in our minds. Love, hate, aversion, attachment and what not. This mind, filled with expectation and hope, creates so many complications. All of us live lives full of negativity and rejection, whereas this crusade demands positivity and faith. It is my humble request to all of you to drop all your baggage and confusions, here and now. All of us have to accept ourselves wholeheartedly. Otherwise, we will not even be able to stand in the battlefield. Yudhishthir, let's begin with you ...'

A deathly silence engulfed the tent. It was quite some time before Yudhishthir started speaking. He looked at each person in the tent. Every face was filled with a vague sense of dejection and discomposure.

Yudhishthir gulped and began speaking in a low voice, with his head lowered, 'I, Yudhishthir, the eldest scion of the Pandav race, accept that perhaps I am the reason why all of you are here. My addiction to gambling has landed all of you in this situation. I am guilty of giving more importance to gambling over my brothers, my wife, my mother and the reputation of my clan. I have paid a heavy price for it! Today, on the eve of the great war, I have realised that I have tolerated injustice by keeping quiet and not speaking out. It was my pledge to never speak a lie, but by not revolting against untruth, I have been a party to lies myself. I pray that justice and dharma win!' His voice was choked. He cleared his throat and began speaking again, 'I am most saddened by the fact that we are fighting this battle on Draupadi's strength. The five Pandavs have made a woman the excuse for this war. I am surprised and distressed ...

'... we Pandavs, well known as illustrious warriors all over Bharatvarsh, are going to battle with our wife as a front. Today, at this very moment, can't we forgive Duryodhan? It was I who chose to gamble; it was I who put Yagyaseni at stake, but it is Duryodhan who is labelled an adharmi—a sinner. Why Krishna? Why this deceit?

'History will certainly remember us as men who considered their wife an object and staked her in a gamble—as men who couldn't protect her dignity. Even if we win this war, history is not going to eulogise us, Krishna!' Yudhishthir fell silent, but his breath could be heard in the tent for a few moments.

There was pin-drop silence yet again. Bheem sat down with his head bowed, twirling his mace.

Krishna got up, sat next to Bheem and placed his hand on his shoulder. Bheem looked at Krishna pleadingly. Krishna's eyes were steady—they had the firmness of command!

'Bheem, what do you have to say?' Krishna's voice was as smooth as butter.

'Nothing, I have nothing to say. I am sure I will kill at least twenty-five to fifty men tomorrow, and the count will increase every day.' Bheem's gaze was focused on his mace and he did not look at Krishna.

'This is a war cry, not acceptance,' Krishna patted Bheem's back. 'Bheemsen! What is burdening you, Vayuputra? Remove the misgivings from your mind as easily as you breathe out and expel impure air!'

Bheem looked up. Krishna's eyes were comforting. Bheem felt the same sense of peace that a small child feels when meeting his mother after a long time.

'Speak out, Bheemsen! Let the windows of your mind open wide. Nothing belongs to us. We have to get into war by letting go of everything, don't we?' Krishna spoke to Bheem as if he was speaking to a small child.

Bheem continued to twirl his mace for some time. 'Yagyaseni, Draupadi, Panchali. She's the only weakness I have,' Bheem said, his voice rising and breaking.

Draupadi looked at Bheem intently. Everyone was stunned.

'Beautiful! This is acceptance,' Krishna said, trying to pacify Bheem.

'The day I saw Yagyaseni for the first time, I felt dejected for not being an archer. Arjun is a fool.'

Everyone was dumbstruck. Bheem's fervour was singeing everyone; Yagyaseni alone was looking at Bheem with affection.

'If I were in Arjun's place, I would never have agreed to share Yagyaseni. She is my weakness, and even the thought of her dishonour makes my blood boil. I am going to destroy the Kaurav army because I have to reach Duryodhan, break his thigh and seek revenge for Draupadi's humiliation.' Bheem's face was red with rage. His breath was rapid and his chest was heaving. He lifted his mace as if he was going out to battle right then.

'If my elder brother hadn't stopped me, I would have ripped Dushasan's hands right there in the rajya sabha at Hastinapur. I would have torn open Duryodhan's chest. I will certainly avenge Yagyaseni's humiliation, but it will not be forgotten. The image of a helpless Yagyaseni pleading, with folded hands, in the rajya sabha is etched deeply in my heart and mind. Injustice has occurred, and the victory of dharma will not be able to erase what is imprinted in time. I love Yagyaseni and I will lay my life down to protect her self-respect.' His voice echoed inside and outside the tent.

Krishna patted Bheem's back again and he calmed down gradually.

Bheem began speaking again with difficulty. 'Had Yagyaseni been only my wife, Hidimba and other women would never have come into my life. Spending twelve months with her once every four years would never have been acceptable to me. I wanted her only for myself.' Bheem's eyes met Draupadi's. An extraordinary thread of trust and love seemed to bind them.

Bheem didn't say anything for some time. Krishna used the opportunity to break the silence and said, 'Parth.'

Arjun looked up, startled. He had been sitting against a pillar with one knee folded and the other leg stretched forward. His waistcloth was dusty. His face reflected perplexity and confusion. Having heard his elder brothers speak, he didn't know what to say. He sat staring at the ground and then slowly looked up at Krishna. He then began to speak in a meek and feeble voice:

'As I begin to speak, so many images swim before my eyes. Pandu baba's death, our arrival in Hastinapur, Guru Dron and his training, Draupadi's swayamvar, the Hastinapur rajya sabha, the gamble and the exile. We had all paid the price and been punished for the gamble, even then why did we join our brother when he decided to gamble yet again? Yagyaseni had to suffer the consequences and we all sat quietly, watching helplessly.' He stopped speaking, took a deep breath and said, 'And despite that, Yagyaseni has stood by us throughout. She roamed around in the jungles, dressed in bark and fulfilled her marital duties. And what did we offer her in return? We sat mutely, watching her being humiliated right in front of our eyes! And today, our egos are hurt because this battle is being fought for avenging Draupadi's humiliation.

'Don't we want to have a kingdom of our own? Don't we desire to rule over Hastinapur? If not, then why the gamble? What was the exile for, and the palace of wax? And what was the purpose of the Ashwamedh Yagya for Indraprasth?

'This is mere politics cloaked as crusade or Dharmayuddh. What are we going to achieve by this war? Will the bloodied land won by killing my own brothers, friends, Pitamah, my uncles and other loved ones establish dharma? I don't understand all this. I don't understand what I am going to achieve by killing my own people tomorrow on the battlefield. What am I going to prove? Will dharma win? And which adharma is going to be vanquished?' Arjun's face clouded. Tears were streaming down his cheeks. Arjun, the great warrior, had been shaken by the quandary of dharma and adharma.

'Is this fair, Madhusudan? Have we too, not been unfair, Madhusudan? Despite having Yagyaseni as my wife, I married Uloopi, Subhadra and others. I have constantly been unjust to everyone. I have no right to fight a war. I will offer you my life, if you so command, but please keep me out of this war.

'I have a lot to say and yet nothing to say. I am dumbfounded. I am hit by thousands of thoughts at times and sometimes, I just can't think. I am going through a strange predicament of indecision.'

He stopped for a moment and continued with lowered eyes, 'I never imagined that being an extraordinary archer would become a curse someday. It seems as if the entire war is being fought on my shoulders. Everyone expects me to decimate the sinners, but those sinners are my own brothers. There is Bheeshma Pitamah, who raised me. My uncle, my grandfather, my friends and my near and dear ones—is it necessary to kill all these people to seek revenge for Draupadi? Is it right? You tell me, Madhusudan, can't Draupadi forgive all of them? Was Duryodhan the only one who was unjust? Can we say that my elder brother Yudhishthir followed his dharma? If not, then why is Duryodhan on the other side? Why should we fight this war? The truth is that all of us have sinned. The fact is that we have no right to punish Duryodhan or Dushasan for Draupadi's humiliation. I am not fit for this war.' He wiped his eyes with his waistcloth and looked at Draupadi. Draupadi's eyes were aflame.

What was her beloved husband saying? She was hurt by Arjun's words. She felt stifled and wanted to storm out of the tent, but it was Krishna's order that no one leave the tent till everyone had spoken their hearts out.

Krishna now turned towards Nakul—the ever-smiling, gentle, humble and childlike Nakul. He seemed to be unaware of the ferocity of the impending moments. There seemed to be no confusion in his mind. He was eager to accept the imminent war with ease and grace. Being a Kshatriya, he wasn't afraid of war. The confidence and solace of having Krishna on his side reflected on his face. He felt calm and secure. Without a hint of hesitation, he said, 'I have nothing to say. I too wanted to see this war averted somehow, but it is inevitable now. I love my wife Draupadi and hence, I will fight for her honour and peace. I will fight for the rights of my brothers. I will fight for the victory of dharma and the defeat of adharma. What else is there to say? I am not scared of death. I am certain that the side you are on is surely going to win ...'

Krishna couldn't help laughing aloud. He was touched by Nakul's simplicity and spontaneity even during such grim moments. He now looked at Sahadev.

Sahadev, who had been sitting silent all this while, folded his hands and greeted Krishna.

'I am not going to say anything. I have nothing to say.' He then added forcefully. 'Whatever I say will become a prediction. I am one of those unfortunate beings who can understand the signs of time.' He hesitated a little and continued looking directly at Krishna, 'You know very well that even those who know the future are helpless. I stand before you, the divine, and realise that whether someone is a sinner or not, his blood is red. I pray that it is best if blood flows only in the veins, and not on this earth. Our appeals reach you but sometimes the answer is "no", and our mind refuses to accept it.

'I am pained by the fact that despite knowing what is going to happen, I cannot express it. Regardless, there is nothing that I need to unburden from my mind. My lord, please pardon me. Liberate me from this trap of plusses and minuses. My life has been a clean slate and I wish to die the same way.'

'Clean slate!' Krishna looked at Sahadev with a slight smile. 'It will be a clean slate on which whatever is written cannot be read, Sahadev. It's your choice! I am not asking for an account of deeds or misdeeds like Chitragupt ... I was just ...'

'I understand what you are referring to, my lord, but I beg you to understand what I am saying. Words are deceptive webs, and people will interpret my words in hundreds of ways. I am aware that I cannot avoid speaking the truth and once I start speaking, it will be a calamity, and that is why I beg for liberation.'

'Calamity has already struck, my dear! How worse can it get?'

'My words, unintentionally, become predictions, and I am scared to make any prediction about this carnage, my lord! I am Panchali's husband and was incapable of protecting her dignity in the rajya sabha. I will fight to restore her respect and dignity. I have nothing more to say.'

'As you wish!'

Krishna's eyes turned towards Draupadi. There seemed to be a tornado of questions in those eyes.

Draupadi's heart seemed to have leapt to her throat. She had fervently wished Krishna wouldn't ask her to speak. Krishna looked at her and said, 'Sakhi!' There were thousands of questions hidden in those two syllables. She didn't want Krishna to ask her anything, and yet she was also eager to say everything that she hadn't expressed till then. It was the same dilemma that she had faced when she had seen Krishna for the first time.

'Sakhi!' Krishna called out yet again and everyone waited for her response.

This was a challenge tougher than her swayamvar!

There was no target to be hit today. She was going to bare her heart to the husbands with whom she had spent a lifetime, and who perhaps, loved her equally with the same intensity. She was the woman because of whom everyone was here. She was the woman because of whom everyone was together. Maharaj Drupad's daughter, born from fire, was so magnificent that she had rattled the likes of Duryodhan and Karna. She was a woman who had persistently fought for her dignity.

Today, her five husbands were keen to hear what was on her mind.

'Me? Am I going to fight the war? Why should I say anything?' The look in Krishna's eyes was unbearable for Draupadi.

'You may not fight the war, but you are the reason for this war!'

'I don't understand.' Draupadi feigned ignorance. A strange fear gripped her. The fear of a small child caught stealing sweetmeats. Her, long, black hair, left untied, flowed down till her feet. Her eyes were shining but were also frightful.

'Bheem was right,' Krishna said. 'This is one amazing woman.'

'I don't understand, Sakha,' Draupadi repeated.

Krishna couldn't help smiling. He said, 'An extraordinary woman like you couldn't understand my question? Will anyone believe this?'

'Sakha, what can I say? I was invoked for seeking revenge. Born of fire, I am a burning lamp myself. What is expected of me?'

'Acceptance ... acknowledgement ...'

'Acceptance? Would I have survived till now without it? I have accepted each and every moment, every situation, every injustice and hurt, sorrow and pain ... my terrible humiliation too!'

'Accepted, I agree. But I want to unburden your mind on the eve of this great battle. I wish and request that you let go of all the desires, sorrow, weaknesses and hurt that you have accumulated.'

'Why are you asking me, Sakha? Is there anything in my mind that is hidden from you?'

'Devi, this is not about you and me.'

'But it is about you and me.' Draupadi's eyes changed. She knew it was time to reveal her most personal secrets. 'After a menstruating woman is disrobed, can anything personal remain, Vaasudev?'

'This is not the moment to express bitterness but one of absolute acceptance—a moment of complete acceptance of every moment, every person and every relationship ...'

'You are right, Madhusudan. I too was waiting for a moment like this perhaps. I have to accept a fact right now.'

Everybody stared at Draupadi's face. The dusky complexion, the dark long hair, the lips shaped like lotus leaves ... big eyes ... and despite being a mother to five sons, the attractive body ...

There was a strange softness, a wonderful sweetness on her face. There was an adolescent simplicity about her. 'Vaasudev ...'

Everybody was eager to hear what she was going to accept, whom she was going to accept.

'When my father decided to call me Krishnaa, I never imagined that the word Krishna would become synonymous with my life. Sakha, you know and understand truth and sensibilities. If, on the eve of the Kurukshetra war, I speak the truth, the war will begin here itself. It is not easy to live with five husbands with the same faithfulness, and if even a thin crack is seen in my devotion ...'

'Our respect for you will not diminish, Panchali,' Arjun said suddenly. '*Preeti parthena shashwatim*. Parth's love is eternal. What do you have to say?'

'To you, Phalgun? And to you, Sakha ... do I have to tell you what goes on in my mind? All of you know what I am thinking, and it will be known to several generations to come.' She stood up.

Her eyes were moist. 'When my five husbands sat helplessly watching me being disrobed, I reached out to you, called to you for help. Our relationship continuously swings between trust and distrust like inhalation and exhalation—even if one stops, life will come to an end.

'I, Drupad's daughter, Krishnaa Draupadi, open the doors to my heart to you in the presence of my five husbands. There is no burden, no pain, no peace and no sorrow either. This thought has been buried in my heart for ages. It has been piercing my heart like shards of glass for years ... Vaasudev, Madhusudan, Sakha, every moment of pain has brought me closer to you, and every time I stood up to fight injustice, I have felt you holding my hand. I have no other desire but to receive the same love from you for many more lives to come.'

A heavy silence pervaded the tent. Each person sat interpreting her words in his own way and dissecting her words at will. But Panchali hadn't finished speaking.

'Sakha, why is it that you are there for us only in times of grief? Is being in pain the only way to have you close to us? Is it mandatory for us to be helpless and struggling to get you? Your mere presence in this meeting organised on the battlefield of Kurukshetra is so calming and soothing! Why do you choose to be our charioteer only during war? Can't you be our mentor at every moment—sad or happy—in our lives? Lord, if a rebirth is possible, I pray that I have the fortune of being your Sakhi and meeting you yet again.'

The memory of his first meeting with Draupadi swam before Krishna's eyes ...

The beautiful, dusky, long-haired sixteen-year-old had lost her heart to Krishna in their first meeting itself. Although every princess aspired to marry the greatest man of all times, Draupadi was different. She was the princess every eligible prince wanted to marry. However, Krishna had come to her swayamvar with a totally different purpose. The incident of the lacquer palace had just taken place. Draupadi was relieved to see Krishna amidst princes like Duryodhan and Karna and kings like Shishupal and Jarasandh. As she sat with her head lowered, she mistook Arjun's dark feet passing her by for Krishna's. She secretly prayed to bless those feet with success at piercing the fish's eye. After successfully piercing the fish's eye with his arrow, when Arjun came and stood in front of her, to be garlanded, Draupadi's heart skipped a beat. It wasn't Krishna! Her eyes had brimmed with tears and she had looked at Krishna with hurt eyes. Draupadi felt as if Krishna had tricked her. Despite knowing everything, Krishna had encouraged Arjun and rejected her; this pierced her heart like a thorn. She had looked up at Krishna, her eyes filled with questions about his rejection.

Krishna hadn't forgotten those eyes even to this day. Who else but Krishna would have known that this woman, born to seek revenge, had such a tender heart. Despite that, this softness, as soothing as a drizzle of cool water, remained trapped in her heart and soaked her. Others could only see her fierceness. Anyone who came close was scorched by her beauty, intelligence and pride. Nobody could touch the tender core of her heart, not even her five husbands. To reach that delicate moistness of the first rain, one needed courage to first pass through her fire and brilliance, and none possessed that kind of fortitude.

Her eyes had reflected anger rather than shame and trepidation when she stood half-naked in the rajya sabha. Dushasan hadn't just tried to disrobe her, but had trampled upon her self-respect. Even today, Yagyaseni was not hurt as much by the fact that her five husbands sat watching her being disrobed in the rajya sabha, but more because Duryodhan had trodden upon her self-respect and dignity.

The ignominy of being made to stand as a helpless, menstruating woman in front of the elders didn't hurt as much as being treated as an object and staked in a game of dice.

She had asked in a voice that had shaken the foundations of the rajya sabha, 'Did my husbands first lose themselves, or me?'

She had questioned the silent braves and elders—the stunned Dhritarashtra, Vidur, Gandhari and Bheeshma Pitamah: 'How can those who have lost themselves put any other person at stake?'

Krishna was reminded of his own words to Draupadi. 'Those who humiliated you will surely be killed by Arjun's piercing arrows. Their wives will cry as you are doing now. It is my promise. The skies may fall, the earth may shatter and the ocean may dry, but my promise to you shall not fail!'

The sound of the Panchajanya conch echoed in Krishna's ears. He felt the trauma of putting the flute away and picking up the conch in every cell of his body. Krishna could foresee the horror of the days following the Kurukshetra war. He knew that what was to come wouldn't be forgotten for centuries.

In those moments, on the eve of the Kurukshetra war, Krishna's voice rang out loud.

'*Yato dharmastato jaya ...*'

'Where there is righteousness, there is victory ...'

When Arjun's chariot entered Dwarka, it was noon. The two-day-long ride had tired the horses and their mouths were frothing. Draupadi's face and hair were covered in dust and Arjun's hands were weak on the reins.

As the chariot passed through the gates of Dwarka, Draupadi was surprised to see the desolate roads. The streets that used to be teeming with people were literally empty with an odd Yadav woman walking by. The doors of the palace were shut tight. It looked as if death had swept through the city.

Draupadi asked Arjun, 'What is the matter, Parth? My mind is filled with ominous thoughts.' Arjun quietly placed his hand on Draupadi's shoulder and turned the chariot towards the palace.

The main palace, with its dazzling golden dome, stood in the middle of the city, surrounded by eight smaller ones for Satyabhama, Jambavati and the other queens. Despite it being lunchtime, the royal kitchens, on the right of the main palace, wore a deserted look. The palace premises, usually buzzing with activities of servants and maids, were covered with a pall of gloom.

The palace guards looked listless. Arjun veered the chariot towards the palace stables. Apart from a few old horses and foals, the stable was almost empty.

Arjun helped Draupadi down the chariot. They were numb and tired after travelling continuously. The whistle of the wind still echoed in their ears. Draupadi began walking towards the main entrance of the palace with faltering steps. The steps were vacant today. Usually, there would be hordes of people waiting to meet Krishna. These steps hadn't been this vacant even when Krishna was away from Dwarka. As she ascended those steps, Draupadi was reminded of the welcome Rukmini had accorded her when she had visited Dwarka soon after Rukmini's wedding. Till then, Draupadi had been welcomed grandly every time she came to Dwarka, but it lacked a woman's touch. Rukmini had welcomed her with a shower of pearls and flowers and called her, 'Vaasudevasya Sakhi ... Vaasudev's Sakhi!' She had said this with folded hands and a mischievous smile on her face.

Rukmini was younger to Draupadi and much younger than Krishna. When she had failed to convince her brother Rukmi against getting her married to Shishupal, Rukmini had written to Krishna. In that letter, sent through a Brahmin named Sudev, Rukmini had written only seven verses articulating her love for Krishna. She had also expressed that if her wedding to Shishupal wasn't stopped, she would take her own life.

Draupadi was in Dwarka when Krishna received Rukmini's letter. He came to her with the letter when she was strolling in the garden. Draupadi could see Rukmini's face in that letter. She could see her mischievous eyes filled with love for Krishna. She could see her own reflection in Rukmini's face—the same innocence, infatuation and intense devotion to Krishna!

Draupadi had said without being sarcastic, 'Even I haven't been so devoted to you, Sakha!'

'Really?' Krishna said with mischief.

'Sakha, this woman is totally fit to be your queen, and it is your duty to abduct her. She is a scholar. Even I have heard about her beauty and knowledge. A woman like her deserves to be the queen of Dwarka.'

After bringing Rukmini to Dwarka, Krishna invited Draupadi to visit and meet her.

'Vaasudevasya Sakhi! My lover's friend, his Sakhi, I welcome you to Dwarka,' Rukmini had said with folded hands.

Standing before Krishna's palace, Draupadi remembered Rukmini's childlike eyes, her smile and the affectionate touch of her hands.

Arjun held Draupadi's hands. She gripped them like a fearful child and ascended the steps of the palace.

Rukmini looked at Draupadi tearfully. Draupadi sat staring at Rukmini, stunned. Rukmini had just finished narrating what had happened. Arjun hadn't spoken a word and stood absent-mindedly by the window. The sun had begun its descent behind the trees. The sky looked like a bloody battlefield, and Arjun stared at it with terror-struck eyes.

Darkness began to sweep over the Dwarka palace. The evening seemed to have brought the message of death to every household of Dwarka. The Yadav men had hugged their wives, bid them goodbye and mounted their golden chariots with majestic horses to leave for Prabhaskshetra just that morning. Only about twelve hours had passed since they had left, and already Dwarka appeared woefully lifeless.

Draupadi looked at Rukmini in amazement. Dwarka seemed like a graveyard without her Sakha.

'So ... now ...?' Draupadi asked Rukmini.

'Time has bared its fangs. The drinking spree must have begun in the evening by now,' Rukmini's voice sounded chilling.

'But Sakha ...'

'Vaasudevasya Sakhi, couldn't you have come earlier?' Rukmini asked Draupadi with a piercing gaze.

'What happens now?'

'You won't be able to meet him. All the Yadavs will be annihilated at Yadavsthali, and the golden era of Dwarka will be over forever,' Rukmini said. Her eyes were like stones and her face was impassive.

'Parth!' Draupadi's voice trembled. Tears rolled down her cheeks, her voice became hoarse and she screamed, 'Parth ...'

Arjun, standing by the window, heard her scream and ran inside, and barely managed to keep her from falling before she fainted. Arjun gently laid her down on a bed nearby. 'Sakha ... Parth ... Prabhas ... Sakha ...' Draupadi mumbled vaguely amid tears.

Rukmini froze looking at Draupadi's state, and her eyes welled up. Her voice trembled as she said, 'There is still time, please try to reach Prabhas. If Panchali is not able to meet the lord in his last moments ...' Rukmini couldn't continue any further.

Arjun stood gazing at Draupadi. This was the woman who loved him intensely. She was the one who had tied the five brothers together with her love and devotion. She had never failed in her duties as a wife. She was the queen of Indraprasth ... and she loved Krishna deeply!

She was unfazed while seeing off her five husbands leaving for the Kurukshetra war. The very same woman lay shattered on hearing the news of Krishna's last journey.

This is what she had meant when she said on the eve of the Kurukshetra war:

'When my father decided to call me Krishnaa, I never imagined that the word Krishna would become synonymous with my life. Sakha, you know and understand truth and sensibilities. If, on the eve of the Kurukshetra war, I speak the truth, the war will begin here itself. It is not easy to live with five husbands with the same faithfulness, and if even a thin crack is seen in my devotion ...'

This was the crack. Despite it being so miniscule, the light escaping it was dazzling enough to blind the eyes.

Arjun was surprised that the brave queen who remained unfazed at the death of her five sons was today devastated by a mere doubt. All the events associated with Draupadi and Krishna flashed before his eyes. All those memories, etched deeply in his heart, seemed to be imploring him, saying—'Go Parth, hurry! If the soul leaves, the body too will perish.'

Draupadi mumbled unclearly, 'Sakha, I will come. I will reach you ... please wait for me ... Sakha, Krishna ...'

Arjun lifted the incoherent Draupadi in his arms. Her bun had come loose and her hair and waistcloth were trailing on the floor. Her lifeless hands were limp by her side. Her bustier had slid down slightly and her cleavage was visible. Her pearl necklaces were askew and swayed with her flowing hair. Her legs had gone limp and were bent at the knees.

Arjun laid her straight in the chariot. Rukmini didn't have the courage to stop them. She prayed: 'Please let her win the race against time and reach Krishna. This will be best for everyone. Please make it happen. Shanti ... shanti ... shanti!'

Krishna opened his eyes and looked all around. The afternoon sun was blazing hot. The large peepal tree shaded him from the fierce sun like the seven-hooded Sheshnag. Jara still sat beside Krishna.

'Did you hear the bells of a chariot?'

'No, my lord, no one seems to have come this way.'

'Delusions!' A sweet smile spread on Krishna's face. 'The mind is so peculiar, isn't it, Jara? It pines for the ones it is waiting for, and strongly believes that they will come ...'

'You are waiting for Arjun, aren't you, my lord?'

'Yes, for Arjun too.'

'Will there be anyone else with him, my lord?'

'Only the visitor knows that ...'

Krishna's eyes were dropping with fatigue and his throat was going dry. Myriad colours drifted before his closed eyes and created countless patterns. Peacock feathers floated down and caressed his face ... Was it the sound of Radha's anklets in the streets of Vrindavan or the sound of Arjun's chariot welcoming Dwarkadheesh at Indraprasth? Were the small bells in Rukmini's necklace tinkling or was it the jangle of the flowers carved in Satyabhama's bracelets? Was it the tinkling of the bangles in Yashoda's hands as she churned butter or was it the magical sound of the gold bangles in Devaki's hands as she stroked his head with her palms ...

Where were all these multitudes of sounds coming from? Krishna closed his eyes and continued to wait.

'What is this you are doing, Sakha?'

'Why? I too should contribute something in this yagya, shouldn't I?'

'But this?' Draupadi asked, sounding shocked.

'Let go of my hands, Sakhi. Everyone is watching.' And Draupadi bashfully let go of Krishna's hands.

When all of them sat on their golden seats in the palace courtyard under the open sky that night, Arjun burst out laughing uncontrollably.

'I have never seen Yagyaseni so shy.'

'What is so funny about it?' Bheemsen asked, confused.

'When I told Sakhi that everyone was watching, she immediately let go of my hand, as if it was some kind of deceit ...'

Arjun was still in splits. 'It was deceit, wasn't it? Despite having five husbands, Panchali openly holds the hand of her Sakha.'

'Oh! He was picking up used plates and leftover food ... shouldn't I have stopped him?'

'Yes, you stopped me and I had the fortune of having these beautiful hands, decorated with henna and decked in diamonds, hold mine! Can anyone be luckier?' Krishna said with a chuckle and Yagyaseni blushed.

Arjun continued to laugh. Yagyaseni continued to feel self conscious, and Bheem sat perplexed.

This was the day of the Rajasuya Yagya at Indraprasth. Draupadi was now the queen of the invincible Pandavs. Indraprasth was unconquerable.

Despite all the fun and banter, Krishna was disturbed about the inescapable calamity. How could he stop the inevitable? He had no answers.

Suddenly, his eyes fell on Sahadev. Sahadev was sitting, quietly gazing at the sky, and as his eyes met Krishna's, he lowered them. The two of them exchanged a lot without saying a word.

'I feel like having some fruit, Sakhi,' Krishna said.

'I will get them right away.' Draupadi got up.

'Aren't there any maids?' Arjun asked, holding Draupadi's hand, as if to stop her.

'No maids for Sakha,' Draupadi said, pulling her hand away.

Sahadev and Krishna exchanged glances yet again, but this time, it was Krishna who lowered his gaze.

Draupadi came back bearing a golden bowl full of fruits. Draupadi's gem-studded earrings shone in the darkness. Her eyes brighter than her earrings, her bun about to fall open, loose strands of hair on her forehead, her sharp nose, beautiful lips and rounded chin, her long, chiselled neck and the striking magnificence of her breasts—she was a sight to behold! She was breathtakingly beautiful. Her lissome waist could fit into two palms. Her bejewelled waistband and her anklets tinkled as she walked towards them.

'Sakha, please have them,' she said, placing the bowl on a stool in front of Krishna. Krishna took the knife from the bowl and began cutting a fruit. The moment his eyes met Sahadev's, the latter laughed, with good reason.

Even before Krishna could hear Sahadev's laughter, the knife pierced Krishna's palm and it started to bleed. Before anybody could react, Draupadi tore the end of her exquisite silk saree and bandaged Krishna's bleeding palm with it. Arjun, Bheem and Yudhishthir were stunned. Sahadev got up laughing and looked at Krishna. No one other than Krishna understood the purport of that laughter. He held Draupadi's hand and said, 'Sakhi ... today, I promise you in the presence of all these people that when the opportunity arises, I will give you as many clothes as there are threads in this piece of cloth.'

Sahadev laughed yet again.

'I will never need that many clothes, Vaasudev. After having lived in the forest, I now prefer clothes made of bark. These luxurious silks irritate my skin. Jewellery too; I find floral ornaments more charming. I don't know anything about the threads in these clothes, but Govind, please promise me that the threads that join us together will remain intact ...'

Krishna held Draupadi's hand affectionately. 'Do you really need this promise, Sakhi!'

'My husbands had lost themselves before they put me at stake. If that is true, who gave them the right to do so? What kind of principle is this? I ask you this question, Pitamah, Maharaj Dhritarashtra and Kaka Vidur—how is this acceptable to you? I am the daughter-in-law of this family. Is the daughter-in-law allowed to be put at stake in a game of dice? Is this the tradition in your family?' Draupadi's roaring, trembling voice reverberated in the rajya sabha. Everyone's already lowered necks bent down even further under the gravity of Draupadi's questions.

'I am asking you; please answer my question,' Draupadi asked piercingly.

'Question? Slaves don't have the right to question. They just have to obey commands. Shut up or else I will tie your mouth with a cloth similar to Mata Gandhari's blindfold!' Duryodhan guffawed aloud.

'You may silence me now, but how will you silence history, Duryodhan?'

'History will remember you as the queen of the Kauravs. Forget all this and your five impotent husbands, the ones who put you at stake like a mere object!'

'How are you any different? You too have won me like an object!'

'That's the power of victory. The vanquished are left with nothing else but humiliation!'

'Duryodhan, I have a question to ask of you. I have a question for every man present here in the rajya sabha today. Did my husbands lose themselves first or did they lose me? Once they had lost themselves, did they have a right to stake me? What does dharma have to say about this? What does your system of justice say?'

'Nobody says anything. Everybody is silent under Duryodhan's majesty and everyone will be quiet for centuries to come.'

'That is what you believe, you scoundrel!'

'One more word and I will disrobe and strip you naked right now!'

'I wish that you do so. You still haven't managed to rattle me enough to curse you, torment me so much that I curse the entire Kuru clan with annihilation.'

Duryodhan's mocking laughter echoed in the rajya sabha.

'You will curse us?'

Karna, who had been silent till then, couldn't resist any more. He opened his mouth to seek revenge for his own humiliation.

'Only Satis or pious women have the power to curse. A woman with five husbands can't by any definition be considered pious. She is called a whore. Panchali—the woman with five husbands!' Karna laughed. Bitterness had seeped into every cell of his body. The words he had heard in the swayamvar haunted him to this day.

'Shut up! My name is Yagyaseni. I am one born out of ceremonial fire. I am as pure and majestic as the flames. Maharaj Drupad's daughter, Draupadi—I am one among the greatest women revered by everyone. Impotent men like you, who can't live faithfully with one wife, can never understand how difficult it is for a woman to live with five husbands with complete fidelity and devotion. It isn't possible for an ordinary woman to live with all her five husbands with equal devotion. It would have been child's play for me to pit the five Pandavs against each other and divide them. But I kept them together with the strength of my love, loyalty, truthfulness and devotion. Despite accepting all conditions, being humiliated time and again and having heard all kinds of barbs and nasty jibes, I never wavered from my faith.

'Just try to imagine what would have happened if I had wavered from my loyalty even for a moment! These five brothers, seated here in front of you, would have drifted in five different directions. The thread that holds the pearls together is never seen. But it is that very thread that keeps the pearls intact and safe. I have achieved the impossible task of keeping everyone together.

'I have never understood why my love for one should lessen if I love another man. Some people have an immense amounts of love to give, and such people can love more than one person at the same time. They can love with abundance and despite that, their love doesn't diminish; it only becomes stronger! Why is there no protest against a mother who loves both her daughters equally? When it is about men or husbands, our society suddenly begins to judge women.

'... and because of this, I have suffered a lot. I have had to stake my self-respect, my femininity and my whole existence at times. I have had to go through trials by fire almost every day to preserve my truth. Nobody in this rajya sabha will understand how demeaning it can be for a faithful woman to prove her fidelity time and again ... And, even now, at this very moment, I am suffering because of my devotion. But what will I achieve? It will make no difference to my loyalty and self-respect. My very existence has been born from the flames of revenge. Being Agniputri, I can, right now, burn down myself and my husbands who staked me like an object.

'Why didn't anyone think about his Kshatriya dharma before dragging a menstruating, unornamented woman into the rajya sabha? I am the daughter-in-law of this family and my honour should be the honour of this family. I ask you, Dhritarashtra baba, Vidur kaka, Guru Dron, all the scholars and brave men present here, weren't the men who staked me in the game of dice from your own family? Why didn't any of you stop them? I, Yagyaseni, stand half-naked and humiliated in this rajya sabha; and my husbands are solely responsible for my condition. They have been unfair to me over and over again and yet, I constantly keep forgiving them. I forgive all my five husbands for my humiliation ... But you, Duryodhan, I will never forgive! Every single arrow in Arjun's quiver and every blow from my Bheem's mace will seek revenge for my humiliation and my tears! You will be on your knees, seeking forgiveness for your loathsome laughter. I will not tie my hair until I rinse it with the blood from your severed thighs—the same thighs that you invited me to sit on! Duryodhan, you have tested a woman's dignity to the limits, and a woman's vengeance is primal. It is very difficult to persuade a woman to seek revenge, Duryodhan. Women stand for forgiveness, affection, love and sensitivity. But when their honour is put to the test, words of love can turn into swords of hate; vengeance is one face of the coin, the other side being forgiveness, affection, love and sensitivity. Today, the venom of revenge has spread into my veins. I will nurture this tree of vengeance every single day with the memories of my humiliation till that day when I get to rinse my hair with your blood. This is Draupadi's, Yagyaseni's promise to you Duryodhan! You will burn in the fire of my vengeance, and so will the entire Kaurav race.'

Draupadi's tears streamed down her nose, cheeks, neck and reached her bosom. Saliva dripped from her lips as she spoke. Trembling with rage, Draupadi's face had become red. Her whole body shook like the branches of a tree stranded in a storm. And then, Draupadi's loud chants echoed all around in the rajya sabha:

'Hey Govind, hey Gopal ... hey Govind, hey Gopal!'

Both her hands were raised. She seemed to be totally unafraid that Dushasan would disrobe her and she would stand naked in the rajya sabha. It was as if her chants were hammering at everyone's heart. The lowered necks of her husbands slowly seemed to rise. Dushasan tugged at the loose end of her saree and looked at Duryodhan. Duryodhan, with a cruel laugh, ordered Dushasan to pull Draupadi's saree.

Dhritarashtra's, Vidur's and Pitamah Bheeshma's faces seemed to be blackened with shame, while Draupadi's chants reverberated like an invisible oracle.

'Hey Govind, hey Gopal ... hey Govind, hey Gopal!' Both her hands were raised and eyes closed in obeisance. Tears continued to stream from her eyes and the intensity of her voice was gradually increasing. Every person present in the rajya sabha was about to witness a miracle right before their eyes. Dushasan continued to pull Draupadi's saree.

Suddenly, her face shone with an unearthly glow. A mesmerising sweetness and honesty came into her voice: 'Hey Govind, hey Gopal ... hey Govind, hey Gopal ...!

An unconscious Draupadi muttered incoherently in Arjun's arms. Arjun laid her down in the seat and raced his chariot. He realised there was very little time left between him and his guru, mentor and Sakha's final moments.

The sun had reached its zenith, high above the banks of the Hiranya. Krishna's eyes were closed, and he seemed to be having a conversation with himself.

'Who are you waiting for, Kanha?'

'No one.'

'Really?'

'I mean ... I already know that the person I am waiting for will not come.'

'So it is true that you are waiting, isn't it?'

'Yes ... but only for the final, unending sleep.'

'Is that all? Hope you are not waiting for someone you left behind long ago?'

Krishna laughed. 'Why would I wait for her? How will she come? She doesn't even know that I ...'

'Do you know how many complaints, incomplete sentences, questions and how much pain she will come with?'

'But only if she comes!'

'Will she come in person? Isn't her touch, her laughter, her sulk, her cajoling, the tinkle of her anklets, her fragrance ... still here?'

'These have always existed in me—always.'

'A conversation has been taking place in your mind constantly—the conversation of yes and no. Haven't I

been a part of all your thoughts, sorrows and happiness?
Then why are you waiting for her?'

'I don't know. The truth is that I am waiting for nothing.
I am just waiting to peacefully merge with infinity, with
the absolute truth, of which I am a part.'

'Truth?' It was as if there was another Krishna, talking
from within. 'But at a time when one among the many
parts of you is going to disappear, is there not one person
you await? You have always spoken the truth ... Why do
you hesitate to confront it?'

'No, no, I am not under any such illusion. But I don't
know why sometimes ...'

Krishna's eyes were still closed. The image of a
mischievous, delicate, fair girl with long black hair and
dancing eyebrows swam before his eyes. She was playful,
and restless like the waters of the Yamuna. She stared
at Krishna through her doe-eyes and asked him, 'Who
do you think you are?' Her face had the faint red glow
of anger and fear. She was drenched to the bone and her
clothes were dripping wet. The drops of water on her
wet hair gleamed like pearls. Her lips trembled in anger.
Her saree was sticking to her skin. Her long, wet skirt
betrayed every line of her body. She was holding a broken
earthen pot in her outstretched hand. It still had a little
water in it. She threw the water at Krishna's face in anger.

'No ... you first tell me who you think you are? I don't
get pots for free. What is this habit you have got into ...
you break the pots of all the village women!' Krishna was
chuckling loudly. He was aware that this anger wouldn't

last long. This was a daily routine. Krishna, Balaram and the other cowherds would hide in the trees with their catapults and break the pots of the gopikas who came to collect water. All of them would be livid. They knew that this could only be Kanha's handiwork, but they would melt under the spell of his innocent excuses, his entreaties and the mellifluous sounds of his flute. But Radha was different. Kanha's enchantment had no effect on her.

And that day, Radha's pot had been broken. Balaram and the other cowherds refused to climb down the tree; they knew that if Radha lost her mind, it would spell doom for them.

'You tell me what you think of yourself?' Radha asked for the third time. Kanha was still laughing. Radha came closer. Kanha's friends knew what was going to follow. Balaram and the cowherds quietly sat on the tree, waiting for a fierce battle between the enraged Radha and Kanha. But Kanha stood his ground without any trace of fear. Radha stared into Kanha's eyes. He was still laughing. Radha smashed the already broken pot on Kanha's head. The little water left in the pot trickled down his face. Kanha coolly sipped the drops of water.

'Oh Radha! The water from your pot is as sweet as nectar!'

'Just shut up!'

'You don't like it?' Krishna continued to laugh and Radha's anger grew with every chuckle of his. The cowherds hiding on the tree were getting nervous. Radha came closer to Kanha and threatened him, 'I am surely going to complain to your mother today.'

'Fine. I will come with you. You won't have to look for me.'

'Aren't you ashamed of yourself, Kanha?'

'Why should I?'

Radha realised that any more argument was pointless, and said, 'Come, buy me a new pot.'

'Sure!' Radha stood looking at Kanha for a moment, staring at his innocent laughter, his mesmerising eyes, dusky complexion and the peacock feather in his curly hair.

'Why does my anger disappear when I look at him? What is so special about him?' Radha questioned herself.

Krishna still stood his ground. 'Come ... come, I will buy you a pot with pictures of peacocks and parrots.'

'I know how to draw. I will paint the pictures myself.'

'You know how to draw peacocks and parrots?' Kanha's eyes were filled with awe.

'Yes, very well. Look at this pot you broke. I had worked so hard to paint it ...'

Kanha picked up one broken piece after the other. Then, he walked slowly towards Radha, handed her his flute and said, 'Paint this for me.'

'Paint on this?' Radha asked wide-eyed. 'On this piece of wood?'

'Silly girl, this is not a piece of wood.'

'Then what is it?' Radha shrugged and looked at the flute.

'This is a flute.'

'A flute? What is it for?'

'This is a musical instrument. When you blow air into it, it comes alive.'

'Get lost! I don't believe you!'

'You don't believe me?'

'Not for a moment. You are a liar and everyone in the village says the same about you.'

'But I don't lie to you.'

'Why?'

'I don't know why, but I don't feel like lying to you. I look at your eyes and just tell the truth.'

'Go, just go ... I don't want to talk to you.'

'You won't talk, but you can listen to the flute, can't you?' There was a yes in Radha's eyes ... a yes filled with curiosity. Even then, she turned her face away and said, 'I don't have time to listen to music played from a piece of wood. Go ahead and play and listen to it yourself.' Radha smoothened her skirt, shook out her wet hair, straightened her shawl and walked away, conscious of her beauty. She must have hardly walked ten steps when the air was filled with a mellifluous sound. It seemed to be drawing her towards itself. There was a strange magnetism, a rare tenderness in it; it was captivating.

Radha didn't turn back, but stopped walking further.

The sound slowly came closer to her. Radha's eyes began to close. The music was casting its spell on her.

'Radha ...' That voice too seemed to be part of that mesmerising music. A hand stretched out towards her hands and it felt as if she was touching a bunch of flowers. Radha didn't know whether this was a dream or reality. All she wanted to do was to float in this river of melody, flowers, fragrance and allure. She was ready to go wherever the river of music was taking her.

The tunes of the flute were piercing every single cell of her body. She was entwined by the magnetism of the music, as if a snake had wound itself around her. But that touch was turning her into wholly new Radha.

'Ma ... Ma ...' A young woman ran out of the kitchen and entered the room. She looked at the woman she had addressed as Ma. She saw a few grey hairs peeping from behind her ears, a slightly furrowed forehead, glistening skin and an elegant, fit body even at this age. Her firm back was covered with a red shawl. Her low bun, tied at the nape of the neck, was still black. A few strands of hair had escaped the bun and hung loosely from her forehead and on her cheeks. Her beautiful eyes were moist as she sat still near the butter churner. Her eyes were focused far on the horizon. Her hands had stopped working the churner.

'Ma ... Ma!' A beautiful young woman was calling out to her, 'Radha Ma, o Radha Ma!'

The old woman was startled and looked up.

'What are you thinking about?'

The old woman caressed the young girl's face with her slightly wrinkled but soft palms.

'Nothing ...'

'You have finished churning the curd already, Ma. What are you sitting here for?'

'What?' Radha still seemed lost.

'I have noticed that you sit deep in thought every day, your eyes well up with tears, time and again. What is it, Ma? Has somebody hurt you?' The young woman now held the hands caressing her cheeks.

'No, no ... it's nothing like that.' Radha eyes were still a little moist.

'Ma, there is surely something bothering you. You just don't want to share it with us. You are worried about something.'

Radha gazed at the young woman. 'You understand my thoughts even if I don't say anything. God forgot to give me a daughter and that's why he sent you.'

'You are changing the topic.' The young woman persisted.

'I don't know why I am so dazed. I constantly feel something inauspicious is going to happen.' She decided to bare her mind to the young girl because she knew that the young woman wouldn't relent otherwise.

'What is it, Ma?' The young woman hesitated a little and stared into Radha's eyes. She could only see serenity and moistness. 'I hope I haven't done anything to hurt you?'

'Oh, no! Not at all, you silly girl!' Radha said. 'Your face, your affection, make me want to live!' The young woman looked at Radha unblinkingly.

'Hope, it's not something Bapu said?'

'No!'

'Then what is it?'

Radha sat silent for a few minutes, watching white clouds float by in the sky. Her lips trembled a little and she said, 'I am finally free of all my debts.'

'Ma ...' The young woman was surprised. Radha was still staring at the sky and seemed to be saying to someone up there, 'You just needed an excuse ... But remember one thing, you won't be able to leave—just the way you couldn't leave Gokul without my permission.'

'Whom are you talking about, Ma?' The young woman asked, looking upwards. The sky seemed to be strewn with dark clouds that were forming myriad shapes. They looked like huge balls of cotton. Radha seemed to be searching for something in those clouds.

'Ma, o Radha Ma!' The young woman broke Radha's reverie.

'What?' Radha stood up abruptly, as if she had stepped on a thorn. She quickly walked towards the kitchen without saying a word.

The young woman, Shubhra, kept staring at Radha, whose gait was as graceful as that of a young girl.

'Shyama!' Radha called from inside the kitchen. Although the young woman's name was Shubhra, her mother-in-law chose to call her Shyama.

Though Shyama did not understand this habit of her mother-in-law's, she still loved her a lot. Radha too unwittingly saw her own youth in the young woman.

It had been three years since Shubhra had married Radha's son. One day, there was a serious fight between her and her husband, Aaryak. No one knew why they had fought, but Shubhra had cried the whole night and hadn't eaten either. Radha tried hard to pacify her. Shubhra's father-in-law, Ayan, too requested her to eat, but Shubhra refused to give in.

Radha too couldn't sleep the whole night. When Radha woke up early the next morning, she found Shubhra still sitting in the verandah, staring blankly at the sky. Her eyes were dry and her face was lined with sorrow. Radha came and sat down beside her. Despite being aware of Radha's presence, Shubhra didn't look at her. Radha sat quietly, caressing Shubhra's head. She loosened Shubhra's bun and began massaging her head with her fingertips. The young woman gently bent down and placed her head on Radha's lap. It immediately became soaked with Shubhra's tears.

The two women sat there for hours together. Neither of them spoke. Finally, it was almost dawn, and the sky had begun to turn red. Shubhra gently lifted her head from Radha's lap, looked straight into her eyes and asked, 'Ma, is love a crime?'

Radha looked at Shubhra, as if she was peering into a mirror.

'No, my child, love can never be a crime.' Both of them were quiet for a few moments. Radha's eyes became moist and she said, caressing Shubhra's cheeks, 'This is the tragedy of a woman's life. Her love is always an offering—just giving without asking. And yet, she has a lot to answer for! My dear, it is not necessary that your lover be your husband, and what is even more distressing is that your husband too may not be your lover ...'

Shubhra took Radha's hands in hers and said, 'Ma, have I ever failed in fulfilling my duties? Have I ever refused to do anything? Have you even, for once, seen me hurt Aaryak? I have served him with all my devotion, my body and soul, but Ma, my mind ...'

'Don't listen to it, my child; the mind is not in anyone's control.'

'Ma, one corner of the mind, drenched by the showers of the first rain, always remains wet, and no warmth or heat is capable of drying it. What can I do, Ma?'

Radha sat quietly, looking at Shubhra. She then moved close and placed Shubhra's head on her chest. Stroking her hair, she said, 'Shyama ...' Shubhra was perplexed. Radha's eyes seemed to be reading the history of centuries in the red sky. Every word was familiar to her, and she must have heard it a million times.

'For a woman, her love is her life breath. It is what keeps her alive but also kills her. My dear girl, love has different meanings for men and women. For men, love is about taking, always taking, while for a woman, it is flowing like a river that pours fresh water into the sea. Like fragrance, the duty of love also is to give. When love flows in one direction like a river within the boundaries of its banks, every drop creates and nurtures life, but when it breaches the banks, it creates havoc. It leaves behind only sludge and mourning. Love is like the air in our fist. The fist is empty and yet full; etched with lines that define our lives and our marriages. The henna on our palms might fade away, but not the lines. These come with the closed fist at birth and follow what they have predestined throughout our lives.'

Radha and her daughter-in-law Shubhra sat talking to each other for a long time and from that day, Shubhra had become Radha's Shyama.

'Shyama ...' Radha called out from inside the house.

'Yes, Ma.' Shubhra got up and entered the house. For the past several days, Radha had been uneasy. The sounds of the flute that she had stopped listening to ever since Kanha left Gokul for Mathura, now constantly followed her all the time—while eating, sleeping, churning curd, feeding the cows and milking them.

Radha sat watching the glowing embers of the firewood; her hands were busy kneading the dough for rotis, but her mind was in turmoil.

Shubhra sat in front of her, cleaning rice, but her eyes constantly kept going back to Radha. She had never seen Radha so deeply immersed in thought. In so many years, Shubhra had never seen Radha's eyes welling up with tears so often. This woman is truly inscrutable! God only knows what is going on in her mind. Shubhra threw away the stones from the plate of rice and looked up at Radha. Radha hadn't put the roti on the pan and had absentmindedly placed her hand on the hot pan. Shubhra rushed to bring butter to apply on Radha's hand. A big red blister had formed on Radha's hand. When Shubhra looked at Radha, Radha lowered her eyes, as if she had been caught red-handed.

'Ma, are you thinking of someone?' The love story of a married woman had been legendary in Gokul until a few years ago. Gossip about Radha had reached Shubhra too, over the years. Radha stood up without saying a word and walked towards her room. She slammed the door shut and sat down on the bed. There was a beautiful, ornate mirror hanging on the wall in front of her. Her eyes fell on the mirror; she stared at her own reflection for a few minutes and burst out crying. The wails coming from Radha's room were heart-rending and brought tears to Shubhra's eyes, but she quietly continued to do her work. She neither stepped out nor knocked on Radha's door.

When Ayan and Aaryak returned home in the evening with their cattle, the house seemed sombre and gloomy. Radha's eyes looked sullen while Shubhra looked like she was carrying a heavy burden on her shoulders. The men thought that the impossible had happened and the women had had a fight, and decided it was better to ignore it.

Having finished dinner and all her chores, Radha sat in the verandah. Aaryak and Ayan were in their rooms. Shubhra came and sat quietly beside Radha. She took Radha's hands in hers and stroked them. She looked at her mother-in-law and asked softly, 'How far is Dwarka from here, Ma?'

Radha pulled her hand away without answering Shubhra's question.

'Ma, I am asking you ...' Shubhra said gently.

The steadiness and firmness in Shubhra's voice shook Radha.

'I don't want to go to Dwarka.'

'Who said anything about going? I am just asking how far it is from here?'

'How would I know?'

'Ma, it was you who had said that a woman and a river have to flow in one direction—if they change directions or breach banks ...'

'My dear, when it rains in the upper reaches, the river loses control over itself and sometimes, breaches the banks inadvertently.' Radha looked up at the sky. 'Even if the whole of Dwarka came to Gokul, it would mean nothing to me.'

'Ma, do you have any apprehension? Are you afraid of something?' Shubhra asked.

Radha slowly turned towards Shubhra and said, 'Everything he said has been happening, and that is what will happen in the future too. If he had taken care of our fears and our safety, feelings and shortcomings, everything would have been different.' Radha turned her eyes towards the sky yet again. 'What would he be worrying about? He must have several tasks and duties ...'

'Ma, whom are you talking about?'

'My child ...' Radha said in a weak but deep voice, as if it was coming from some distant cave. 'Don't ask his name. If I mention his name, the kadamba tree will shed all its leaves, the Yamuna will break its banks and flood Gokul and Mathura, the Govardhan hill will shake and all these fields we have tilled so painstakingly will turn upside down.' Radha clamped her ears with her palms and said, 'I can't bear this sound any more. Who is playing the flute so loudly? Shut it down! Stop the music! My blood will spill out of my veins. My head is splitting, and my heart might just stop beating ... please stop the flute!'

The melodies of the flute got louder and seemed to move closer to her. Radha was drowning under its spell.

'Radha!' That voice calling out to her too seemed to be a part of the same spell, the same music. A hand extended towards her hands. Its touch seemed soft, like a bunch of flowers. Radha was unaware if it was a dream or reality. She did not want to know either, all she wanted to do was float on this river of the melody. She just wanted to float along the rising, falling, crashing, frothing waters and go wherever they took her. The notes of the flute were piercing her soul and entrapping her like a snake.

Shubhra thought of asking Radha where the sound of the flute was coming from, but she decided it was unnecessary. Suddenly, she too could hear the sounds of the flute and they seemed to be penetrating every cell of her body. Blood was rushing through her veins and her heart was beating hard. It looked as if the whole of Gokul was bewitched by the music.

Shubhra made Radha lie down, with her head in her lap. She loosened Radha's bun and began caressing her long hair. Both of them sat drenching their hearts with tears and cried uncontrollably, while their husbands slept unaware that the waters of the Yamuna had breached its banks and reached their house.

The melodies of the flute seemed to be cracking the walls of the house and gushing through the veins of the two women.

Krishna lay under the peepal tree with his eyes closed. His gaze roamed all over the narrow by lanes of Gokul, the palaces of Indraprasth and Dwarka. Draupadi's lustrous, perpetually enquiring eyes seemed to be looking at Krishna from the sky, like the bright afternoon sun, and asking him, 'Whom are you thinking about, at this moment?'

Rukmini's devoted, loving eyes, always eager to see Krishna, glistened in the river water. Her eyes, moist with tears, seemed to be caressing Krishna's feet lovingly and asking him, 'Does it hurt a lot, my lord?'

As deep as the Yamuna, as mischievous and restless as a fish, as dark as a monsoon cloud, the mildly angry eyes of Radha bent close over Krishna's face, like the leaves of the peepal tree and swayed gently, saying, 'Kanha, you lied to me, didn't you? You cheated! You didn't turn up finally!'

The three faces were merging into one another, and Krishna was trying to separate them like the waters of the three rivers, but failed. Radha, Rukmini and Draupadi's tears coursed down and merged like the confluence of the Hiranya, Kapila and Saraswati. He just couldn't separate the three.

Krishna opened his eyes. It was afternoon now, and the sun's brightness seemed to increase and decrease along with the rising and ebbing of the rivers. The branches of the peepal tree swayed in the cool breeze. Krishna's eyes were waiting for the voice that could wake him from his stupor and make him hear his own words ...

Sargaanaamaadirantashcha madhyam chaivaaham arjuna
Adhyaatmavidyaa vidyaanaam vaadah pravadataamaham

Aksharaanaamakaaro'smi dwandwah saamaasikasya cha
Ahamevaakshayah kaalo dhaataaham vishwatomukhah

Dando damayataamasmi neetirasmi jigeeshataam
Maunam chaivaasmi guhyaanaam jnaanam jnaanavataamaham

O Arjun! I am the beginning, middle and end of all creation; among the sciences, I am the science of the self; I am the logic of the conversationalists.

Among the letters of the alphabet, I am the letter A, and the dual among compounds. I am verily inexhaustible or everlasting time; I am the dispenser of the fruits of actions, I am omniscient.

Among the punishers, I am the sceptre; among those who seek victory, I am statesmanship; among secrets, I am silence; among knowers, I am knowledge.

Daruk, who had gone to receive Arjun, hadn't returned yet. And how could he—he got to know only after he had reached Hastinapur that Arjun and Draupadi had already arrived at Dwarka.

But where was Krishna? If he was not in Dwarka, not in Gokul, neither in Hastinapur, nor in Indraprasth, then where was he?

For the first time ever, Krishna wondered where he was. In an attempt to be omnipresent, he hadn't reached anywhere!

The light of the full moon played on the waves of the Yamuna. The gurgling waters would alternate between a dazzling silver and pitch black within moments. The bright moonlight, filtering in through the kadamba trees, was lending an ethereal glow to Radha's face. She sat with her eyes closed, her head resting on Krishna's chest. Her bun had come loose and Krishna stroked her hair with his long and slender fingers. His other hand was entwined in Radha's hand and rested on her chest.

'Shall I go, Kanha?' The tears from Radha's shut eyes streamed down her cheeks.

Krishna wiped her tears ever so gently and asked, 'You have to go, don't you? Will I ever have the fortune of seeing the rising sun in your eyes?'

'Kanhaiya, my sunrise is tied to someone else's bed. I don't know if I must consider it my fortune or misfortune, but I cannot desert someone, and snatching someone away is not one of your skills.'

'I am bound by my word. I have no choice.'

'My own time is not mine,' replied Radha.

'You will go today, and I too will have to go sometime; I will go.'

'I know that you will.'

'Won't you stop me?'

'If you won't go just because I say so, then why would you go at all? I know Kanha, you will leave soon; each one of us has to reach our destined place. I have to go to my home and you to yours.'

'Turn this side ... towards the light.'

'Why?'

'Your eyes are moist.'

'That is what you feel, because your eyes are tearful.'

'Will you cry when I leave?'

'Will you feel happy if I do?'

'Is it even possible that I'd be happy to see you cry?'

'This has been true till now, Kanha! You trouble me, make me cry, break my pots, beckon me with the music from your flute and then go and hide somewhere.'

'That was just play, Radha.'

'And what is this?'

'This is the truth.'

'Your play and your truth—where do *I* fit into all this, Kanha? What about me?'

'You are a part of me, Radha. You are my play and my truth. What I cannot experience explicitly, I experience through you, Radha.'

'Kanha ...' Radha said in a sharp and piercing voice, 'it is you who will decide everything, isn't it? Our love was your decision; your departure is your decision. My loneliness and tears are also for you to decide. The fact that I won't be able to forget you, will wait for you every moment of my life, is also your decision?'

Krishna leaned in closer, held Radha's hands, and kissed them. All of a sudden, Radha could hear the strains of the flute. Both of them were lost in the moment and glided along, mesmerised by the melodies of the flute.

Suddenly, Radha pulled her hand away and said, 'Shall I say something, Kanha?' and began talking without waiting for his response. 'Sometimes, the traveller himself becomes the path he travels on. He doesn't understand whether he is the wanderer or the path. Kanha, you are certainly going, but do remember to remain a traveller and not become the path that leads to nowhere.'

'Radha, I am the one who flies in the sky. My relationship with this earth is going to be cut off. The dust of time will stick on my palms in such a way that when I try to wipe a dull mirror, it will get dirtier.' Krishna's voice was drenched with tears but his eyes were dry and focused on the emptiness far away.

'Why do you have to go? You have Gokul, your cows and your mother.' Radha hesitated a bit and said, 'I am here too. What else do you need?'

'Me? Where do I want anything? I am going to distribute whatever I came with and leave.'

'Leave? What do you mean? Where are you going?' Radha asked.

'Forward, forward and further away. I don't have the luxury or the right to look back. I am time myself. I am incapable of turning back, Radhike! Even if I want to, or if you want me to!'

'I just don't understand you, at times. In any case, you always do what you decide to do. Tell me, have you ever lived for someone else? What you say is truth and what you do is karma. Wow, Kanha!' Radha said with sarcasm. Her voice was as deep and as dark as the waters of the Yamuna.

'I am independent, that's the truth. Only an independent person can come and go as he pleases. I am going because I want to. I came because I had no other alternative. Radha, those who are independent have to carry a huge responsibility, that of liberating others. Only the liberated can liberate other people. Have you ever thought what would happen to the liberation of others if I myself got bound? I know you aren't selfish, and I can never be so, because when there is no self, how can I be selfish?'

'Everything here will be so dull and desolate without you.'

'I am here. I will be here. It's the mind that travels, comes and goes, my dear! There is nothing like coming and going. It's just the time between two points, and our existence is somewhere between those two points. Right now, you and I are sitting entwined with each other. That is the only truth of this moment. The moment that just passed is the one we came from and the one about to come is where we are headed; these are the two points between which we travel. Every moment is one of departure, my dear. That we will all depart is certain, but exactly when—no one knows the answer to this question and that is what makes this journey so fascinating, and fun. Do you understand?'

'Kanha, I just understand one thing; I won't be able to live without you.'

'My love, life is eternal. It continuously flows like the waters of the Yamuna, sometimes dark and sometimes sparkling, yet flowing ceaselessly, whether I exist or not.'

Radha rested her head on Krishna's chest yet again, but this time, her incessant tears were drenching his chest. Krishna sat caressing her back, looking far into infinity.

The time for departure from Gokul had to come sometime or the other. He knew this well and had made up his mind; he had to reach his last point, that too within a certain period.

The moment Draupadi came to know that Krishna had left Dwarka and gone to Prabhaskshetra, she had screamed in a broken voice: 'Parth ...' Arjun's heart had skipped a beat on hearing Draupadi's heart-wrenching cry.

He ran towards her and managed to catch her just before she fainted. He laid her gently on the bed. Draupadi's eyes closed and she mumbled unconsciously, 'Sakha ... Parth ... Prabhas ... hey Gopal.' Tears were rolling down her eyes.

Arjun picked her up and ran to his chariot in one breath. He had realised that his guru, Sakha and mentor had very little time left, and they had a long, long way to go before he could meet Krishna. He laid Draupadi gently on the chariot, took the reins in his hands and sped off. It appeared as if the horses too had realised that they had to leave even the wind behind and race in the direction decided by Arjun. After going some distance, Arjun realised that the land route to Prabhas would be too long, and decided that he could reach much faster by taking a boat to Somnath. He turned the chariot towards the sea.

There was a lone boat on the seashore. While boarding the golden boats, perhaps the Yadavs must have ignored the wooden one. Or, Krishna himself must have left the boat there to make it possible for Arjun and Draupadi to reach him! Arjun picked up the unconscious Draupadi. The sands on the shore still had footsteps of some of the Yadavs who had just left for Prabhas. Several footsteps had been erased by the high tide overnight, but the divine footsteps with the lotus symbol were intact, and Arjun realised that they belonged to none other than his dear Sakha, Krishna. Arjun tried to wake Draupadi up saying, 'Yagyaseni, wake up. Yagyaseni! Look, these are Krishna's footprints. It's not too long since he left from here. Do the waves of the mighty ocean have the power to wipe away his footprints! He is time himself—nothing can happen to him. Wake up, Yagyaseni and see ...'

'Govind ... Gopal ... Govind ...' Draupadi mumbled indistinctly and gently opened her eyes.

Draupadi bent down devoutly to place her head on Krishna's divine footprints. Her tears continued unabated. Her lips spontaneously uttered yet again:

'Twadiyam vastu govindam tubhyameva samarpaye'.

Once Arjun and Draupadi had left, the palace looked desolate and dark to Rukmini. She felt dwarfed and inadequate before Draupadi's devotion to Krishna.

'Why did I allow Krishna to leave? Why didn't I go with him? Why did I agree with him?' Numerous questions arose in Rukmini's mind. Till date, she hadn't been able to understand how a woman with five husbands could love Krishna, and it gnawed at her constantly.

'She must be one extraordinary woman,' Rukmini thought. Krishna's love for Draupadi had rubbed off on Rukmini too. There was no place for envy in Rukmini like other ordinary women.

Krishna used to say, 'If we observe the personalities of men and women carefully, we find that men live their lives immersed in their egos and women in envy. It is true that envy is the dormant form of egoism, while egoism is active envy.'

About Draupadi, Krishna had said, 'This woman is capable of living in love devoid of envy, and is far superior to her five husbands in many ways. They have been in intense pain. They have been continuously fighting an internal battle because of her, but Draupadi has remained unaffected and peaceful. She was able to come out of her extremely strange circumstances unscathed, and the adoration and devotion for the people she loved remained unbroken and unquestionable.'

Whenever Rukmini complained about Satyabhama or any of his other queens, Krishna would say, 'The misunderstandings we have are all created by ourselves. We believe love is possible only between two people. Love is like a flower and can suddenly bloom for anyone, anytime. It has no bonds and limitations. Because of our strong bindings, we refuse to allow love to bloom and are trapped to live life without it. We humans are strange indeed! We also refuse to let go of our ownership of love. We accept our loveless, empty lives, but cannot accept the fact that the person we loved can get love from someone else.'

And today, Rukmini had witnessed before her a love that meant only surrender. There were no questions, no expectations, no sorrow, no pain—all that existed was an undisputed, complete, constantly flowing, living love.

That is why their love remains strong and intact to this day. Rukmini, who called Draupadi Vaasudevasya Sakhi, could never imagine that this Sakhi would be so close, so dear to her husband.

After Draupadi left, Rukmini felt that she had made a big mistake by not going with Krishna and suddenly began preparing to go to Prabhas. It's all right if I didn't go with Krishna; I can always follow him! Even otherwise, it is a wife's duty to follow her husband, and today, when everyone is walking towards him, why should I, his wife, his queen, be left behind? What am I doing here?

She came out of the palace. Will I be able to meet Krishna? Will I reach there on time? Rukmini's mind was filled with doubts. Her lips prayed as she descended the steps of the palace, 'O God! Let my lord have peace wherever he is. Let no sorrow or pain touch him, let all his suffering be mine.'

Rukmini walked fast and reached the main square. The marble-floored, tree-lined square and the beautiful, landscaped palace premises had never looked so desolate and lifeless before. There was a beautiful fountain, surrounded by a small pond with blooming lotuses, in the middle of the square. Whenever Krishna was in town and the rajya sabha was in session, this place teemed with people. This is where Krishna had welcomed his dear friend, Sudama. He had come running barefoot, right from the palace steps to the centre of the square to meet him. All those visuals swam before Rukmini's eyes. How many festivals and celebrations this square had witnessed! All the citizens would assemble there; it would be festooned with flowers and ashoka leaves. Krishna would participate wholeheartedly in every occasion. Krishna, who had made every moment of his life a celebration, was now preparing for the celebration of his own death!

Rukmini had spent innumerable full moon nights sitting there with Krishna. Words would disappear, and there would be nothing to say in those moments. Krishna made every moment he spent with Rukmini memorable. She had seen Krishna and Draupadi sit there and talk late into the night. Rukmini would look out of the window and wonder what the subject of their conversation may have been ... Once in a while, she would feel a slight tinge of jealousy. Seeing her own husband share his deepest feelings and thoughts with another woman so effortlessly and uninhibitedly made her feel inadequate and small. Why wasn't she that close to her loved one? Rukmini would often be plagued by such thoughts.

But she had never mentioned this to Krishna.

Once, when Draupadi was in Dwarka with the Pandavs, Krishna had come to Rukmini's palace. Seeing Rukmini awake at midnight, Krishna had asked, 'Why are you still awake, my dear?'

'I was waiting for you, you seem to have spent quite some time with your Sakhi—I thought you would come only at dawn.'

Krishna had burst out laughing. 'My dear, no matter how much time I spend with my Sakhi, it is never enough.'

'I see,' Rukmini said. 'We have to make do with whatever little time is left after your meeting with her, isn't it?' Krishna came close to her and said, 'My love, your voice sounds a little bitter today. Are you feeling jealous of Sakhi?'

Rukmini's eyes welled up with tears, 'No, I am not jealous of anyone. Your absence hurts me!'

'Yes, my dear. My absence hurts my own self at times. That is why I have gradually started moving towards my liberation.'

Rukmini was perplexed. 'Liberation?'

'Yes, my love. I have begun the process of detaching my mind from all mortal relationships and merging it with the supreme being.'

'But, my lord, you have always lived a life of detachment—like that of a lotus, which blooms in water but remains untouched by the sludge around it.'

'You know and understand, and yet complain about my absence tormenting you. My dear, I am completely yours and I equally belong to everyone else. I never hold back on giving. It's just that your expectations exceed my affection and that is when questions arise, my absence hurts ... I have no authority over my birth, my life and my death. My birth took place for the establishment of good; that is my duty, my goal and the essence of my existence.

'Not only Yagyaseni, everyone is worried about the rehabilitation and revival post the carnage. Being a woman, she worries more and is agitated. She has lost her sons. Victory gave her nothing but the satisfaction of having taken revenge ... yet, she remains the queen of Bharatvarsh. You are a mother. Can't you understand her pain? What is the future of this huge kingdom? Isn't it natural for her to be worried? Despite being the wife of five husbands, she is sad and lonely. She shares her pain, agony, her questions and aspirations only with me. She has immense respect and reverence for me. And here you are doubting your trust, complaining about the absence of your husband?'

Rukmini stood stunned for a while, and then hugged Krishna tight, as if she wanted to merge with him.

She was the consort of the lord himself! Any traces of doubt that she had vanished when she realised that the queen of Bharatvarsh held her husband in such high esteem and was so devoted to him.

Rukmini walked past the square. Satyabhama's massive palace with its huge windows with vines hanging from them and the gleaming gem-studded dome on top, stood to her right. Satyabhama's palace reflected her aesthetic sense. Hers was the most beautiful palace, and she had the maximum number of maids.

Satyabhama believed that one of the most effective ways to attract Krishna was with her beauty and charm. She was the youngest among all his queens and hence, Krishna pampered her a lot.

Krishna was attracted to Rukmini's patience and maturity. He had a lot of respect for Rukmini because of her large-heartedness and generosity, and though Satyabhama didn't show it openly, she was certainly jealous of Rukmini. Krishna's understanding with Rukmini and their effortless communication made Satyabhama feel that she wasn't as close to Krishna as

Rukmini, that she was less dear. This wasn't true, but it made Satyabhama envious.

Suddenly, Rukmini's eyes wandered towards the windows of Satyabhama's palace. She saw Satyabhama standing unadorned and lifeless at the window. She was in a white saree, devoid of her earrings and necklaces. Her lustrous hair was loose and hanging on her back. The smile, which played on her lips constantly, was lost and her eyes were stony. Satyabhama, who was beautiful and usually so full of life, seemed like a lifeless statue at the window.

Rukmini's heart filled with pain on seeing Satyabhama. She felt like running to her and hugging her. She wanted to bless her with love and affection.

Satyabhama's eyes suddenly fell on Rukmini, but her expression didn't change and she stood as if she didn't know her at all. For some reason, Rukmini decided that it would be better not to disturb Satyabhama's solitude, and she walked forward. She had to reach her lord. She had hardly walked about twenty steps when she heard a voice, 'Didi ... didi ...' It was Satyabhama. She came running, held Rukmini by her shoulders and turned her around. Staring deep into Rukmini's eyes, she asked, 'Is our lord not going to come back?' Rukmini was stunned. Satyabhama's eyes were hollow, as dry as a desert. Her eyes reflected the pain of one who had been deceived and abandoned.

Rukmini lowered her eyes; she didn't know what to say.

'Our lord, is he not going to come back? Please tell me, didi ...' Satyabhama asked again.

Rukmini had no choice but to tell her the truth. She gently lowered Satyabhama's hands from her shoulders, pulled her close and held her in a tight embrace.

'Yes, our lord has gone to Prabhaskshetra, and from there—to heaven.'

'How? How is it possible?' Satyabhama asked in disbelief. Her eyes were filled with misery. She couldn't accept that Krishna had left without taking her leave. 'Didi, what did I do wrong? Why did my lord leave like that?'

'He is on his final journey and no one can accompany anyone on this journey.'

'But I was his dearest, his closest, wasn't I?' Satyabhama asked, wishing that if Rukmini agreed, all her shortcomings, all the malice could be done away with.

'Yes, you were ...' Rukmini held Satyabhama to her chest and stroked her hair.

'Who else was dearer and closer to the lord than you? You were his life, his companion, his lover,' Rukmini said in a gentle voice, as if consoling a sulking child.

All of a sudden, Satyabhama burst out crying.

'Please forgive me, didi. I have always been envious of you. Your proximity and your identification with my lord hurt me. I was jealous of you being his queen consort and because of all this, I could never come close to him. He came to you when he was leaving on his final journey and informed you, but ...' She sobbed uncontrollably.

All the impurity and misgivings in her heart were getting washed away with her tears. Truth had sprung up in her mind like the rising sun. Rukmini's status and place had become clear to Satyabhama, and she felt herself to be insignificant in Krishna's life.

Rukmini related to Satyabhama what Krishna had told her. 'I am completely yours and I equally belong to everyone else. I never hold back on giving, it's just that your expectations exceed my affection and that is when questions arise, and my absence hurts. I have no authority over my birth, my life and my death. My birth took place for the establishment of good; that is my duty, my goal and the essence of my existence!'

Satyabhama's mind was getting cleansed. She had, for the first time, understood Krishna, with whom she had spent her life. Satyabhama had found the Krishna she had been constantly looking for; but it was only now, when he had left!

Perhaps, this is what it meant to be God. One couldn't find him when one looked for him, asked for him, or aspired for him. He manifested himself as truth from your soul, your heart and your mind, and pervaded your every cell.

Krishna's Satya had found her 'satya'—her truth—today. Satyabhama had become Krishna's *ardhangini* or life companion, in the true sense, only today. Rukmini consoled Satyabhama and told her about her journey to Prabhas.

'Will you come with me?' Rukmini asked.

'No, didi, I will stay here in Dwarka. Krishna's memories reside here; his fragrance permeates Dwarka. The days he spent here are still alive ... I will live with all this. I spent days and nights with Krishna, but couldn't find him. Now, I will find him for sure. His footsteps are imprinted on the stones of this palace. These domes echo his voice and I can still see him sitting by the palace window. I can still visualise him celebrating Janmashtami in this square. I am going to recall these memories in a whole new way now. I will relive every single moment I spent with my lord all over again. I will not leave Dwarka till my last breath, because my lord lived here, lives here and will live here for eternity!'

Leaving Satyabhama behind, Rukmini began walking rapidly through the streets of Dwarka. She suddenly heard the sound of the wheels of Krishna's chariot. She knew that sound very well. She would stand for hours at the palace window, waiting to hear the tinkle of the silver bells tied to the chariot. And the day the sounds reached the courtyard of her palace, it would be a celebration for her.

'Maharani, maharani!' She heard Daruk calling out to her. Turning around, she saw Daruk in Krishna's chariot. For a moment, she innocently imagined that Krishna had come back, but the chariot was empty.

'Where is my lord?' Rukmini asked.

'Where are Mata Draupadi and Parth?' Daruk asked in return.

'Why? What about them?'

'I have come to take them to Prabhas.'

And not me? The question reached the tip of her tongue, but she checked herself.

'Come, let's go, Ma. Otherwise ...' Daruk stopped mid-sentence. Rukmini could feel something ominous was going to happen. She sat in the chariot without asking any questions and they raced towards the shores of Dwarka.

'Why are we headed in this direction?' Rukmini asked.

'Ma, we can reach Prabhaskshetra faster by the sea route. There is still a possibility that we will be able to meet our lord,' Daruk's voice trembled.

'What do you mean?' Rukmini's voice was choked. She knew what Daruk meant.

She could see the forthcoming moments clearly. Daruk's voice, the speed of his chariot and the apprehensions in her heart made Rukmini extremely restless. When they reached the sea shore, there wasn't a single boat in sight.

'Let me arrange for a boat.' Daruk rushed away.

The sea was turbulent and wave after wave was crashing on the shore and washing away footprints of the Yadavs each time.

Rukmini suddenly sat next to a set of familiar footprints. Tears rolled down her eyes. They were the same feet that her long hair touched every day. These were the feet she had worshipped with sandalwood paste. These were the same feet that she had trusted and walked away with, leaving everything behind. They belonged to her lord, Krishna! The footprints were deep and filled with water. Her tears were flowing into the footprints.

Daruk came and stood close to her. His eyes were wide with astonishment. Rukmini's tears were disappearing into the water-filled footprints, but not a single tear flowed out of the small pools. Krishna's footprints were accepting and absorbing everything and everyone with the same love, respect and affection. That was how his entire life had been.

'Ma, the boat is ready. Let's go.'

Rukmini stood up. She bent down and bowed to the footprints. She covered her head with the end of her saree to protect herself from the harsh afternoon sun and sat in the boat. The boat began sailing towards the shores of Somnath.

By the time Arjun and Draupadi's boat reached the shores of Somnath, the receding afternoon was casting its yellow glow on the sea and turning it golden. Since the afternoon tides had ebbed, they had to anchor their boat at a little distance. Draupadi got off the boat and began walking fast, water splashing all around her. She was finding it difficult to walk in the shallow waters; Arjun held her hand and they reached the shore together.

The imposing Somnath temple, built by Krishna himself, was right in front of them, standing majestically, with its gleaming, gem-studded dome. Draupadi had visited the temple a few times with the Pandavs. She had great faith in Lord Somnath, the presiding deity of the temple. It was believed that he fulfilled everyone's wishes.

Draupadi didn't have enough time to go to the temple, but she closed her eyes and prayed, 'O Shiv! Shambho! Krishna has accepted one and all unconditionally. Please accept him with respect and affection and grant him a peaceful and painless journey ... I have nothing more to ask.' And then, she mumbled as if she was talking to Krishna himself, 'Govind, you have given us so much peace, affection, respect and harmony. I offer all this to you. I don't know whether I will be able to reach you or if you will accept me or not, but at this very moment, I accept you completely and offer to you all the relationships you have given me. I pray for your liberation. My only wish is that you don't face any hesitation or unhappiness in the moment when you give up your body and merge with the divine. I am aware that I will need the same prayer for myself as well, because you give back to us everything we offer you, and we have to accept everything that you give us. This is the truth, the end, the beginning and this is consciousness ...' *'Twadiyam vastu govindam tubhyamev samarpaye.'*

She closed her eyes and prayed to the Shivling. She opened her eyes when Arjun placed his hand on her shoulder. It seemed as if everything had fallen silent. The agitation, anxiety and discomfort on Draupadi's face had vanished and had been replaced by the glow of calm and wholehearted acceptance. Merging with the divine was the ultimate goal for everyone and at the same time, the dawn of a new beginning. Wasn't this the next phase in the unending cycle of the soul discarding one attire and wearing another?

When Arjun looked at Draupadi, he could see Krishna's reflection in her eyes. The chariot standing in the middle of the Kurukshetra battlefield, Arjun, who had lost even before the battle began, all brothers and cousins standing on the other side, and his own people fighting on the side of dharma ... and Krishna's words at that moment ...

Vasamsi jirnani yatha vihaya, navani grhnati naro 'parani
Tatha sarirani vihaya jirnany anyani samyati navani dehi

As a person puts on new garments, giving up old ones, similarly, the soul accepts new material bodies, giving up the old and useless ones.

They were just a few minutes away from Prabhaskshetra. Since they didn't have a chariot, Draupadi and Arjun had to walk. Just a short distance from the Somnath temple, they could see the corpses of Yadavs scattered all around. Many of the Yadavs, who had run in that direction while fighting or to save themselves, had perished because of excessive bleeding from their wounds. Arjun shivered at the pitiable sight of the once mighty and strong race. He began separating their mangled bodies and covered them with their clothes. He placed their severed limbs close to their bodies, and performed the last rites of those whom Krishna hadn't cremated. They were fortunate to attain liberation at

Arjun's hands. Gradually, he began to realise the purpose
of his journey to Prabhaskshetra. Perhaps, the tasks left
incomplete by the lord were destined to be completed by
Arjun. When Arjun reached Prabhaskshetra, there were
innumerable funeral pyres ablaze, and the smoke from
the burning bodies of the mighty Yadavs was creating
varied patterns in the air.

Arjun collected the ashes from all the pyres and looked
around. He saw a large number of wine glasses, vessels
and pots of alcohol strewn around. Realising that it would
be inappropriate to carry the ashes in those pots, he tied
them in his waistcloth.

'What are you doing, Parth?'

'Many of these Yadavs have been cremated by Krishna
himself, but he has left the sacred task of immersing the
ashes to me. The confluence of the three rivers is close, I
will immerse these ashes there and pray that their souls
rest in peace,' replied Arjun.

'But where is Sakha?' Draupadi had been hiding her
restlessness for long. 'We have come here to meet Sakha.'

'We haven't come; we have been called by Sakha,
to complete the tasks he couldn't finish,' Arjun said.
He continued, 'I am sure Sakha will not be here in
Prabhaskshetra. He must have been very hurt and pained
to see all this, he must be in some temple or sitting under
some tree nearby.'

'But when will we meet him?' Draupadi asked.

'When he wishes ...' Arjun said with utmost faith.
'He himself will come to meet us when he so desires.

Our duty is more important now. One finds the lord the moment his duties are completed. And he is obligated to come. When a task is done conscientiously with utmost devotion, results are bound to be conducive.'

'Parth, I don't know why but I have a feeling that Sakha is waiting for us; we have to reach him right away.'

'He never waits for anyone, but it is us who wait for him to call us, for him to allow us to come close to him.'

Arjun had, by then, collected all the ashes and tied them up in his waistcloth. 'Come dear, let's go.'

Draupadi was upset. Time would be lost in going to the Sangam and then finding Sakha. Despite her patience, she was irritated, panicking and getting angry at Arjun's behaviour.

'Parth, please find Sakha. I will not go back without meeting him.'

'He too won't leave without meeting you,' Arjun said casually, with a gentle smile. 'Otherwise, would he have called you all the way here? Calm down, my dear! You will surely meet him!' Saying so, Arjun placed the bundle of ashes on his shoulder and started walking.

Draupadi plodded behind Arjun, finding it difficult to carry her own weight.

The two of them proceeded towards the confluence.

Krishna's eyes seemed to be looking for his final moments, far in the sky. His life seemed to be waiting for something. What was the wait for? Draupadi, Arjun,

Rukmini, Radha or for Lord Shiv himself, who had been waiting to take him along for quite some time? Krishna's body seemed to be turning into a peacock feather and his flute seemed to be playing its last melody. All ready and eager to go, yet waiting, holding his breath in his fist for some reason. But for whom? He didn't know the answer yet.

Even though the earth had become hot due to the blazing afternoon sun, the cool breeze on the banks of the confluence made the heat bearable. The branches of the peepal tree swayed in the breeze. Krishna asked Jara one more time, 'Can you see anyone?'

Jara's silence conveyed to him that the person or people he was waiting for hadn't come yet. Will I have to go without taking leave from my loved ones? The question arose in Krishna's mind, and he got the answer almost instantly: I have already taken leave from the most important people in my life, and they all have let me go. If I had been bound to them, I would have never reached this far. They liberated me wholeheartedly, and here I am, sitting without a trace of burden, without any worries or turmoil plaguing my mind. It is time for me to spread my wings and fly towards liberation with a free heart and an empty mind.

He seemed to be talking to himself. 'Waiting is a waste. Waiting for someone or something, every moment of one's life, is not living; it is craving. Instead of living to fulfil every single desire, it is better to accept whatever we get. It is more important to breathe life into every breath—that is the biggest truth; who knows it better than I? People who live today with the expectation that something will happen tomorrow and live tomorrow in the anticipation that something will happen the day after, will never be truly able to live life. The only true moment is the present. Those who live for tomorrow are tied to the future and forget the present. Such people never experience life in real terms.

In their dying moments, these people will say that they only wished to live. Their biggest pain will be the absence of anything to look forward to. If they were to see a glimmer of expectation, they would even tolerate death. Maybe that is why the dying ask, 'Does rebirth happen? I won't die forever, will I?'

And that is when Krishna was reminded of his own words:

Na hi prapasyami mamapanudyad
Yacchokamuchhosanam indriyanam
Avapya bhumavasapatnamarddham
Rajyam suranamapi cadhipatyam

I can find no means to drive away this grief which is drying up my senses. I will not be able to dispel it even if I win a prosperous, unrivalled kingdom on earth with sovereignty like the demigods in heaven.

Was living life completely free of desires just a sham, Krishna thought. While he was taking the last few breaths of his life, what was this intense desire, expectation and deep longing that was seeping through every pore of his being?

The Triveni Sangam was now visible in the distance.

The three rivers, Hiranya, Kapila and Saraswati, streaming from three directions, flow with a sense of surrender and empty their sweet waters into the sea. They flow unquestioningly and readily lose their sweetness, and accept the salty identity of sea water. Despite this, why don't they let go of their desire to merge with the sea, Draupadi thought. Are women also destined to flow in a single direction, restricted between two banks? Eventually, are they also supposed to give up all their sweetness, desires, emotions and aspirations for the sake of men and relinquish their own identities? Why is a woman's life like this? Why isn't she allowed a mind of her own? Why is she not allowed to raise questions and express herself? Draupadi's eyes clouded over and began to wander among the trees on the banks of the confluence. She was desperate to see that face, the one that was synonymous with her entire life.

Why is my mind so agitated? Despite having been so closely associated with Sakha, why am I getting so disturbed? Why am I not ready to accept that if he himself has called me all the way to meet him, he would certainly wait for me? Now, when the moment of meeting is so close, why is my mind so restless and full of doubt, Draupadi thought, staring at the vast expanse of sand on the banks of the rivers. The rays of the receding afternoon sun were dancing on the river waters. The gushing waters of the Hiranya were glistening like molten gold. The white and black rocks and stones under the clear waters of the Saraswati river were visible even in the distance. The gurgling of the Kapila was rivalling the turmoil in Draupadi's mind. Suddenly, Arjun's eyes fell on Jara. He was sitting with folded hands, facing the other side. The end of a yellow waistcloth was visible near Jara. Arjun silently led Draupadi by her hand without saying a word. Now Draupadi too could see the yellow patch of cloth.

Draupadi's bare feet were burning while walking on the sands of the riverbank. Her loose hair was flying behind her. Despite the tremendous pain she was experiencing with every step she took on the sand, Draupadi ran breathlessly in the direction of the yellow piece of cloth.

For some reason, Draupadi missed seeing a big rock on the sand. The end of her saree caught in her toe and she fell face down on the rock, hurting her forehead. Blood spouted out of the wound. Her face became red with blood. Her feet were mechanically dragging her towards the peepal tree. Her eyes were transfixed on the yellow fabric. She mumbled, 'Hey Govind, hey Gopal, hey Govind, hey Gopal ...'

Arjun, walking a few steps behind, thought of stopping her, but he knew that after seeing the yellow waistcloth covered in mud, Draupadi wouldn't stop even for a second. It was futile to hold her back. Seeing her fall on the rock, a scream escaped his lips, 'Panchali!'

Krishna smiled with his eyes closed and thought, the mind plays such games! The name of the person that I am waiting for is echoing all around me.

And just then, Jara said, 'Prabhu, they have arrived!'

'Really?' Krishna was still not convinced. 'What do you mean by they?' Krishna thought: I have called out to so many people. Who would have heard my voice first? Who would have reached first? He sat up with great effort and looked back.

Draupadi, with her dishevelled hair, her saree in disarray and her bloodstained face, had almost reached the tree.

'Sakha!' She wailed her heart out.

'I knew you would come. I was certain that my friend wouldn't let my body go without proper rites,' Krishna said to Arjun.

'And what about me? Did you not call me?'

'Phalgun and you are one and the same for me, Sakhi; I don't see you as two separate people. You both are one for me, extraordinary and special!'

Draupadi sat near Krishna's feet, tears flowing down her eyes. Her tears were getting mixed with her sweat and blood and flowed down right till her breasts. She realised what had happened the moment she saw Krishna's wounded toe. It was clear to her that not much time was left. If only one could stop the flow of time.

'I will not let you go. You just can't go.' Draupadi took Krishna's hand in hers.

'Leaving is how everyone sees it; where am I going anyway? It is just another journey. Once a person's time is up, the next journey has to begin. You know very well, Sakhi, even then you ask.'

'Why hasn't my time come? Put an end to my time too.'

'Is that in my control, Sakhi? Everyone is bound to wait for their time. I have done the same.'

Arjun placed his head at Krishna's feet and burst out crying. 'We will be left alone ... empty. Madhusudan, our lives have no meaning without you.' His voice was choked. The blood from Krishna's toe was being washed away by Arjun's tears.

Krishna stretched out his hand and began stroking Arjun's head. Draupadi still sat holding his other hand. Krishna smiled and closed his eyes and then said in a soft voice filled with pain, 'I neither have the energy nor the time to narrate the Gita all over again. Get up, Parth, rise and focus on your goal.'

'Goal? Is there any goal left to be achieved any more, my lord?'

'Liberation! Yours and everyone else's! All the other goals were transient and evanescent. Your real goal is right in front of you. Become free, Arjun!' Krishna freed his hand from Draupadi's and folded his hands together, 'And free me too! Until your mind is in mine, my mind too cannot be free.'

Arjun looked up and said, 'My lord, you are free—formless, stoic and detached ...'

'Yet human,' Krishna said. 'Who is free from the duties of the body?'

'Even you?' Draupadi asked. Her eyes reflected a strange yearning. They had the same question that she had when she met Krishna for the first time in Panchal as a sixteen-year-old girl. That question remained unanswered.

'Krishnaa!'

Every cell in Draupadi's body felt satiated on hearing Krishna address her thus. She just wanted to disappear deep into the earth at that very moment. Her life and her birth had found meaning in that address.

Arjun looked at Draupadi. There was a sense of amity in her eyes as she looked at Krishna. Arjun held her gently by the shoulders recognising the intensity of her emotions. He got up and began walking towards the Kapila, wanting to leave them alone.

'Parth,' Draupadi called out to him, but Arjun continued walking sedately, disregarding her voice.

'Krishnaa ...' Krishna said again. 'Love is not about receiving or gaining. To pray for others' well-being and to work for it is also love.'

'No! Not for a woman.'

'I am not a woman.' A mischievous smile played on Krishna's lips.

'But I am a complete woman. A desirable woman for many men, a devoted and perfect one for my husbands ...

yet, it feels like that is not enough; it keeps rankling me. What is lacking in me? Tell me, Sakha.'

'Desirable! What you desire becomes desirable, doesn't it? But why would I desire you when you were already always with me? I never looked at you as a woman or saw your femininity. For me, it was always about your individuality and personality. Perhaps, our relationship is one between just two human beings, not what exists between man and woman.'

'Don't speak for both of us! I had asked you for love. I have desired you ever since I saw you for the first time in Panchal. I desired you even during the swayamvar ceremony, I wanted you to win. But you didn't even care to participate! You left me to struggle in an incomplete and inadequate world ... all alone!'

'It was you who had said, *twadiyam vastu govindam* ... You have probably accepted the incompleteness I gave you wholeheartedly, and that is why, in this moment, you are offering it back to me, so that it becomes a part of me too.'

'You are known to be the complete one! Poorna Purushottam! You are an epitome of completeness. How can a complete person like you speak about incompleteness? If our venerated lord, considered an incarnation, who lived a life of completeness, accepts incompleteness in his last moments, the entire world will be shaken, Sakha,' Draupadi's voice had unintentionally become a little bitter, as she wiped her tears and steadied herself.

'Acceptance is my dharma, my duty, Sakhi. Whether we talk about completeness or incompleteness, they are both the same, in a way. Where incompleteness ends, completeness begins, and where completeness doesn't reach, everything is incomplete. Where completeness parts ways, incompleteness prevails. Although they mean exactly the opposite, in truth they merge into one another because life is a study of contrasts.'

'Words—words yet again! Why don't you, for once, go beyond words and let the truth reach me. That will be my liberation, Sakha. My sorrows, humiliations, my truths and falsehoods—all of these will be put to rest with just one word of acceptance from you.'

'Have I ever refused anything, Sakhi? My life has been that of simple, undisguised acceptance.'

'No, you did not accept me, Sakha.'

Krishna laughed and said, 'Sakhi, how can one accept oneself? You are a part of my existence. It's possible that your incompleteness has given me my completeness! These little imperfections are what finally give birth to completeness ...'

'Have you ever loved me or not? This question has been tormenting me. It pierces and punctures my entire being every time I think about it. Please tell me, Sakha; tell me without bringing ethics between us and leave aside morality for a moment. Forget that I am your friend's wife and tell me whether you have ever loved me?'

'Yes, I have ... I have loved you deeply. But for me, love does not mean being a spouse. I don't believe marriage is a consequence of love. For me, love is not like a stream that flows unidirectionally, between two banks. I consider love to be life force that pervades, like air, all creation, and an undeniable necessity of our existence. It exists in a closed fist as well as in a closed room. Life is not possible without it even for a moment and yet, living beings need not be aware of its existence. Sakhi, my love for you is a prayer for your well-being, a wish for your prosperity, it is a prayer for the protection of your self-respect, for your happiness. My love is the answers to your prayers, and it lies in my sincere efforts to fulfil all your desires. Sakhi, love for me doesn't mean touching you or even living with you. Does love mean living under one roof? For me, love means to stand under the open sky and looking up, imagining your smile! Sakhi, I have loved you endlessly, and it's been so natural and spontaneous. I love you even at this moment, and this love will exist even after my body perishes. People who associate the body with love are incomplete. Just for one moment, dissociate the body from love in the real sense. You will realise that the Krishna you love, or the Krishna whose love you complain of being inadequate, that Krishna is not a body; he is the pulsating love alive in your imagination! You love the Krishna of your imagination. The Krishna you love is not Rukmini's husband, neither Devaki's son nor Arjun's friend. He is only your Krishna, who belongs to you alone. You are totally his, and he is entirely yours, Sakhi, the Krishna you love loves you intensely too. Have faith; what you asked for was always yours, is yours and nobody can ever take it away from you!'

'Sakha!' Draupadi looked at him with enraptured eyes. 'This is the most blessed moment of my life!'

'So, can I take your leave now?'

'Do you *have* to go?'

'I was always here and will always be here, but the soul has to complete its bodily duties before it leaves. This is one of them, Sakhi. If your mind was entwined with mine; how could my mind be free? And without freeing the mind, where can my soul go? Sakhi, I had a responsibility towards you and your love for me ...'

'My love will pull you back to this earth, Sakha. I will meet you again in human form.'

'That is your attachment speaking, Sakhi.'

'So be it! I am attached to you, Sakha, because I am human.'

'Am I God either? You are the only one who didn't allow me to become God.'

'Sakha, why are you putting me in a quandary? Tell me before we part: what direction is my destiny going to take?'

'Your destiny is linked with five names, Sakhi! Why are you trapping me with these questions? Calm down. There is a vast, pure, formless, unobjectifiable expanse of peace beyond this world of questions and answers. That peace has invited me today; yours too has to come some day.'

'When, Sakha? When will I get my invitation? This body has become a burden for me. Every moment I have lived thus far stings me constantly. I want to go beyond relationships, pass through the pores of time, go beyond time and see me, see my bare self.'

'Sakhi, how will you transcend time if you still have desires left in you? One needs to become lighter than air to do that. You will have to drop all your burdens right here. You will have to erase all the lines on your palms. You will have to wipe all the images and memories etched in your mind and clean up your slate. That is when time will spread its arms wide and call you. I am going at this moment, piercing through all the pores of time, towards a dazzling radiance that is a part of me or that I am a part of. We are all a part of this radiance, and it will merge us with itself at the appropriate time.'

'Sakha, I Panchali, Draupadi, Drupadputri, Pandavpatni, Kurukulvadhu free you from the bonds of my love.' She then said in a choked voice,

'Twadiyam vastu govindam tubhyamev samarpaye'.

Those words echoed from all ten directions around the confluence. Krishna gently closed his eyes. Draupadi too closed her eyes and chanted under her breath:

Om poornam-adah poornam-idam poornaath poorna-mudachyate
Poornasya poorna-maadaaya poorna-mevaa vashishyate

Everything in this universe is complete and infinite. Anything created out of something that is complete is also complete.

When something is removed from this infinite universe,
infinity still remains.

Seeing the waters of Kapila rushing towards the sea, a
thought struck Arjun: This river must have had such a
long journey, traversed a long distance, carrying within its
heart so many apprehensions and questions with it. There
must have been so many turns, ups and downs along the
way, but as it nears the sea, it calms down. All its doubts
vanish and all questions seem to get answered. Draupadi
is like the Kapila river. Even her doubts and questions
have disappeared. Her face glows with divine peace. On
the battlefield of Kurukshetra, Krishna had answered all
my questions and helped my mind become clear, steady
and quiet. It appears that removing apprehensions
and doubts is Sakha's ultimate duty. But now that he's
leaving, who will answer our questions henceforth? Who
will calm and comfort us?

As if Krishna himself was answering Arjun's question,
Arjun's heart seemed to say,

'*Uddhared atmanatmanam, natmanam avasadayet*
Atmaiva hy atmano bandhur, atmaiva ripur atmanah'

'A man must elevate himself by his own mind, not
degrade himself. The mind is the friend of the
conditioned soul, and its enemy as well.'

Arjun began walking in Krishna's direction. Both Draupadi and Krishna were sitting with their eyes shut. Their faces were serene and peaceful. It looked as if a terrible storm had passed over without causing any damage. Arjun too sat down quietly near them. He closed his eyes and caressed Krishna's feet with his hand. With every movement of Arjun's hand, Krishna's pain seemed to lessen. His face became more and more relaxed. Yet, something seemed to gnaw at Krishna. Who was binding him even now? Whose fears were becoming hurdles on his final journey? Whom was he waiting for? What questions remained to be answered?

When Rukmini got off the boat on the shores of Somnath and saw Arjun's boat, she was certain that Arjun and Draupadi must have gone in Krishna's direction. But which direction was that? She had no idea.

Krishna had told her about the circumstances leading to the annihilation of the Yadavs at Prabhaskshetra, but she had never imagined that things would be so terrifying and devastating. Although Rukmini couldn't see the corpses as she ran towards the path leading from the Somnath temple to Prabhaskshetra, the burning pyres, clothes, vessels and chariots told her the horrifying story.

Today, my lord was all alone while watching his own brothers, friends, sons, grandsons and his loved ones perish one by one right in front of his eyes. How would he have dealt with the grief?

'This is Satyaki's garland. I can recognise it,' Daruk
said. Picking up a bloodstained waistcloth, he said, 'This
is Kritivarma.' And then, he recognised and identified
the clothes and ornaments belonging to Aniruddh,
Charudeshna, Pradyumna, Anuj, Gad and many other
Yadavs. Crowns, garlands, necklaces, armbands and
blood-soaked clothes lay scattered all around. Daruk
picked them one by one, and wailed heart-rendingly.

Rukmini searched for the vaijayanti garland and yellow
waistcloth among all the clothes and ornaments, praying
all the while that she wouldn't find them.

Daruk, who had been running helter-skelter like a
lunatic, suddenly collapsed on the ground. He picked up a
sandal. It was made of sandalwood with fine carvings on
the edges. Seeing it, a scream escaped Rukmini's mouth,
'Lord!' She ran and snatched it from Daruk's hand and
pressed it to her chest, eyes and forehead. She then began
looking around for the other sandal, but couldn't spot it
anywhere.

'Lord! How much you would have suffered! Is this
sandal too like the clothes and ornaments of the Yadavs?'

'Ma! Here ... here is the other sandal!'

Rukmini took the other sandal from Daruk with
trembling hands. The front part of the sandal was
bloodstained. She touched it to her chest and forehead.

'Lord, if only you had permitted me to come with
you ... I would have taken all your pains upon myself. I
wouldn't have allowed even the shadow of suffering to
come anywhere near you.

'What could have happened? Why would it have happened? Who would have done it?' Such questions began to plague Rukmini's mind. Tears began flowing down her eyes and washing away the blood from Krishna's sandals.

'Where is my lord? Where can I look for him?' Rukmini was getting agitated. Daruk gently held her hand and helped her stand up. She was still holding the sandals close to her heart and staring ahead, stunned. Daruk, walking ahead while holding her hands, was following the drops of blood on the ground. There was a little puddle of blood at the place where they had found the second sandal. From the bloodstains on the ground, Daruk guessed that the painful feet would have walked really slowly.

Our lord couldn't have injured himself, Daruk thought. Even in the fierce battle of Kurukshetra, not a single weapon had been able to touch Krishna. Daruk had witnessed that miracle himself. 'Who had the gall to cause so much pain to my lord? I will tear him to pieces if he comes anywhere near me.' Daruk was seething with rage. He continued to walk holding Rukmini's hand, following the trail of blood.

'Ma, don't worry. Our lord is safe wherever he is.'

Rukmini said with a choked voice and eyes brimming with tears, 'I can see that from these bloodstained sandals. Why are you giving me false hopes, Daruk? The lord had told me while leaving Dwarka that all his earthly duties are over. He must have left his body long ago. To even think that my perfect, detached husband would be waiting, still bound by worldly ties, will be a sign of our ignorance, Daruk!'

'Ma, our lord just cannot go like this.'

'He had taken leave when he left Dwarka. He just has to attain samadhi and merge with the divine. This is such an easy and effortless task for him! Do you think he would be suffering in pain and extending his final moments? He must be in a hurry to unite with the supreme consciousness.' Rukmini continued in a hollow and empty voice, 'That is why he left me behind. While taking the wedding vows, he had said *"neti charaami"*. What happened to his promise? He has embarked on his path of liberation and left me to suffer alone in his absence. Tell me, Daruk, am I not capable of walking the path of liberation with him?'

'Why are you tormenting yourself so, Ma? Swami will never leave without fulfilling his responsibilities. The doubts arising in your mind are a sign that you are destined to meet our lord once. He is not so selfish to liberate himself before he clears all your doubts and shows you the path of liberation. Please listen to me, Ma; please walk fast, these drops of blood are guiding us in the direction of our lord.'

'That is right, Daruk. You seem to have understood him better than I did. The fire raging in my heart is trying to tell me that he is waiting to answer all my questions. If he had really left, he would have erased all my doubts and freed my mind. Come on, Daruk, let's hurry.'

Suddenly, her tired legs seemed to have grown wings, and she began walking really fast. It appeared as if the breeze carried Krishna's fragrance with it. So she stopped looking at the blood drops on the ground and blindly ran towards the confluence, as if she could hear Krishna's voice. She shouted, 'Wait, my lord! I am not very far away. I am headed in your direction. I will be there in just a few minutes. Please wait for me!'

A tearful face seemed to appear in the waves of the Kapila river and say to Krishna, 'There is so much to ask, so much to say, my lord! It feels like we have hardly spoken through our long years of togetherness. Time beckoned and you decided to leave. That is when it struck me that I have a lot to say to you, there is so much I have to hear from you. Our conversation is incomplete, Swami, please wait.'

Krishna opened his eyes, and on seeing the anticipation on his face, Draupadi asked, 'Sakha, is someone going to come? Whom is your heart waiting for?'

'Sakhi, someone's sorrow is tormenting me, and it is so severe that I cannot leave without mitigating it.'

'Sakha, who is it? It is a fact that everyone is saddened by your parting. We are all so dependent on you that just the thought of your absence is enough to tear us apart. But who is this person whose pain has bound your soul thus and is holding you back?'

'Who else can it be, Sakhi? My wife is very distressed. I had taken her leave when I left Dwarka, but it was incomplete. There was a desperate pleading in her eyes, asking me not to leave. That is tying me down. Her face appears before me time and again—her tearful eyes, open arms and trembling lips, the lines on her forehead, want to say something to me. She is not at peace.'

'When we went to Dwarka ...'

'You went to Dwarka? Then why didn't Rukmini come with you? Didn't Satyabhama insist on coming with you?'

'We didn't have much time, Sakha. I myself have barely managed to get here before it is too late!'

'She will surely come, Draupadi. Rukmini is a learned lady; she understands the scriptures. She is extremely sensitive and knows that till her mind is entwined with mine, I cannot leave in peace. She will certainly come. She will come to liberate herself, and once she is liberated, she will free me too.

Rukmini reached closer to the confluence. She could see Draupadi sitting at Krishna's feet. She could see Jara sitting silently with his hands folded. Jara thought, this is a man who is aware of everything. I have seen his divine from. Won't all these people, who are sitting around him and shedding tears, know that he is God? Even before Jara could make sense of Draupadi and Arjun's arrival, Rukmini came running and collapsed at Krishna's feet. Her face awash with sweat, was exactly as Krishna had described. Her eyes were begging him not to leave. She wanted to stop him from leaving. Her face was drawn.

Her moist eyes, her open arms and trembling lips, the lines on her forehead and her furrowed eyebrows were anxious to say something.

She bent down and placed her head at Krishna's feet. The vermilion in the parting of her hair had smudged because of sweat and her forehead had turned red. When her head touched his feet, his blood mixed with the vermilion and the colour on her forehead became darker.

'What has happened to you, my lord? Why did this happen? What for? Why did you ...?'

'My love, I had told you while leaving Dwarka that our time together was over. You allowed me to leave but not wholeheartedly. There was an instinct that wanted to bind me, didn't want me to go, and maybe that is why I sat here waiting for you, and you have come all the way here to see me off,' Krishna said with a smile and gestured for her to come closer. She moved closer to him. Krishna lifted his hand with great difficulty and placed it on her shoulder.

'My dear, wipe your tears. You are the daughter of a Kshatriya. It doesn't augur well for your royal lineage to shed tears when the husband is leaving. It is a Kshatriya woman's duty and dharma to see the husband off courageously with a smile.'

'That is when the husband is leaving for war. This is no war, my lord!'

'Yes, this too is a war, my dear—a battle between life and death. The body is unwilling to let go and the universe pulls the soul towards itself. How can I go if you don't see me off with a smile?'

'Lord, if it's a war that the wife sees off her husband for, she knows that he may return, and that she may get an opportunity to be a part of his victory procession. Here ...' Rukmini's voice was choked. She couldn't say anything more.

The sun was moving slowly towards the west. Its rays were now slanting, and the shadows of the people sitting under the peepal tree were getting longer. Filtering through the branches of the peepal tree, its multi-hued rays were more soothing now. The three rivers were turning golden.

'You are an erudite scholar; you know the scriptures. You are aware of the mortal nature of the human body, and yet ... Our relationship was one between two souls.'

'Was? My lord! Does that mean our relationship is over?'

'Our relationships cease to exist once the body is gone. The very reason we perform last rites is to help the departed soul leave the body and free itself from all ties, attachments and emotions associated with it. Once the soul leaves this body that people identify as Krishna, what remains is nothing but a piece of wood or a fistful of soil. The face that you recognise and love as Krishna is radiant and beautiful but alive only till the breath remains. Once the soul departs, it will lose its beauty, and you will find it difficult to love it any more, my dear. That is the reason why our religion gives so much importance to the performance of the last rites. All impure, lifeless and soiled things are burnt to ashes by fire. Fire engulfs everything and removes all impurities, whether in gold or in our souls.'

Seeing Rukmini's eyes, Krishna was reminded of the evenings he had spent with her. Countless moments from their blissful marital life, laid on the foundation of her love, her intelligence and maturity, swam before Krishna's eyes. Seeing the undulating waves in the three rivers at the confluence, gleaming under the evening sun, he was reminded of the lamps lit in Rukmini's palace.

'But, prabhu, in all these years, I am not sure if my words ever reached your soul and helped me understand the real you. Whenever you met me, only some part of you met me, as if you were divided into many fragments. Even when you were in my arms, you were preoccupied with the problems, questions and troubles of other people ... you were never completely alone, my lord. There was always someone present even in your solitude. Someone whom I couldn't see, couldn't know, couldn't touch but could always feel the presence of. You could never be completely mine.'

Krishna burst out laughing. 'Women can be so transparent! Men can never be like that. It is said that it is impossible to fathom a woman's mind. Women's minds are like rivers; the water runs very deep, and yet, it is clear and pure. One can see the smallest of the pebbles at the bottom. Do you believe that I will understand your pain and your passion only when you express them in words?'

'But my lord, you have never spoken about this. You never gave me the time I needed. Tell me, what did I ever ask for? The status of a queen, a place on the throne, clothes, jewellery? I could have got all that in Shishupala's palace as well. I didn't write to you for all this. I risked my reputation and wrote to the greatest man in Aryavart because I wanted to live with him. I wanted to live with you as your wife, devote every moment of my life to you, merge my existence with yours, forget myself and become Krishna.'

'Then why this remorse? What are all these misgivings for? You have lived as Krishna, my love. And living as Krishna means to forget one's ego and identity. Even otherwise, everyone has a right over my time, anyone can meet me, anytime. That is the purpose of my life. You don't love any particular person—you just love, and gradually become love yourself. Sweetheart, when love becomes restricted to one person, it becomes like stagnant water or a locked room that becomes stale and dirty with time. That someone is mine or I belong to someone is nothing but ego. And love has nothing to do with ego.'

'But, my lord, is it too much for a woman to expect that the time she spends with her husband be totally hers? Was it too unreasonable of me to have expected you to remove all your worries, responsibilities and apprehensions like a crown and leave it outside my room?'

Krishna was moved on seeing Rukmini's tears. He thought, what do women ask for after all—love. Nothing but boundless, ceaseless, undivided love. It is really very easy to make women happy. Their expectations are minimal or trifling. Perhaps men are incapable of understanding this.

Krishna looked at Rukmini and said, 'My dear, what you are describing is bondage, whereas marriage is not bondage but consonance. My responsibilities, my worries and my apprehensions are a part of my being. Did you want me to come to you as an incomplete being? My completeness is possible only because of these questions, responsibilities, and the people who have surrendered to me. If I remove all these, I myself will become incomplete. Devi, two people love some precious, invisible object, which they bring to life through words. They are mutually independent and therefore capable of opening up to the other. There is no room for fear. They are like seeds that are closed and hence cannot merge into one another, unlike blooms that can be together.'

While Krishna and Rukmini were speaking to each other, Daruk ran and gathered some medicinal herbs. He pounded them with a stone and made a paste. He was about to pull out the arrow and apply the paste on Krishna's wounded toe, when Krishna said, 'Let it be, bhai, it's of no use. Let the arrow be there. I will be able to keep my body and soul together only until the arrow remains pierced in my toe. It is now time for me to transcend pain and move to formlessness. No amount of herbs can cure the wounds on my body.'

'But, my lord ...' Daruk wanted to say something.

'You have obliged me greatly by bringing Rukmini here. If I hadn't met her, my soul wouldn't have been fully free. You have been my charioteer all your life. I am indebted to you,' Krishna said with folded hands.

'I am grateful to you, my lord, for giving me the opportunity to serve you. My life's purpose has been accomplished.'

'You are a pure-hearted and virtuous man. You have been with me till my last moments. You have been faithful. You are free, Daruk. Go on your own path.'

'My path is with you, my lord. Where else will I go?' Daruk broke down.

Krishna placed his hand on Daruk's head. 'May you live long, Daruk. May all your wishes come true! God will take care of you.'

Rukmini sat listening to Krishna and Daruk's conversation. Arjun and Draupadi sat like statues. Each one of them was praying for Krishna's peace and his pain to subside. Rukmini then said, 'Prabhu, I cannot stop you from being liberated, but it would be unjust if you left me behind.'

'My dear, one has to walk that path alone. We had become one the moment we held hands. The question of letting go of your hands doesn't arise.'

'Prabhu! These are words of wisdom. What is the connection between love and wisdom? Words are incapable of expressing love. Love is a feeling, an experience which is extremely personal. You may say anything, but what I have experienced is my truth, my lord, and how can you understand my truth? My thirst, my loneliness and my isolation are mine, aren't they? Were you a part of them?'

The sun slowly descended towards the horizon. The darkness after sunset was going to be distressful, terrifying. Maybe destiny was aware of this and was trying to keep the impending darkness at bay for as long as it could.

'All of us have to carry the burden of our loneliness ourselves, but dear, there is a vast difference between solitude and loneliness. Once you mistake solitude for loneliness, the whole context changes. Solitude is beautiful and carries grandeur and positivity. Loneliness is a sign of wretchedness and negativity and is ominous, but it is also natural; nobody can escape from it. Each one of us comes into this world alone and we have to go on our last journey alone.'

'Then why do people get married? Why do they create families? Why do they build relationships like brothers, friends, relatives and other loved ones?'

'Solitude is our fundamental nature, my dear, but we are unaware of it, or don't want to know and fail to know ourselves. People who know and recognise solitude make friends with it, and nothing else can be more blissful. Solitude allows us to be alone and at the same time, be with everyone.'

'And what about love? More than one love is impossible for a woman. For her, it is her man who is the centre of her universe, and the focus of her happiness ...' Rukmini suddenly remembered Draupadi's presence there, and added, 'Not everyone can be as capable as Draupadi. I am just an ordinary woman who loves only one man and expects happiness from him alone.'

'My dear, you are not ordinary and cannot be so. How can Krishna's wife be ordinary? I am not saying this out of conceit or arrogance. Like I told Arjun—I am the Airavat among elephants, the peepal among trees, the Kamdhenu among cows and the Ganga among rivers, and I am Rukmini among women! Priye, you are sublime, and that is why, you are the best part of my exceptional life. Love is not dependent on material objects. Love is the light of the soul. Love becomes boundless when it is all pervasive. When love spreads its wings wide, the span of our existence widens ...' Krishna was finding it difficult to talk and closed his eyes. His breath was becoming laboured and his voice was feeble. The incessant bleeding from his foot was weakening his body.

He continued after a pause, 'People who think marriages are made in heaven have a lot of expectations and believe that marriage is not love or that the love before marriage was something totally different. But love is actually a very deep understanding in which someone makes you complete in some way. The presence of someone gives you a well-rounded personality and enhances it. Love gives you the freedom to be yourself. Priye, how can you be happy and at peace, if your happiness and sorrow is dependent on someone else?

'Priye, the time we spent together was the best time of our lives. We were happy together and we shared our lives. We made each other so happy. If you look at our life this way, you will realise that we have been so fortunate.'

As if a bright light filled Rukmini's and Draupadi's minds. The dark clouds of despair seemed to scatter and Rukmini calmed down and sat looking at Krishna's face. Seeing this, Draupadi too felt comforted. It was as if this conversation had washed away Rukmini's dejection.

He was her husband, her lord, and he loved and respected her so much. The moments she spent with him had been so unique, priceless and timeless! All of a sudden, the moments Rukmini had found meaningless and hollow felt complete, fragrant and lively. They now seemed to dance around her with gay abandon. Her face filled with the satisfaction of having had a marvellous conjugal life.

'Lord, today you have removed the dark shadows of emptiness in my mind with your hands and spread the light of clarity. Lord, now when I look back, I realise that what I had understood as neglect was actually an opportunity given to me. What I considered to be your reticence, and despaired about, was nothing but your effort to keep me away from pain. What I complained to be shortage of time was actually your dedication to the service of others. Yet, whenever I felt lonely, you gave me a chance to come closer to you, every single time. You are so far removed from the men who consider their wives to be mere objects or just bodies. A wife becomes a friend from the seventh step she takes with her husband on her wedding day. You have proven this to me, lord! Please forgive me. I underestimated your benevolence and suffered constantly.'

'That is the real problem. We refuse to understand the perspective of others. We just overlook what someone is saying or wanting to say and prejudge them, and end up weakening the most beautiful and precious relationships. Logic is the man inherent in every person, while the mind is the woman. One should use logic to fight wars, but whenever sensitivity is needed, we should pay heed to the mind. A man is a man and a woman is a woman. There is a vast difference between the way they think, behave and live life. Women should retain their individual identities and instead of creating friction, focus on improving their emotional maturity and enhance their distinctive femininity. The best way for someone to avoid a clash between masculine logic and the feminine mind is to keep the eyes open and experience what is seen and then reason about it. If one can do this, marital discord will never arise. My dear, I loved you a lot. Your devotion is very valuable and I respect it immensely. If I am ever born again, I would pray for you to be my wife.'

Rukmini burst out crying. She seemed to be cleansing her heart with her tears. Despite living with Krishna for so many years, she had not understood him. Krishna caressed her back gently, as if he was saying, 'Remove all the toxins from your mind. Become pure and free. Please liberate me because until your mind liberates me, I will not be free from my responsibilities towards you, and my final journey cannot begin ...'

'My lord! I offer you everything you have given me ... *Twadiyam vastu govindam tubhyamev samarpaye.*' Rukmini wiped her tears and looked up at Krishna. His eyes were closed and his face was peaceful. She placed her palm on Krishna's chest. Krishna pressed both her hands to his chest.

'There is still some time, I have to reside in this body a little longer. There are still some unanswered questions. Someone's eyes are looking at me and saying, "Kanha, are you leaving? Won't you think about me even today?"'

'Radha ...' Rukmini's heart stopped for a moment.

'Will she come?' Draupadi wondered.

'Ma, why are you crying so bitterly?'

'Where am I crying?' Radha wiped her tears.

'Don't try to hide anything from me. Is there anything that is hidden from me? Are you thinking about someone?'

'Have I ever forgotten him? He has been with me in every moment of my life and never gave me a chance to miss him. He is thinking of me today.'

'Where could he be?'

'How do I know? When has he ever thought about me ever since he left Gokul?'

Radha suddenly felt that she shouldn't have said that and tried to get up. Shubhra stopped her, saying, 'Can we forget someone just because they have forgotten us?'

'Shyama, I don't have time to talk about all this. I have a lot of work to do.' Radha stood up.

'Ma, please take care. It shouldn't happen that someone's soul remains unsatisfied without meeting you ...'

Radha's voice was choked and trembling with emotion. She said, 'I don't understand why you support him so much! You don't even know him.'

Shubhra's eyes were full of mischief when she said, 'Who says that I don't know him? I have been seeing him in your eyes, every day. His name is connected with mine. Every time you call me Shyama instead of Shubhra, it feels like I am in Dwarka.'

'What have I got to do with Dwarka?' Radha looked away.

'He lives in Dwarka and everything that is associated with him drifts around there.'

It was as if Shubhra wasn't planning to leave Radha alone today. But Radha too seemed to have decided not to give in. 'I don't know him. I have heard that he is a king, the king of the golden city of Dwarka. I have also heard that he talks about knowledge, wisdom, yoga and devotion these days. The one I loved is still here— in the bylanes of Gokul, on the banks of the Yamuna, hiding among the trees, with his herd of cows, and in Ma Yashoda's eyes ...'

'Ma, what if he comes here ... to meet you?'

'Are you mad? The one who has left never comes back. If he had to come back, why would he have left in the first place? Despite all these contradictions, he lives in me. He is my existence. He has no name or form.'

Shubhra kept staring at Radha. This woman, who had followed the path of dharma all her life, was an ideal wife and an extraordinary mother who took care of everyone. She spent every moment of her life ensuring that everyone was well. She had never looked back. She just kept walking forward.

Today, the old woman had reached a point in her life where she felt as if her feet were chained heavily and she was unable to move forward. Not only that, she repeatedly looked back, as if someone was calling out to her. And yet the old woman's eyes looked like that of a sixteen-year-old. Like a teenager who had just fallen in love, whose youth had blossomed just recently and coloured her like a rainbow!

'Ma, what if he comes to meet you?'

'Let me tell you one thing: I have shut the doors of Gokul so tight that no one can leave this place and anyone who has left Gokul cannot return here.'

'But why, Ma? I have seen how you have suffered without him. I have seen you waiting for him every moment of your life.'

'It's not necessary that someone will come just because we wait for them, isn't it? And just because someone is expected, should we wait for them? We wait because we cannot see the person.'

'So we wait for the person who is not visible, right?'

Radha's eyes seemed to be lost in the past. 'You ask too many questions! When relationships end, all debts are redeemed and one wants to be free from all bondage, transactions and desires, to merge with the divine. I cannot say for sure that I am free from all my debts, but I must say that I am ready to offer whatever is required of me to rid me of my debts. Moreover, if I don't return what he has given me, how will he be free to go? He is my creditor for this life and many lives to come. I have always tried to give him everything he has ever asked for, because whatever he asks for belongs to him anyway.'

'Ma, can I ask you something?' It was as if Shubhra was bent upon peeking into Radha's heart today and determined to accept and absorb her pain and sorrows.

Radha, who was lonely and continuously talking to herself, knew that Shubhra always achieved what she decided upon. By being constantly close to Radha, Shubhra was helping her reach the deepest recesses of her mind. There were so many things that Radha hesitated to talk about on her own. Today, Shubhra had opened the doors of the dark room where Radha had locked away that name and so many moments of her life. And now, every moment of Radha's life had become resplendent. As she answered Shubhra's questions, it appeared as if she was answering her own mind, and she would be completely natural and true with her answers.

It was like Shubhra was Radha's alter ego.

Radha's mind had split in two halves. One, where she was Ayan's wife, Aaryak's mother, a milkmaid of Gokul; and the other, where she was a woman who was one with Krishna, whose existence meant nothing without him. She breathed Krishna's name and her blood flowed in the name of Krishna. Her eyes saw only Krishna and she spoke to him every moment of her life … Yet, Ayan's wife never had to face any moral questions. She served Ayan with all her mind, speech and actions. She was totally dedicated as his wife and never fell short as a lover either.

'Ma, why did you live two lives, being in one body?'

'Body? My body perished long ago. The moment he left Gokul, my life left this body. I am just biding my time, waiting for his call that will liberate me.'

Shubhra took Radha's hands in hers and asked her very sincerely, 'Ma, didn't you ever feel like going to Dwarka? Did you never want to know what he does, how he lives and who he lives with? Who are the people closest to him?'

'No,' Radha said abruptly.

'Why?'

'Because I know that once I get the answers, I won't be able to leave Dwarka and return. It's not in my nature to leave my own space and settle elsewhere, and it is not in his nature either to accept me from anywhere but my own space.'

'But Ma, this dissatisfaction, this loneliness, the agony of waiting to meet him, this pain—what do you achieve by all this?'

'Peace. Happiness is accepting what destiny has laid out for us. We are all arrogant fools who feel we can do anything. Our meeting was destined. Our parting was also decided the moment we met. Every moment is born to pass. We suffer in the attempt to hold on to time. I couldn't have stopped him from going, but what you call my loneliness and my anguish are my joy and a symbol of my association with him. If he had forgotten me, it wouldn't have been very difficult for me to forget him either. This is like fire that dies if you don't add fuel. I am aware and my soul is aware that he has constantly been adding fuel to it, and that is why, it is still burning bright.'

'Ma, hasn't Bapu ever asked you anything?'

'He knows, he is aware that his wife belongs only to him. He knows that she is completely devoted, faithful, and lives peacefully within the four walls of his house. He has nothing to do with this other woman who lives within me and is aware that she loves someone else in her own way.'

'Still, isn't it difficult for a man to accept that?'

'Why only for one? It is equally difficult for both men. To know that someone loves your wife so much, or to love someone else's wife so intensely—both are not easy to accept. And Shyama, even otherwise, love is not easy to experience—there is so much restlessness, lamentation and pain associated with it.'

'But, Ma, it is only love that can give us happiness, isn't it?'

At this question, as if every cell in Radha's body became a flute and Krishna's lips touched her every pore, for her whole body reverberated with a magical melody. All the moments she had spent with Kanha came alive.

'Yes, I am happy and peaceful only because of love. He remembers me wherever he is. He loves me. For me, this knowledge is more joyful and romantic than being with him.'

'If that is the case then what am I seeing for the past several days? Why have you been so despondent? What is troubling you? What is this yearning that torments you so much?'

'I have to liberate someone. If I don't become free, how will he be liberated? And how will he be peaceful without liberation? I am the peace in his life, his charm, his music and the melody of his life. He expects to take leave from me and I have to bid him farewell ... I just have to comfort him. That is my duty, my dharma.'

Draupadi looked at Krishna lying with his eyes closed. His expressions were changing every moment, and it looked as if he was talking to someone. The colour of his face too changed every instant. For one moment, his face would have a smile as if he was remembering some sweet memory and in the next moment, his face would darken with deep anguish. Rukmini, Daruk, Arjun, Draupadi and Jara sat around him. Despite the presence of all these people, Krishna looked all alone and was talking to himself. His eyes were shut, and the image of a beautiful, mischievous, delicate, long-haired girl floated before his eyes. She was as sprightly as the waters of the Yamuna. She stared at him through her clear, gazelle-like eyes, and asked him, 'What is holding you back now? Go ... go if you want.'

'This soul is waiting just to meet you, I will have to hold on to this body till you come.'

'Your wait is a waste. I am not going to come.'

'You used to say this every day and then you would come, drawn by the melody of my flute, remember?'

'No, I don't remember anything.' Her face was red with indignation.

'Oh, come now. How will I go if you don't come?' Krishna pleaded with Radhika.

The evening sun had turned a deep saffron. The spot where the rivers met the sea was waiting for the sun to set. The waters of the rivers looked like a carpet of blazing marigold flowers. The sky seemed to be wrapped in saffron and ready to bid farewell to the sun in a saintly manner.

Krishna's face too took on the hues of the setting sun. With his eyes closed, Krishna continued his conversation with the floating image of Radha ...

'How can I come? Our paths branched off and we moved in opposite directions the moment you left Gokul. Now, if I desire to come to you, I will have to walk my path and yours as well. We have come too far away from each other, Kanha.'

'Only those who have let go of each other's hand get separated. We may have walked in opposite directions, but we never left each other's hand. Whatever the direction may have been, our situation hasn't changed.'

'Kanha, you have been clever since childhood. You are a master at trapping me with your words. You cajoled and convinced me when you had to leave then, and now you are calling me with your wordplay. But remember, I am no longer the naive girl you could once trick with your words.'

'For me, you are still the same. I left you and Gokul, but your image in my eyes has remained unchanged. I can still see the same sulking, fighting Radha who was crazy for me.'

'Because you made that Radha dance to your tune at will.'

'Then you make me dance now.' Krishna's face lit up with a mischievous smile, as if he was enjoying his banter with Radha just as much as before.

'There is magic in your fingers, Kanha. The entire Aryavart dances to your tune.' Radha shrugged her shoulders.

Krishna laughed aloud.

'Radha, the fragrance of your touch is intact on my fingertips to this day. Whenever I smell my fingertips, I can feel the scent of your skin.'

'And what about your queens, all sixteen thousand one hundred and eight of them?'

'They are my wives, my better halves. But none of the sixteen thousand one hundred and eight names are taken together with mine, Radhike. All over the world, we are addressed as Radha-Krishna. Your name comes before mine.'

'These are mere words. Have you ever called out to me during all these years?'

'How could I? You have been with me every single moment. Why would I miss you when my existence is one with yours. I am incomplete without you.'

'And that is why you left me and went away?' Suddenly, the Yamuna appeared in Radha's eyes. Krishna lifted his hands to wipe her eyes, but then held back. Where was she?

Her memory was so vivid and strong that he could feel her presence there.

'Yes, that is why I had left. If I had continued to be with you, I would have lived in completeness. I wouldn't have tried to find anything, search for anything at all. All my duties and my activities would have centred around you, Radhe.'

'Did you ever give a thought to what would have happened to me? You lied to me and left. You said you would come back for me.'

'Where did I ever leave? If I had gone, I would have certainly returned. I had left my entire being with you, Radha. At this moment, I am looking for that Krishna. I have to take him back with me. Please return that Krishna to me.'

'He is not yours; he is mine. You just said that you had left that Krishna behind in Gokul. It was I who protected him all these years. Do you think I will hand him over to you just like that? Get lost! Everything cannot be as per your whims and fancies, Kanha.'

'My dear Radhike, this is the only thing I ask of you,' Krishna said in gullible, boyish voice. It was as if Radha was enticing a young Krishna with a pot of butter, and he was determined to get it by any means.

'But this is all I have and if I give this away, what will I have left with me?' Radha's voice was imploring and obstinate at the same time. It was like a child refusing to give away its favourite toy. Radha pressed Krishna's memory to her chest, not wanting to part with it.

Krishna began explaining to Radha in a serious tone, 'We are the only ones who can complete the circles of each other's lives. Till today, we have been living for each other within a single circle, pining for each other. The universe labelled me as Poorna Purushottam and placed me on a pedestal. But you are the most complete woman who made me so. How can my existence be imagined without you, Radha? Whatever little femininity and gentleness I have within me is all you. Whatever is pure, authentic, clear and strong, is you, Radha. The masonry that forms this body is based on your essence. You are my reality. You are the purport of my entire life. You are my worldly form. You are my consciousness that resides in this creation that has kept me untouched, intact and pure till now.'

'Kanha, you have become a great man. You speak of profound things. I am a simple woman who understands the language of the heart.'

'True. I have become entangled in knowledge and politics, and have forgotten the sacred fragrance of Brajbhoomi. You have brought that scent with you. I feel as if I am sitting on the banks of the Yamuna with my hands in yours. The moonlight straining through the kadamba trees is caressing your face.'

'Kanha, come away with me. Let me take you back to Braj, far away from here. Let's go back to the beauty of the small village, the hearts as pure as raindrops, the herds of cows and the taste of butter churned by your mother.'

'Radhike, how is that possible? It is too late now ...'

'No, it is not. Everyone is waiting for you even now. Everything is just the way it was. All the dancing, singing, playing, looting, losing, sulking, cow grazing, pleading, envying and pot-breaking stand still there. Come with me, Kanha.'

'Radhike, my destiny is just the opposite. I cannot retrace the path that I have traversed once. I move from the source towards expansion, I flow like a stream. But you are Radha. You can flow from the expansive world towards the source. You are fortunate to have drenched the base desires of mankind in the colours of love.'

Innumerable images appeared and vanished before Krishna's eyes during the conversation. The torrential rains of Gokul, raindrops dripping from the kadamba leaves, white and red lotuses blooming on the Yamuna, the huge lotus leaves not allowing a single drop to stick to them, dancing peacocks, the tinkle of bells tied to cows' necks, their painted horns, the sounds of butter being churned in backyards, the anxious eyes of a perpetually waiting mother and the blazing red bindi on her forehead, his own peacock feather and the empty room where he would be locked by his mother ...

With every image, a distinct expression would appear on Krishna's face, and then disappear.

Draupadi and Rukmini sat watching the play of expressions on Krishna's face. He seemed to be wandering in Brajbhoomi. A little Krishna was running all around, troubling his mother. Sometimes, he would break Radha's pot and hide in the kadamba tree; at other times, he would sit on the tree with Sudama, getting drenched and trembling in the rain.

'Kanha, tell me something.'
    'Yes, my dear.'

'Whatever you lived, how much ever you lived, was it all real? Or were you deceiting yourself and others?'

'No, I never cheated anyone, but I must say that I lived the way I wanted to. My duties and my actions kept pulling me, while my mind was asking for something else altogether. At times, people have found me to be unjust, but I did nothing out of selfishness.'

'Kanha, you were so simple, sweet and naive. How did you get trapped in this maze of politics, knowledge, intrigues and manoeuvres?'

'This question has arisen in my mind often. I was reminded of it even in the middle of the Kurukshetra war. I was reminded of my flute in the midst of the clang of weapons, the trumpeting elephants, the trotting horses, the screams of dying soldiers and the sound of the Panchajanya conch. But going back was impossible for me.'

'But it wasn't conceivable that you wouldn't have come back to me, Kanha.'

'Why didn't you ever come to meet me? To see how I was doing? To check if I was happy?'

'You are the one who left Gokul and went away ... so, one of us had to stay back in Gokul, isn't it? Your karma and my dharma ... how could we have been together, Kanhaiya?'

'Radha, I don't know whether you will believe me, but, at times, I used to feel like leaving everything and running back to Gokul. I just wanted to give up the politics, the responsibilities, the throne, and go back to you.'

'Yes, I do believe you, because many a time, when I sat alone on the banks of the Yamuna, I have seen whirlpools form on the surface of the water. I have felt someone sitting beside me and sighing deeply, silently sharing his travails with me.'

'Where else could I go? Whenever I found the foundation of my faith in truth shake, I thought about you. These eyes of yours have kept me from turning away from life. I have fulfilled all my duties, shouldered all my responsibilities on the power and strength of your eyes.'

He fell silent for a few moments and then changed the subject, asking, 'Radhike, hope everything is fine. Your husband, your children ... are you happy?'

'Kanha, I don't know why, but I am cursed to be happy. I am able to find my peace in any situation, anywhere.'

The sun started dipping towards the horizon. It was looking like a flaming ball of fire standing between the sea and the sky. The sea breeze turned cool and blew in the direction of the peepal tree. Everyone sat watching Krishna immersed in his past.

'Radha, I feel very good to know that you are happy.' Radha's eyes had an unfathomable expression. It had never happened that Krishna was unable to understand Radha, but now, her eyes looked so languid and cold that Krishna felt very sad.

'Don't look at me so morosely. I truly wish for your happiness.'

'My peace is all around me, Kanha. My husband and my children are my responsibility, my dharma. My peace is not due to them. Your love, your memories and the times I spent with you are what define my happiness. Kanha, won't I feel sad if you ask me if I am happy? You are the only one who knows me inside out, and the other is Shyama ...'

'Shyama?'

'Why do I hear a hint of jealousy in your voice? Shyama is my son Aaryak's wife.'

'If someone other than me knows you so deeply, I am bound to be jealous. I am the only one who resides in you.'

'Everyone calls you God, and you talk like an ordinary human being?'

'Radhike, you are the only one with whom I become simple and ordinary. I become free of all the layers that conceal me, and I reach my past. You are free to threaten me, berate me, fight with me ... you are the only one who has the liberty to do this and have complete right over me. You are my foundation. Never pluck me out of yourself, Radhike, even when I am not there.'

The tears that Radha had been holding back for so long flowed unabated now. Her voice trembled and she said to Krishna, angrily, 'You have spoken the truth only now. Couldn't you say it all this time? Where do you have to go?'

'From the place I have come ... where else?'

'Where have you come from? Gokul? Come, I have come to take you with me.'

♣

Krishna's eyes were closed, but he chuckled aloud. Draupadi, Arjun, Rukmini and Daruk had never seen him laugh like that. The childlike, mischievous, uninhibited laugh made Krishna's face fresh and alive, as if his life had been steeped in nectar! Everyone knew who Krishna was talking to. Draupadi and Rukmini felt elated at the thought of Radha's good fortune. Such laughter could be only for Radha.

'Tell me, where have you come from?' asked Radha. Krishna's voice reverberated like the sound of the Panchajanya conch. Draupadi, Rukmini, Daruk and Jara were immersed in that divine voice. Arjun was reminded of the voice he had heard in the battlefield of Kurukshetra. Krishna was speaking with his eyes closed,

> 'I didn't come from the east,
> I didn't come from the west,
> I didn't come from the north,
> I didn't come from above,
> I didn't come from below,
> I didn't come from any direction or country,
> I never came, I was always here.
> I am and will be!'

'Stop it! I don't want to hear all this.'

'All right then! I will go back to where I was even before I entered my mother Devaki's womb, and before I was brought to Gokul on that dark new moon night in the month of Shravan.'

'Then why don't you go? What are you waiting for? Or do you want to tease me, trouble me, make me cry as always?' Tears streamed down her eyes. 'What pleasure do you derive by leaving me and going time and again! I am so angry that I feel like tying you to this peepal tree.'

'You have already bound me so much. How much more do you want to bind me? And even if you do, I will go ... I have to go, my dear. You were the one who was holding me back till now. Please free me so that I can go.'

'Go now. I will not stop you.'

'Do you promise?'

'Kanha, don't make me angry now.'

'You look so lovely when you are angry.'

'So lovely ...' said Radha, mimicking Krishna. 'That is why you are leaving me.'

'Yes, that is precisely why I am leaving. If you keep loving me thus, I will never be able to leave. I will have to be tied like this for centuries; do you know that?'

'I just don't understand what you say.'

'Do I myself understand all this fully? That is the reason I have to undertake this journey. May I go?'

'All right ... go and never come back again.' Radha turned her back. Krishna felt as if he was standing next to Radha.

'Say that again ...' Krishna mumbled with his eyes shut, lying under the peepal tree.

'Yes ... go and never come back here ever again.'

Krishna's eyes welled up. He looked at Radha tenderly. He could see her back clearly behind his closed eyes. He felt so close to her that he could touch her. He thought of placing his raised hands on Radha's shoulders, but changed his mind and just stood still. He could picture the entire scene in his mind's eye. Suddenly Radha's back felt so distant that it was beyond his reach. He kept his hand raised and said, '*Tathastu*! So be it!' His voice was broken. Tears streamed from his eyes, washing away Radha's image gradually. Radha, with her back turned towards Krishna, seemed to be walking away slowly. She turned around and looked at Krishna once. She said to Krishna with tearful eyes, 'Go, Kanha go, and don't ever come back. I offer back to you everything you have given me, and I free your mind that is tied with me, because binding someone is not in my nature. I didn't shackle you then, why will I do it now? Go Kanha ... go away.'

She walked away.

Krishna opened his eyes. Draupadi, Arjun, Daruk, Rukmini and Jara sat close to him. There was silence all around. The sun was setting far in the horizon. There was just a fine saffron line separating the sea and the sky. Krishna took a deep breath and closed his eyes. It was as if he had unburdened himself from the weight of the precious load he had been carrying until that moment. He murmured very feebly:

'Now, there is no bondage, no desire, no expectation, no debt ... There are no questions, no duties, no struggle and no waiting for anyone. I am becoming more alive than the earth, lighter than air, brighter than light, clearer than water and more expansive than the sky. I am able to see my path, my direction. A big ball of light is beckoning me towards itself.'

Thousands of Brahmin priests seemed to be chanting, and their chants echoed all around—

Mamaivamso jiva-loke jiva-bhutah sanatanah
Manah-sasthanindriyani prakrti-sthani karsati

The living entities in this conditioned world are my eternal, fragmental parts. Due to this conditioned life, they are struggling very hard with the six senses, which include the mind.

His breathing became slow and shallow. His face had a glow of peace and dazzled with divine radiance. The sun set far in the horizon. A bright ball of light seemed to have spread inside the sea as well, and the water turned molten gold.

Krishna folded his hands and took a deep breath. The people sitting around him were witnessing the divine merging with the supreme consciousness.

A voice reverberated—

Nainam chindanti sastrani nainam dahati pavakah
Na cainam kledayanty apo na sosayati marutah

Acchedyo 'yam adahyo 'yam, akledyo 'sosya eva ca
Nityah sarva-gatah sthanur, acalo 'yam sanatanah

Jatasya hi dhruvo mrtyur dhruvam janma mrtasya ca
Tasmad apariharye' rthe na tvam socitum arhasi

Avyaktadini bhutani vyakta-madhyani bharata
Avyakta-nidhanany eva tatra ka paridevana

The soul can never be cut into pieces by any weapon, nor can it be burnt by fire, nor moistened by water, nor withered by the wind.

This individual soul is unbreakable and insoluble, and can be neither burnt nor dried. It is everlasting, all pervading, unchangeable, immovable and eternally the same.

For one who has taken birth, death is certain, and for one who is dead, birth is certain. Therefore, in the unavoidable discharge of your duty, you should not lament.

All created beings are unmanifest in their beginning, manifest in their interim state and unmanifest again when they are annihilated. So what is the need for lamentation?

Made in the USA
Columbia, SC
01 May 2021

37195768R00162